UNTAMED

THE ELEMENTAL SAGA
BOOK TWO

JESSICA RUDDICK

Chapter 1

SOFT SNORES EMANATED from the bed next to me, and in my drowsy state, I thought it was Lena. As sunshine peeked through the cheap hotel curtains and I became more alert, reality crashed down as it had done every morning for the past four days.

Since Lena had been taken.

Not wanting to make any noise, I sat up slowly and eased my legs over the side of the bed. Though Michelle had taken to spending the nights in my hotel room, I could count on one hand the number of hours she'd actually slept in the last four days.

Of course, I could say the same for myself. With Lena gone, a piece of my soul was missing.

Testing had been officially canceled, and almost all the other elementals had returned home—all of them except the families of the six.

Lena Brandt.

Aniyah Williams.

Shana Kowalski.

Alexis Quigley.

Isabella Garcia-Cruz.

Emma Perkins.

I hadn't heard most of their names before, but now they were forever etched in my memory.

Closing my eyes, I stretched, making my body long. Power zinged from my pointed toes to my fingertips. My power had always been omnipresent under the surface, but recently it had become difficult to ignore.

As I lifted my body off the bed, the coils in the mattress squeaked. Michelle's body jerked, but she remained asleep.

Whew.

Mike appeared in the open doorway that adjoined our rooms. "Good morning." His eyes were bloodshot, and his face was covered in stubble. He hadn't slept much either.

I put my finger to my lips and pointed to Michelle.

His gaze—filled with both adoration and sadness—shifted to his wife's form. "I convinced her to take a sleeping pill. She won't be waking up anytime soon."

"What about you?" I asked. "You need to sleep too."

His smile didn't reach his eyes. "I'll be okay. Do you want to go down and get breakfast?"

Nodding, I went to my suitcase to find some clothes that were somewhat clean, which was becoming harder by the day. We hadn't anticipated being in Florida so long, and none of us had taken the time to hunt down a laundromat.

"Just give me a few minutes."

"I'll meet you in the hall in twenty." Mike pulled the door closed to give me privacy.

As I rooted around in my suitcase, my fingers brushed the phone hidden among the clothes. I'd only used it once, and the memory of those two minutes made my heart pound and my mouth go dry.

Carly Levitt—my mother—had sounded so normal, not like someone who was responsible for the deaths of so many. I'd replayed the previous day's conversation a thousand times in my head, but I'd yet to make sense of it.

"What do you want from me?" I asked. "Why did you find me after all this time?"

She took a shaky breath. "I never expected to hear your voice. I thought you were dead."

I had news for her—*everyone* had thought she was dead. And no one was happy to discover she was alive, not even me. My feelings were complicated at best.

"Why?"

She paused. "Can you meet me? There's a lot to talk about, and I don't want to do it over the phone."

Suddenly doubting my grand idea to enlist my evil, supposed-to-be-dead mother's help, I'd ended the call.

The bitter disappointment had been hard to swallow, but I didn't know what I'd expected. There would be no happy reunion, not under normal circumstances and especially not now. My short conversation had resulted in more questions than answers.

Why did she think I was dead?

Where has she been for the last fifteen years?

Why show up now?

How did she learn I was alive?

Where is she?

What does she want from me?

After I'd gotten my wits about me, I'd hurriedly powered down the phone, hoping I hadn't missed a tracking app in my initial inspection of it.

Putting Carly out of my mind, I carried my clothes to the bathroom and took a quick shower. When I emerged fifteen minutes later with dripping hair, Michelle was still softly snoring, so I tiptoed out of the room and gently closed the door behind me.

Aidan was leaning against the wall outside my room.

My heart pounded, but this time for an entirely different reason. It was because of Aidan, the boy who'd started out like a brother to me but had grown to be so much more.

But that was before.

My life was divided into *BLWT* and *ALWT*—*Before Lena was Taken* and *After Lena was Taken*. I'd thought learning that Carly Levitt was not only my mother but also alive would cause the largest seismic shift in my life, but I had been wrong.

Lena being taken was so much bigger than that.

Aidan's blue eyes met mine, and for a split second, they were filled with pain and sadness. Then his expression turned neutral, and he donned the mask I'd gotten used to seeing the last few days.

"Hey." I tucked my hands in my pockets, not sure what I should do with them. What I wanted to do was put them on Aidan's cheeks and force him to look at me, to tell me what was going on inside his head.

After I'd finished talking to Carly, my first instinct had been to turn to Aidan, both to tell him about the conversation and to ask him to double-check the phone, but I didn't want our first interaction in three days to be him berating me. The wall he'd erected between us hurt enough as it was.

"Hey." He cleared his throat. "I told Mike I'd walk you downstairs."

"Oh. Okay."

He gestured for me to walk ahead of him toward the elevator. He trailed half a step behind in proper guardian fashion.

Before we'd kissed, I had worried about our relationship being irreparably damaged if we failed in our attempt to move beyond being friends. I'd been right to worry but not for the reason I'd thought. It wasn't our kiss that had ruined everything. Of course, I never could have predicted the kidnapping of six elemental girls right from under everyone's noses.

Aidan hadn't predicted it either, and I knew him well enough to know he blamed himself for not doing the impossible.

I punched the elevator button, and the doors opened immediately. He once again motioned for me to go ahead of him.

What a gentleman.

He could be, but that wasn't what his actions were about. They were about avoidance.

Hypocrite. He'd once called me out for hiding from my problems, but that was *BLWT*. Everything was different now.

He pressed the button for the lobby and leaned against the wall with his arms crossed.

Staring at him, I willed him to look at me. With everything else going on, I couldn't handle one more second of weirdness with Aidan.

I impulsively pushed the Stop button, and the elevator jerked to a halt.

Aidan straightened. "What are you doing?"

"Are we going to talk about this?" I asked quietly.

Working his jaw, he trained his gaze over my head on the wall behind me.

"*Look* at me." I hated how needy I sounded, but I was desperate. I *needed* him, even if we regressed back to our old, casual, antagonistic banter instead of continuing our new romantic involvement. I was barely hanging on, and he probably was too. So why couldn't we hang on together?

He didn't respond. It was as if I hadn't spoken.

"Please," I said softly.

His eyes met mine, and the rawness in them caused my breath to hitch. He hadn't really looked at me in days. For the first time, I noticed his appearance resembled Mike's—his cheeks were unshaven, and his eyes were bloodshot. His hair seemed to have grown in the last few days. He usually rocked the slightly mussed-up look, but at the moment, he simply appeared bedraggled.

He was hurting way more than he let on.

Stepping toward him, I reached for his hand.

He allowed me to hold it for only a second before yanking it away. "We can't."

"I'm not trying to..." I didn't know how to finish that sentence because I wasn't sure what I was actually trying to do, or *not* do. All I knew was that I wanted his comfort and for him to allow me to comfort him. "Don't push me away."

"It has to be this way."

"Why? It's okay to—"

"It's not." The air thickened, and the space somehow increased between us in the tiny elevator. His shoulders sagged, and his voice softened. "I can't. You're a distraction, and I can't help but think if I hadn't—if *we* hadn't—then maybe Lena would be here. Maybe they would all be here."

"There were guardians all over," I said quietly. "This isn't all on you." I didn't bother trying to convince him it wasn't his fault. Since he was a guardian, technically some of the blame *was* his, but he shared it with guardians much more experienced than him. *No one* had seen it coming.

His tone hardened again. "Lena's gone, and that's on me."

I shook my head. "It's not."

He blew out a breath. "I'm not going to argue with you. But here's a fact—I can't *be with you* and protect you. Because when I'm with you, it's all I can do to keep my head on straight. Because you're..." He scrubbed his hands over his face then leaned past me to reach the elevator buttons. The car resumed its descent.

"Aidan—"

"Do us both a favor and keep your distance."

I flattened my back against the wall, granting his request and putting as much physical distance between us as I could in the small space. That wasn't what he meant, but I still did it for my sake. He couldn't have hurt me more if he'd slapped me. At least then I would have been able to defend myself.

But there was no defense against his argument. With those words, I lost the other most important person in my life.

AFTER DEPOSITING ME in Mike's care, Aidan hightailed it out of the room. Mike looked back and forth between me and the trail Aidan had blazed. He knew something was up, but he was also smart—and kind—enough not to mention it. Breakfast was silent with both of us pushing our food around our plates. We wanted to put on a good show for the other one, but it was a lost cause. Neither of us was kidding the other.

We dumped our plates in the trash and headed back to our rooms. I wished we had somewhere else to go, but we'd been told repeatedly "the guardians are handling it" and "there is nothing you can do."

With all due respect to Vic, Suze, and Aidan, the guardians were *not* handling it. Or if they were, no one was sharing the news. We'd been forced into waiting around, which was maddening.

When I opened the door to my room, I was surprised to see that Michelle was awake. I was even more surprised to see Councilwoman West sitting in the sole chair in the room. I hesitated, wanting to tuck my tail between my legs and run in the opposite direction. I hadn't talked with Aidan's mom since she'd visited us and given me a preview of testing. Never had I thought her intentions were benevolent, but it was only when I learned the truth about my parentage that I understood her ulterior motives... sort of.

She had wanted to see how powerful I was because other than Mike and Michelle, she was one of only two other people who had known Carly was my mother. But what she planned to do with that knowledge, I had no idea. Thank God she couldn't see the currents of power running through me.

Michelle sat on the edge of the bed, wearing pajama pants and one of Mike's T-shirts that swallowed her thin frame. Her hands were clasped between her knees, the knuckles white.

I sighed. As much as I wanted to run, I wouldn't leave Michelle.

"Mike," I called to him. He'd stopped at his own door. When he looked up, I jerked my head to indicate he should come into my room. His eyebrows rose, but he abandoned his room without question.

When I walked into the room, the councilwoman turned her cold, appraising gaze in my direction. Though she wore her customary suit, her hair wasn't pulled back as slickly as usual, and her makeup did little to cover the circles under her eyes. I was perversely glad to see the girls' disappearance had affected her too. Maybe she was capable of emotion after all.

As I stepped into the room, I realized the two women weren't alone. Aidan leaned against the wall in the far corner. *Damn.* I wasn't ready to see him again, but it was inevitable. With Vic and Suze gone investigating the kidnapping, Aidan had remained at the hotel to guard us.

"Do you have leads?" Mike asked hurriedly, going to sit next to his wife. He wrapped his arm around her shoulders.

West sighed. "Unfortunately, no. Not really." She laughed bitterly. "The official council statement is 'the matter is being investigated,' but frankly, we don't have anything."

I blinked at her candor. While I hadn't expected her to be forthcoming with information, I definitely hadn't expected her to admit there was none.

"We need to go to the police," Michelle said, repeating the plea she'd already made many times.

"You know we can't." West crossed her legs. "I'm sick inside about those girls, but involving the police would only create more problems."

"But—"

"*No,*" West firmly silenced Michelle's protest. "They're going to want to know why we were gathered at the orchard. They're going to see the damage from the fire and ask lots of questions." Her eyes flicked to me for a moment, and I focused on the carpet. The police would want to know how we'd put the fire out, but we certainly couldn't tell them the truth—that I'd commanded the clouds to unleash rain. "There's no way we could involve them without exposing elementals."

Anger flared within me. Lena and five other girls were gone. Nothing was more important than getting them back. Who cared if the world found out about us? Maybe that would be a blessing. The secrecy was so tiring.

I balled my hands into fists. "It would be worth it."

"We'd risk more than exposure," Aidan said. Speaking up was a rare thing for him to do with his mother in attendance. "The police would question why we waited so long to report them missing. I don't know the exact legal ramifications, but there would be some. Mike and Michelle—and all the other parents—would most likely be brought up on charges."

"He's right," West confirmed. "It's called Caylee's law. The parents would face prison time."

My body shook with anger. "Michelle wanted to call the police the day it happened, and you—"

"Sophie," Mike said. "What's done is done. Fighting amongst ourselves won't help."

Narrowing my eyes at West, I crossed my arms and leaned against the dresser. Mike was right. We needed to focus on finding Lena. And when we found her, then we could hash out the council's asinine actions.

"Why are you here?" I asked, wanting her to get to the point so we could remedy that fact as soon as possible. Her presence wasn't helping anyone. And despite my row with Aidan, I still had his back where his mother was concerned. I always would.

"Partially because of what we just talked about. We need to keep the girls' disappearance discreet."

I frowned at her. It wasn't as if we were shouting it to the world on social media. We hadn't reported it to the police, and she'd made it abundantly clear we couldn't do that at this late date. How much more discreet did she want us to be?

Mike nodded, as though he understood what West was implying.

West's expression was kind. "We're readying accommodations for the families. We'd considered using our already established safe houses, but we thought it might be helpful for the families to be close together, so it's taking longer to find a suitable location."

"Wait," I protested. "Why can't we go home?" As I asked the question, the councilwoman's reasoning dawned on me. Though we hadn't reported Lena's disappearance to the police, people at home would notice she wasn't around. For instance, there were truancy laws. Without proper documentation for our absences—which were racking up—the school would be forced to report us.

But it wasn't going to come to that. It *couldn't*. Because they would find Lena before it became an issue. I refused to accept otherwise. It was the only thing keeping me sane.

West ignored my question. "We'll arrange for some of your personal items to be shipped if you'll make us a list. The girls will need to be withdrawn from school. Sophie can finish her senior year as a homeschooled student."

There were still six months left in my senior year. This *could not* drag on that long. What was the council thinking? They had to realize the kind of message this sent.

One of little hope.

West reached into the satchel at her feet and pulled out a file folder. She handed it to Mike. "The cover story we've come up with for the affected families is a temporary move to care for a sick relative. This contains all of the documentation you need."

"This is so messed up," I muttered.

I couldn't help it—my gaze shifted to Aidan. One look at him told me his thoughts were the same as mine—it seemed as though the council was already throwing in the towel. I didn't understand how they could. Three of the girls were the daughters of council members. I wished Agent Kowalski were there instead of West. With her daughter among the missing, she would understand the council was wasting time arranging for cover stories and whatnot. Every elemental with a brain should have been contributing to the rescue efforts without worrying about secrecy and stealth.

The kidnapped girls didn't have the luxury of time. According to every true crime show or podcast I'd ever seen or listened to, the longer it took to find them, the less likely they would be found alive.

Except this wasn't a normal kidnapping.

We all avoided discussing the possibility I was all too familiar with—what if the girls were taken by witch hunters? My witch hunter kidnappers had planned to kill me the same day they took me. As far as I knew, the guardians hadn't made any progress in discovering who was behind that scheme. The four perpetrators couldn't have been acting alone. Though witch hunters hadn't been an active threat since the incident that had killed Aidan's sister and Lena's parents, my kidnapping was proof the hateful groups were still out there and willing to act against us.

The council's current actions made me wonder if that was the predominant theory. The possibility of the girls being taken by witch hunters was too frightening, so I'd refused to consider it.

It was more than that, though. The six girls who were taken all showed signs of great strength, which led me to believe they had been specifically targeted. For instance, Kennedy and Lena had been together, yet only Lena was taken. Kennedy's powers were weak. So the logical conclusion was the girls were taken for their value and not for some malicious witch-hunter sacrifice.

That was still horrible, but at least it meant the girls would be kept alive.

"Is there anything else?" Aidan asked.

I shot him a grateful look. I was as eager to be rid of his mother as he was.

"Yes." West gave me a level stare. "I want to talk to you about your mother."

I stared back at her, not quite sure how to respond. West not only had knowledge of my parentage, she was the one who'd arranged for Lloyd and Belinda—who I'd thought of as my grandparents until a few weeks ago—to raise me.

It had been surprisingly easy for me to shift to thinking of them in terms of their first names. We'd never been close. Three months after Belinda died of cancer, Lloyd had received a similar diagnosis and been given six months to live. He'd lasted three. I hadn't been there for that because by that point, West had swooped in again and arranged for me to live with Mike and Michelle.

But I still wasn't clear why she had done all that. Mike and Michelle had told me the council had planned to use two-year-old me as leverage against Carly, but they hadn't known specifics. How cold-hearted did a person have to be to use a toddler as a bargaining tool? What had the council hoped to accomplish? And if they'd been successful, would they really have returned me to my monster of a mother? I wish I knew their end game.

I had so many questions that only West could answer—*if* she could be trusted to tell the truth.

Fat chance.

"Why?" It was the simplest question and the most pertinent. Even though I wanted answers to different questions, they weren't important at the moment. There would be time for those later.

"It can't be a coincidence that she showed up shortly before the girls were taken."

That thought had crossed my mind as well. It made me even sicker to my stomach than the list of crimes my mother was accused of and the even longer list of her victims.

When I'd spoken to her, the relief and joy were evident in her voice. She'd gone to a lot of trouble to get in touch with me. It didn't make sense for her to jeopardize a possible reunion by taking Lena. She wasn't stupid—she had to know that would be a deal breaker for me.

Unless she's manipulating you, the devil on my shoulder taunted. A large dose of skepticism and distrust where Carly was concerned was prudent, but the little girl in me was desperate to believe her mother simply wanted to reconnect.

I know... totally messed up.

"What does that have to do with me?" I asked.

No one knew I'd contacted her. Besides, I'd only talked to her for two minutes; I didn't have any more information than

I'd had before. I couldn't tell West anything she didn't already know.

Except I could easily contact Carly again. It took all my willpower to keep my eyes from darting over to where the phone was buried in my suitcase. Turning it over was the "right" thing to do, but nothing the council had done in the last few days—or *ever*, for that matter—convinced me they would use it to our advantage. I'd never been a fan of West's, and frankly, my fragile trust in her was shattered after learning she'd lied to me my entire life.

"Has she contacted you?" West asked.

"No." Technically, it wasn't a lie because I'd called her. But still, my face burned as I spoke the semi-truth. "Do you think she's involved?"

West paused. "Like I said, it's quite a coincidence she reappeared right before this happened."

Her vagueness told me what I suspected—the council and the investigating guardians were grasping at straws. Carly's reappearance made her an easy suspect.

"That's why it doesn't make sense for it to be her," I said slowly. "Why would she show herself right before she planned to pull this off?"

"Maybe she didn't intend to be seen," West countered.

Aidan shifted. "She didn't do a great job of disguising herself at the movie theater."

"Maybe she's out of practice." West sounded exasperated.

I shook my head. "I don't think so. I think she wanted to be seen."

"Why?" Michelle peered at me suspiciously. Despite her distraught state, her motherly something's-up radar must have been wailing.

Carefully keeping my expression neutral, I once again forced myself not to look toward the hidden phone. I couldn't answer the question without giving away my secret, which I wasn't willing to do. Not wanting to outright lie, I shrugged.

West stood, a clear signal the conversation was done. "You two didn't know Carly," she said, looking at Aidan and me. Her tone was dismissive. "Don't presume to understand her motives."

And you do? I wanted to fire back. If the council's file on Carly was any indication, *no one* knew or understood her—no one still alive anyway.

"I'm sure if Carly tries to contact Sophie, she'll let us know." Mike looked at me. "Right?"

"Of course."

Michelle exchanged a concerned look with Mike. I hoped my comments defending Carly in a roundabout way hadn't worried her. I didn't have misplaced devotion—it was logic. Also, I didn't want guardians wasting time investigating dead ends. Carly wasn't a dead end, but not in the way they thought. She had contacts and resources the council didn't. Or God, at least I hoped she did.

My mind was already scheming to find a way to be alone so I could contact her again. Carly had once been an elemental criminal mastermind. Sure, she'd been out of the elemental public eye for the last fifteen years, but guardians who were supposedly on top of all the latest intel had come up empty. Carly had managed to track me down, so she still had some skills.

I glanced at Aidan, my instinct telling me to seek out his help, but his closed-off expression kicked my instinct to the curb. He'd already made it perfectly clear he wanted nothing to do with me. Michelle's mama-bear tendency wouldn't let me contact Carly, and Mike would side with his wife.

I was on my own. And it was time to confront my mommy issues head-on.

Chapter 2

AFTER WEST LEFT, Michelle started straightening manically. Our adjoined space was a mess because keeping hotel rooms clean was not high on the priority list, but something about the councilwoman's visit lit a fire under Michelle. Perhaps my "defense"—and I was using that term lightly—of Carly had snapped her out of desolation. Perhaps it had made her remember she still had one foster daughter left.

"While I'm in the shower, could you gather up all the dirty clothes and put them in here?" She tossed me a pillowcase she'd stripped off the bed. "There's a small laundromat in the hotel next door."

"No problem." I fumbled around with the clothes sitting on top of my bag until she'd disappeared into the bathroom. I unearthed the phone and tucked it in my pocket. Then I stuffed every piece of clothing I wasn't wearing in the bag. My hand stopped mid-reach for Lena's pajamas. Shaking, it hovered over the pink fabric, and tears gathered in my eyes.

The energy inside me became erratic, as if it were as disturbed by Lena's absence as I was. That wasn't possible—my power wasn't a sentient being—but I had no better description.

It consumed me from the inside, and if I didn't do something about the pressure, I would explode.

I grabbed Lena's clothes and stuffed them in the bag. Then I turned toward the bed and flexed my fingers. A gust of wind flew forth, and the covers slammed against the headboard. On the nightstand, the lampshade rattled, so I focused the air more toward the center of the bed. A small tan circle appeared in the center of the wooden headboard that was nailed to the wall. Only when it grew bigger did I realize what it was—the air was sandblasting the finish off the wood.

Shit.

Lowering my hands, I peered across the room at the damage. *Damn, damn, damn.* All I'd wanted to do was expend some energy in a harmless and inconspicuous way. The mark was definitely noticeable, but at least its cause wouldn't be obvious. I hoped we wouldn't be charged for the damage when we checked out. The shame of it was I only felt marginally better.

Hearing the water turn off in the bathroom, I mindlessly stuffed the rest of Lena's clothes in the bag.

Michelle emerged from her shower. "Do you want to come with me?"

I hesitated. Normally, I would help her, but fate was handing me the perfect opportunity to make my secret phone call. It had to be a sign.

Noticing my hesitation, Michelle put her hand on my forearm and squeezed. "It's okay if you don't want to sit in the laundromat for two hours. Mike can go with me."

I paused and spoke slowly. "Are you sure? I—"

I started to say *I'll go*, but I couldn't. I hated thinking I was letting Michelle down, but nothing was more important than finding Lena.

"Stay," she said. "Watch some TV or something. Veg out. I know this is stressful for you too."

Guilt squeezed my heart. She was putting on a brave face for my benefit, and I was using it to deceive her.

"Okay," I croaked.

"But don't go anywhere by yourself," Michelle warned as she opened the adjoining door. "I'm going to lock this from our side. You do the same. And keep the safety bar on the outside door. I would say don't open the door for anyone, not even room service, but this hotel isn't nice enough for that." She gave me a wry smile.

"Don't worry," I said. "I'm just going to lie down for a while."

As soon as she left, I stared at the phone, second-guessing myself. I'd learned about Cruel Carly when I moved in with Mike and Michelle at age ten. Everything I'd ever heard about her told me I should crush the phone and throw it in the nearest dumpster. But I'd already spoken to her once, and nothing bad had happened. Besides, these were extenuating circumstances.

Still, doubt cloaked my thoughts. Maybe grief was clouding my judgment, pushing me toward impulsive actions that were too far on the wrong side of a calculated risk.

It *was* terribly coincidental that Carly had shown up at the same time the girls were taken. I hated to give consideration to West's accusation, but I would have been a fool to ignore it. If Carly was involved, though, that was all the more reason to contact her—she could be a direct line to Lena.

Without any further fanfare, I powered on the phone and immediately noticed the battery was low. *Dang it.* For better or worse, that would force me to keep the conversation short.

With shaking fingers, I pressed on the preprogrammed number. It rang four times before a robotic voice told me to leave a message. *Damn.*

I put the phone on the nightstand and stared at it. Perhaps fate wasn't trying to tell me something after all. But I would be hard-pressed to get another perfect opportunity, so I decided to wait ten minutes and try again. In the meantime, I connected the phone to my charger. At least that problem was solved.

A knock on the door had me nearly jumping out of my skin. Jeez... if my hands weren't shaking before, they sure as hell were now. I crept over to the door and peered through the peephole. Aidan stood in the hall, looking as if he would rather be anywhere but there.

A week ago, the sight of Aidan on the other side of my hotel room door would have thrilled me, but now I could practically feel his discomfort penetrating the door. It hurt.

"Sophie, I can hear you," Aidan said. "Let me in."

I slowly backed away from the peephole. "I don't think that's a good idea." Yet I wanted to be in his presence, even though he'd made it clear he didn't want to be in mine. It was so messed up. Even after that, I would still rather have him around than not. But my potential hurt feelings weren't important at the moment. I needed to keep my wits about me if I was going to try calling Carly again in another eight minutes.

"Sophie," Aidan said again. "I want to talk to you. Please don't make me do it through the door."

He would too. *Damn.* He knew Mike and Michelle were gone, and while he might not have cared about everyone else at the hotel hearing our business, I didn't want that.

I opened the door a crack. "What do you want?"

His guarded expression cracked a little. "Are you going to let me in?"

Sighing, I closed the door so I could undo the safety bar. Then I opened it and retreated farther into the room to sit on the edge of the bed. He locked the door behind him and leaned against it, tucking his hands in his pockets. I didn't know why he had made such a big deal about me letting him in if he was going to stay as far away from me as possible.

Guess he's doing himself a favor and keeping his distance. Hurt filled my chest again. I grabbed a pillow and hugged it, using it like a shield. "What do you want?"

"I'm sorry." He looked miserable, and part of me felt a tinge of satisfaction. "I haven't handled things well. I never wanted to hurt you."

"But you did." Maybe my bluntness was heartless because Lena's disappearance had hurt him too, but I was done skirting around the truth with him.

"I'm sorry," he repeated. "But what I said was true. I can't protect you and be with you."

I closed my eyes and immediately remembered kissing him, the feel of his body pressed against mine, being wrapped in his arms. It was cruel that I'd been cut off so soon after experiencing him for the first time.

And despite everything else going on around me, despite his rejection, I still wanted him.

"I don't agree."

"It doesn't matter. I'm not willing to take the risk."

"Soon, I'll be eighteen, and soon after that, I'll be a guardian myself." Even as I said it, I wasn't certain it was true anymore. "I don't need you to protect me."

His expression shifted, and for a brief moment, a flicker of hope shone in his eyes before it was replaced with hardness. "You were already taken by witch hunters once."

I cringed at his harsh reminder of my failing. "That was before. I was naive and stupid, but I'm not now." *Says the girl who called Cruel Carly on her own.*

"Now that everyone knows what you're capable of, you're not safe. If rogues took Lena and those girls, they'll be after you next."

I narrowed my eyes at him. "I'd like to see them try."

While being strong put a target on my back, it was also the reason anyone would be stupid to try to take me. I'd used my powers to defend myself once, and I wasn't afraid to do it again. Life—my life, Lena's life, *anyone's* life—was more important than keeping elementals a secret. If I was going to be hunted because of my abilities, then I was sure as hell willing to use them to defend myself.

Considering their use set a spark to them and they burned hot before settling back into a low, uncomfortable simmer. I desperately needed to get control over them, but it wasn't as if I could ask Michelle to work with me when she was so grief-stricken. I tried my best to ignore the buzz beneath my skin.

Aidan started pacing and cracking his knuckles one at a time. "Your powers are useless if you're drugged."

I scowled. He was right. I'd made a stupid mistake before because I hadn't taken my safety seriously. I would have liked to say that something like that could never happen to me again, but I didn't have eyes in the back of my head. What was to stop someone from sticking me with a needle while in the middle of a crowd?

Aidan. That was what.

I hated that he had a point. But that didn't mean his entire argument was valid.

"Do you think the girls were drugged?" I asked. There was no evidence of it, but that didn't mean anything except their kidnappers were more effective than mine had been. Other than the ATV tracks, they'd left nothing behind.

Our eyes met, each of us pondering the grimness of the situation. I didn't know which was worse—a girl using her powers to inflict harm or having the option taken away by drugs.

"I honestly don't know. But even if they weren't, can you see Lena using her powers against someone?"

He had another good point. Lena hated using her powers and would be loath to use them against another person, even in self-defense. But she wasn't the only one taken. For all their sakes, I hoped they were still together.

"She might if one of the other girls was in danger," I mused. "I don't know the other girls, but they're all powerful, right? Maybe one of them would be more likely to use them."

Out of the six, odds were that one would be more like me—not sweet like Lena—and be ruthless.

I still hadn't recovered from killing Phyllis, one of my kidnappers. I coped by not thinking about it, but every once in a while, the memory would sneak up on me, like when I smelled burned popcorn. It was a cold, stark, entirely unpleasant slap in the face.

My stance on using my powers to defend myself was controversial among elementals. Many believed we should never use our gifts to cause harm, no matter the cost. But what trumped everything—always—was not being discovered. I couldn't bring myself to agree, but I would never wish my experience on anyone.

"Anyway..." Aidan blew out a breath as he took a step backward. "I'll leave you alone now. I just wanted to apologize."

So we were back to that. After everything I'd been through recently, I didn't have it in me to put up with his bullshit.

"I don't accept."

His jaw fell open. "That's not how it works."

I shrugged. "Since when do I play by the rules? Although I'm pretty sure that's not actually a rule."

A ghost of a smile graced his lips before fading. "This isn't a game, Sophie."

The blasé attitude I was faking dissipated. "Don't you think I know that? Lena—*my sister*—is gone."

His expression remained neutral, and I would have thought him unaffected if not for the thickness in his voice. "I don't want to lose you too."

I wanted to wrap my arms around him, to comfort him and feel loved in return, but I stayed where I was. "You're not going to lose me."

Except he had in a way—he had tossed away what I'd offered him. He didn't realize that by shoring up on his efforts to not lose me, he'd already lost a big part of me.

But it wasn't too late to get it back. To get *us* back.

"Yeah." He paused and ran his hands over his hair, making it stick up at odd angles. "I'll—"

The ring of the phone sitting on the nightstand cut off whatever he was going to say. My eyes widened as I looked at it. *Shit.* I'd forgotten to turn it off while it charged.

Only one person had that number.

"Are you going to answer that?" Aidan gestured to the phone. "Wait, whose phone is that? You didn't get a new one, did you?"

"Not exactly," I muttered.

Mercifully, the phone stopped ringing. I stared at Aidan, unable to keep the guilty look off my face. The phone started ringing again, and he narrowed his eyes at me.

I snatched the phone with the intent of silencing it.

"Answer it," Aidan said. "It must be important."

Shit, shit, shit.

"Not until you promise to trust me," I said quickly. "And not to freak out."

Saying nothing, Aidan crossed his arms.

I should have ignored the call and tried to get in touch with Carly later, but since Aidan already knew something was up, I wouldn't have been able to keep the secret much longer anyway.

Making a split-second decision and hoping I wasn't royally screwing up, I hit the button to accept the call. "Hello?"

"Sophie." Carly sounded relieved, but I couldn't help but notice how weird my name sounded coming from her. It was as if it didn't flow or something.

I'd had a script prepared—I was going to ask her if she still had contacts from her old life and if she would be willing to reach out to them. But with Aidan there, my brain was frazzled, and I couldn't form the questions.

"Sophie?" Again, my name sounded strange, almost as if she didn't like saying it. "Are you still there?"

"Yeah, sorry." I took a deep breath and turned my back to Aidan, though I could feel his gaze boring a hole in the back of my head. "Are you still in contact with any other elementals? Rogues?"

I cringed after saying that last word. I wondered if they called themselves that or if it was a derogatory term EA elementals had come up with.

There was a long pause, and for a moment, I wondered if she'd hung up.

"I'm sorry about Lena." Her condolences were a punch to the stomach.

"What do you know about it?" I practically spat the words. Maybe Councilwoman West was right. Maybe Carly was involved. How else would she know?

She sighed. "Nothing. Just that she and five other girls were taken."

"Who told you?"

"That's not important."

"It might be."

"Trust me. It's not."

"Trust you? Really?" I couldn't keep the venom out of my tone, an unwise move if I wanted her to help me. But she was the last person I should trust. *What am I doing?*

Carly paused again. "I don't want to cause trouble for the person who told me, but they weren't involved."

"Who was involved?"

"I don't know."

"Then I'm wasting my time here." *This was a mistake.*

"Wait! Don't hang up. Meet me. Just once. That's all I ask."

All she asks? Somehow, I doubted it would end there. But I was curious about her motives.

"I don't—"

"I can meet you anywhere. I'm only an hour away."

"How do you know where I am?"

"I know you're near Orlando. The council isn't as good at keeping secrets as they think they are."

That was news to me. They'd managed to keep all kinds of secrets from me. Yet the fact that they were inept wasn't surprising.

An emphatic "no" was ready to roll off my tongue, but something made me stop. She was dangling a carrot in front of me that was hard to refuse. If I never met my mother face-to-face, I would always wonder about...*everything*.

My gaze landed on Lena's calculus textbook that was still sitting on the desk where she'd left it. The sight of it snapped me back to reality. I'd come to realize the reunion with my mother was inevitable—I wouldn't be able to resist the temptation forever. But it was not the right time.

"No."

"I might be able to help you," she said quickly. "I can help you find information about the kidnapping."

Aidan's presence was a weight behind me. He circled around so that I was forced to stare right at him. His expression held carefully contained fury.

I swallowed. He was pissed. And he would be even more pissed when I requested his help. But I couldn't do this without him. Though it was a long shot, if meeting Carly might lead to Lena, it was a shot worth taking.

I returned my attention back to the phone call. "I'll text you a time and place."

Chapter 3

"WHAT IN THE ever-loving hell?" Aidan growled as soon as I took the phone away from my ear.

Shit. I'd expected his reaction, but that didn't make it more pleasant.

"It's not what you think." *Lame, lame, lame.*

"Oh, I think it's exactly what I think." Glaring at me, he crossed his arms. "Tell me that wasn't Carly."

"I can't." Though he was angrier than I'd ever seen him, I was relieved not to have to lie to him. I hadn't realized how much the secret was weighing on me. Sure, I'd hidden things from my family before, like when I'd snuck out of the house to go to a party, but never anything important.

Rubbing his hands over his hair, Aidan spun away from me. "What the hell, Sophie?"

"I'll do whatever it takes to get Lena back, even consorting with the devil." Okay, that was a little dramatic, but it was true. "You can't tell anyone."

"You can't be serious."

I closed the distance between us and put my hand on his arm. "Promise me."

He looked down at my hand for a moment before returning his gaze to mine. My hand burned on his skin, but I didn't remove it.

"Didn't you just promise to tell Michelle and my mother if Carly contacted you?"

I shrugged. "Technically, I contacted her first. She just returned my call."

Snorting, he stepped back, and my hand fell off his arm. "You realize Carly is number one on the council's suspect list."

"On the *council's* list, but not yours," I said slowly, honing in on his semantics. "Or any other guardian for that matter."

He paused as he debated what to say. "I can't speak for others, but no, I don't think she's behind it. Like you said, why would she show herself right before doing something like this when she'd managed to stay off the radar for fifteen years? But there's still no way I'm okay with this."

His hard *no* had a small crack, giving me the opening I needed. All I had to do was drive a wedge in it and keep pressing. Surely Aidan would see the value in my reasoning if he would only give it a chance.

"Hear me out."

He sat on the edge of the bed. "Talk fast."

Despite his command, I took a second to gather my thoughts. "Do the guardians have any leads?"

"No." With that one word, his shoulders hunched over. "I don't understand it. They're no closer to finding them than they were four days ago."

"That's exactly my point. The council put the best guardians on this, and they have nothing. *Nothing.* The more time passes, the more likely..." I couldn't bring myself to say it because it wasn't a possibility. Hope of finding Lena was the only thing keeping me from breaking down into a sobbing basket case.

"I know," Aidan agreed quietly.

"The council is so damn by the book. We need to think outside the lines and use all our resources."

"I wouldn't call Carly a resource."

"I would. You once said yourself that rogues are still out there. Carly has got to know some of them. Or at least she used to. She's our in. Heck, the guardians probably don't even know these people exist."

"You have a point, but we can't trust Carly."

I made a face. "I don't. How could you think I do?"

He put his hands out, palms up. "I don't know. Maybe because you've been having secret phone calls with her on a secret phone that you told nobody about. How did you get it anyway?" When he put it that way, I definitely sounded guilty.

"She mailed it to me," I explained. "It was in the batch of mail Michelle took out of the mailbox on the way out."

"You've had the phone for a week, and you didn't say anything?" Outrage pitched his voice up.

"I didn't open the package until after we'd been here a few days." Though truthful, it was a weak excuse.

"You could have told me."

I contemplated his tone, trying to determine if my actions had hurt him. With the way he'd been avoiding me, I wasn't sure what he expected? His behavior hadn't welcomed my confidence. But *BLWT*, I had no excuse for keeping it from him.

"I would have," I said, wondering if my words were true. "Eventually. But you would have insisted I turn it over to the council."

"Because it's the right thing to do."

"The *right* thing isn't necessarily the *best* thing in every situation." I clenched and unclenched my fists. Our conversation was going in circles. "I want to meet with Carly to see if she can help us. That's all. But I don't want to be stupid about it either."

"So you want my help." He cocked his head and gave me a scrutinizing stare. "If I hadn't been here when she called, would you have tried to do this without me?"

"I don't know, but probably." I hoped honesty was the best policy. "I'll do anything to get Lena back."

"Damn it, Sophie, don't you think I would too?" He stood and took a step toward me before stopping himself. He stared down at his feet. "But I don't want to lose you in the process." His strained tone tore at my heart, but even though I wanted to, I couldn't reach him. He'd shut me out.

"Then help me."

Aidan put his hands over his face and groaned then let out a curse.

He was in.

I SHAMELESSLY EAVESDROPPED as Aidan pleaded my case to my foster parents—something about an outing being good for my emotional health. *So clinical.* I nearly snorted and gave myself away. I knew what would be good for my emotional health—getting Lena back. So I guessed this qualified in a roundabout way.

Aidan was a smooth liar, better than I'd expected given his penchant for truth and justice and all that. Then again, he was a guardian, and the council was all about keeping secrets, which most likely required lying from time to time. It made me wonder how many times he'd lied to me over the years without me being the wiser.

Best not to think about that.

I was grateful Aidan was able to get me out from under Michelle's watchful eye. It sure beat climbing out the window, which I'd been known to do. Mike handed Aidan the keys of the rental car, even though Aidan wasn't supposed to drive it at age nineteen. We set off immediately, and I scrambled to come up with a plan. I wished I'd had more time to think, but time wasn't on our side. I also didn't want to give Aidan a chance to change his mind.

I strapped myself into the passenger's seat of the Nissan Altima. It felt weird to ride with Aidan in a vehicle other than his Explorer.

"Where should we meet?" I asked. It would have been easier to figure that out back home, where we knew the lay of the land. I'd never spent any time in Orlando, and Aidan hadn't been there since he was nine, which was no help.

"Somewhere public and busy."

Disney World immediately came to mind. But park tickets were expensive, and I wouldn't want a meeting with Carly to ruin my first experience at the happiest place on Earth, so I settled on Disney Springs. After pulling up a map of the shopping plaza, I randomly picked The LEGO Store for our meeting place.

I told Aidan the plan as I texted Carly. She immediately texted back: *I'll be there.*

As I stared at the text, my palms grew slick. Reality sank in—the meeting was really happening. In theory, I was gung ho about meeting Carly face-to-face, but now that it was no longer an abstract idea, my bravado faltered.

Aidan pulled to a stop at a red light and used the break to set his GPS. He glanced over at me. "Are you okay?"

"Fine," I replied, but my voice came out squeaky. I cleared my throat. "Fine."

He wasn't convinced, but he didn't press the issue. "How do you want to handle this?"

The question caught me off guard. I'd expected him to try to run the show since he was the guardian. Plus, being in charge was his thing.

"What are your thoughts?" I was sure he had plenty, and I had none. Being en route to meet my evil mother was wreaking havoc on my thought processes.

"There's a few ways we can do this. I could hang back so she doesn't—"

I shook my head. "Carly isn't stupid. She must realize I'm not coming alone. Also, she already knows who you are. You can't keep me in sight without her seeing you. There's no point trying to hide."

"True," he said. "I'd prefer for both of us to talk to her. And I'll feel more comfortable keeping you in arm's reach."

An absurd and inappropriate thought about being in his arm's reach popped into my mind. *I'd like to be within his everything's reach.*

I mentally smacked myself in the head. *Get yourself together, Sophie.*

Maybe Aidan had been right about not being able to concentrate in one another's company. *Nonsense.* My mind was simply trying to distract me from what was currently bothering me—coming face-to-face with my supposed-to-be-dead devil of a mother.

"No. She'll be more willing to talk if you're not there."

"How do you know that?"

I gave Aidan the side-eye. I didn't know Carly, but I knew him. And he was definitely going to play the overbearing bodyguard. He wouldn't be able to stop himself.

"Just a hunch. I'm not saying you should leave me alone. Just sit a distance away to give us the illusion of privacy. She can know you're there."

"I'm meeting her."

"Aidan—"

"And then I'll step back. But she needs to know what's at stake if she messes with you."

His logic made no sense. He was levelheaded except when it came to me, and he was armed. I had no desire to find out how quickly the situation would escalate if he thought Carly intended me harm. For the second time in just the last minute, I worried that Aidan's reasons for brushing me aside were correct.

But our not being together did nothing to quench the tension and emotion between us. Though the hurt he'd inflicted lingered, my feelings for him remained strong. And if I could peer into his heart, I expected I would see a mirror image. He would simply have to learn to "keep his head on straight" as he'd so eloquently put it. Either that or find a way to erase his feelings for me.

I voted for keeping his head on straight.

We parked and headed toward The LEGO Store. Through the store windows, I could see children playing with the colored blocks. As we passed the door, we were nearly mowed down by an apologetic mother who was pulling her screaming kid out of the store. *Yikes.*

For a split second, I worried I'd made the wrong choice of location. Children surrounded us, and if the stuff hit the fan...

I shook off the unpleasant thought. My gut told me Carly wished me no harm. I couldn't guarantee she didn't have other nefarious intentions, but I was certain of my safety. She wouldn't do anything to jeopardize our meeting.

All business, Aidan scanned the area, reviewing the vicinity and dismissing those who weren't worth his notice. I'd seen him do that many times.

If our reason for being there were different, I might've asked him to give me the rundown on each individual. Aidan was amazing at assessing people.

He was pretty much amazing at everything. It used to irritate me because Aidan seemed so perfect. Now I realized he wasn't perfect in all ways—just the ones that mattered to me.

Hurt unexpectedly slapped at me, making me suck in a breath. He'd rejected me because he doubted his ability to protect me, but he was too stupid to see that his concern made him the best one for the job. He would give his life before letting anything happen to me. But he was too hardheaded to realize that.

I glanced at my phone. "We still have twenty minutes."

We found a bench and sat. My nerves grew with every minute that passed. The lack of conversation between Aidan and me didn't help. It wasn't an uncomfortable silence exactly, but it wasn't like it used to be.

"Thank you," I said, needing to say something. "I know you aren't wild about being here, but I appreciate it."

He didn't look at me as he spoke. "I'd much rather be here than have you try to do this alone."

It wasn't the "you're welcome" I was looking for, but I wasn't sure what I expected. If the council found out about this, Aidan would most likely lose his position as a guardian. I'd put him in a tough situation without a second thought about the consequences… or even a first thought. I had tunnel vision where Lena was concerned

Though there was space between us on the bench, when Aidan shifted, his knee touched mine. He quickly adjusted, putting more room between us, so he wouldn't accidentally touch me again.

Ouch. Watching other couples strolling hand in hand while they window-shopped filled me with jealousy. I wondered if I would ever get to enjoy something so simple.

No, because your life will never be simple, my inner voice taunted me. Being an elemental inherently complicated everything. But it didn't have to. The council made things needlessly difficult. Or perhaps I was simply naive and not ready to accept the truth.

I blew out a breath. Everything about the situation sucked—Aidan and I were at odds, Lena was missing, and my evil mother was due to arrive any minute.

Actually, at least one thing didn't suck—it was December, and the weather was beautiful, not too hot and not too cold. *Perfect.* Hopefully, I would be able to come back to Orlando someday when I could enjoy it.

My phone chimed with a text: *5 minutes.*

"She's almost here."

Aidan stood. "Good."

Reluctantly, I stood as well. My knees were jelly, but the rest of me vibrated in anticipation.

I spotted her right away. Swallowing, I met her gaze, and her gait slowed. Her hand went to her mouth as though she were choked up. I started to step forward but stopped myself. Letting her come to me made me feel as if I were the one in control, even if I wasn't positive it was true.

Her hair was no longer the red it had been at the movie theater. Heck, that could have been a wig for all I knew. Now it was toss-up between light brown and dark blond. I wondered if that was a purposeful choice so that anyone describing her would have a difficult time pinpointing her hair color. She wore jeans and flip-flops, just like every other tourist. She could blend into a crowd and disappear, no doubt the reason behind her nondescript look.

When she got within ten feet of us, my power buzzed beneath my skin as though it had been awoken. The lure of it was so enticing, I had to close my eyes for a moment as I swayed on my feet.

Aidan gripped my elbow. "Are you okay?"

I nodded. "Do you feel anything?" I whispered.

His mouth pressed into a firm line, and he shook his head. But this was crazy. Aidan was the one who could sense elemental power, not me. So I didn't understand why it felt as if my power were trying to burst through my skin like a magnet desperate to meet its mate.

Carly stopped two feet away from us and removed her sunglasses. The sight of her eyes was startling, not because they were spectacular or odd, but because it was like staring into my own. Hers were hazel while mine were brown, but the shape of them was the same.

I realized she was shorter than me, only a few inches, but somehow it seemed significant. Her height had probably been in the files I'd read, but if it was, I didn't remember. I assumed she would be taller than me because she was the parent, the adult. It was stupid because obviously I knew adults could be shorter than me—many of my teachers at school were—but meeting this woman made me feel like a child. Her smaller stature reminded me that I was no child, and as Aidan had said, this was no game.

"Sophie." She reached out her hand then abruptly pulled it back, realizing her faux pas.

I may have been ready to talk to her, but I didn't want her touching me, especially when my power was having such a strange reaction to being in her proximity.

"Carly," I said, and she cringed. But what did she expect? I sure as hell wasn't calling her "Mom." If I'd thought about it, I would have called her Ms. Levitt from the beginning just to be ornery.

She shifted her attention to Aidan. "You must be Aidan."

"I have nothing to say to you." He coolly assessed her, probably trying to determine if she was armed. Then he nodded to me. "I'll be watching." He waited for me to nod back before stepping away as we'd arranged.

Carly and I turned back toward one another, neither of us speaking. I think we both needed a moment to gain our bearings. I certainly did. As if meeting my supposed-to-be-dead evil mother wasn't jarring enough, I also had my misbehaving power to deal with. I'd never heard of anything like that happening, and I wondered if she felt it too, but there was no way I was asking.

"You're beautiful," she said softly.

That was the first thing she chose to say to me? My resolve softened at the compliment before hardening again. I wasn't looking for her approval.

It would be difficult to believe any explanations or apologies she made, but at the same time, I wanted to. I wanted her to use whatever magic words she could to exonerate her. Even though Michelle was my mom for all intents and purposes, my blood mother was standing in front of me. Was it too much to hope that it had all been a mistake and that maybe she wasn't evil after all?

Yes, it was. I couldn't let my errant hopes cloud my judgment. I wouldn't engage in any conversation that didn't involve getting Lena back.

I gestured to the path in front of me. "Let's walk." We started off, and Aidan kept pace a short distance behind.

The physical activity dispelled some of the awkwardness because it gave us something to do other than stare at one another. Still, I glanced at her out of the corner of my eye. It was surreal to be walking next to the living and breathing Cruel Carly... who also happened to be my mother.

But that wasn't why we were there. That might have been why *she* was there, but I had other priorities. I was having a hard time staying focused. *Damn it.* I was better than that. *Tighten up.*

"What do you know about the kidnapping?" I asked.

"Not a lot," she admitted. "But apparently, everyone has heard that six girls were taken from the testing site."

The council had made it clear we needed to keep the kidnapping hidden from regular people, but were they trying to hide it from other elementals? It would have been impossible. Too many people had been around when the girls went missing.

"Is that all?" If so, our meeting was a waste of time.

"Whoever did it has a lot of nerve."

I could've told her that. It was another reason I didn't think witch hunters were responsible. If all witch hunters were like the ones I encountered, then they were cowards. It had taken four of them to kidnap me. No way would they have been brave enough to risk facing hundreds of elementals.

"Do you know any rogue elementals with a lot of nerve?" I asked.

She didn't bat an eye. "A few come to mind."

"Really?" Her quick answer shocked me. I had begun to suspect she had nothing, that she would've claimed anything to get me to meet her. "Who?"

"I don't want to say."

I stopped. Maybe my suspicion was correct after all. "Then why the hell are we here?"

Carly's mouth thinned. She must have realized I was only there for information and not a tearful reunion. Hopefully, she understood that I would be out of there when she stopped being useful. "Some of these people have been kind to me in the last decade," she said. "I'm not going to return the favor by making them prime suspects."

Kind to her how? By keeping her existence a secret?

"But you said—"

She chuckled. "Honor among thieves, my dear."

My power rippled through my veins, reminding me it was there. It seemed as pissed as I was. Speaking of rogue elementals with a lot of nerve, I was walking right beside one. I could have double-crossed her and brought more than Aidan with me. If I had, she would have been in guardian custody at that moment. But she must have known that. Either she was confident in her abilities to evade capture, or she was confident in her assessment of me. She hadn't even asked me to keep the meeting secret. She'd known I would. I was beginning to think she knew more about me than I knew about her.

Screw her.

"I don't give a damn about your honor. I care about saving Lena and those girls. The youngest one is eleven. Did you know that?"

Her expression sobered. "No, I didn't. And I'm sorry for it. Of all people, I understand what it's like to have my daughter taken from me."

My stomach tightened, and sympathy reared its unwelcome head before I stuffed it away.

"Losing me was your fault," I snapped. "They wouldn't have taken me if you hadn't been doing all that evil stuff. It was for my own good. What happened to those girls isn't the same." I couldn't believe I'd just used the "it was for my own good" line Mike and Michelle had given me back when I learned the truth. But I couldn't help but wonder what my life would have been like if I'd stayed with Carly and she'd "lived." What kind of person would I have become?

It scared me. I already had intense urges and powers that were quickly becoming more than I could control. What if I'd had her influence my whole life?

She tilted her head. "What do you know about what I supposedly did?"

I rolled my eyes at her language. She could cut the crap. No one had framed her. She wasn't the victim.

"Enough. Anyway, that's not why we're here." That was true, and I also didn't have it in me to hear her talk about her exploits. When I'd tried reading a written account, I had closed the document, unable to face it. I hadn't wanted to know the gruesome details, and I still didn't.

She twirled her sunglasses in her hands. "Believe it or not, I want to help you, but it's not that simple."

"Yes, it is. Give me names. That would help."

She shook her head. "The minute word gets out that I turned over names to the council, I'm as good as dead. Besides that, if those people aren't the perpetrators, you would have lost valuable resources."

I tried to wrap my head around the fact that she was protecting people's identities because they'd been kind to her, yet she seemed certain they would kill her. Essentially, she was protecting herself. *So much for honor.*

"Resources? What do you mean?"

"I don't think any of the people I associate with are involved, but some of them probably have information that could help us find who is."

Help *us*? Hell no. She wasn't part of this.

"Tell me who they are, and I'll talk to them."

She narrowed her eyes at me, and I swore I saw disappointment in them. It stung for a moment before I reminded myself I didn't care what she thought. Besides, she couldn't seriously think I would want to work with her.

"They won't talk to you."

"I'll tell them I'm your..." I trailed off, not wanting to say the words aloud. "I'll explain who I am."

"They won't just take your word for it." She shook her head at my naiveté. "Besides, you don't want these people knowing who you are. Like I said, they've been kind to me, but your secret would not be safe. Word would get around. Fifteen years ago, my enemies used you to hurt me. They'll do it again."

"The EA—"

"Not the EA." She sounded exasperated. "There's more to the elemental world than the EA, despite what the council would have you believe."

Her irritation pissed me off. *Forgive me for not thinking like a criminal.* But what pissed me off even more was that she'd voiced the same concerns I had with the council. I didn't know what to think about the fact that we shared that opinion. I tucked it away to dissect later.

"Then what do you suggest? You said you want to help me. So do it."

"We'll question them together."

I stared at her incredulously. "You can't be serious."

She stepped forward, invading my personal space to grasp my hand. I yanked it away.

I looked over my shoulder, and sure enough, Aidan was ready to swoop in. I waved him off.

Carly's expression was filled with sadness. "I lost fifteen years with my daughter. There's no way I can get those years back, but I'd at least like to get to know you. You also must have a lot of questions."

Of course I did, but I wouldn't give her the satisfaction of admitting it. I glanced over my shoulder again at Aidan to make sure he was still far enough away that he couldn't clearly hear our conversation. "That's not going to happen," I hissed.

"I'm not a monster," she said.

"Bullshit."

"Now you're just spouting off the council's rhetoric. I know what they call me—Cruel Carly. Are you so indoctrinated that you can't think for yourself?"

Her barb hit the mark, and I had to stop myself from recoiling. "The facts speak for themselves."

She laughed. "Don't you know it's the victors who write the history books? I'm not claiming innocence, but there are two sides to every story. I'd like the opportunity to tell mine to my daughter."

My immediate inclination was to tell her not to refer to me as her daughter, but her words gave me pause. Like she said, there was no way she was innocent, but unlike the EA council, I believed right and wrong existed on a sliding scale. I also didn't agree with a lot of the council's policies and decisions, especially lately.

And it would be nice to learn my mother wasn't as evil as she had been made out to be.

I closed my eyes. I couldn't believe I was actually considering such a crazy scheme. Everything had fallen into place for our meeting, but there was no way I would be able to get away again so easily, *if* I even wanted to.

The longer I stayed with Carly, the more my power itched. It was excruciating, and I didn't understand why. There was no reason for me to call it into action. I shook and flapped my hands, as if my power was water that could fly off. My earlier use of power hadn't drained my strength at all.

God, I missed Lena. I wished she were there so I could talk to her about all this stuff. She was the only one who might understand. But she was the whole reason I was there. Because she was missing. A sob rose in my throat as an image of her bound, gagged, and scared floated through my mind. What had she been through in the last few days? What would she continue to endure until she was rescued? I'd purposefully tried not to think about it because the resulting grief and anguish wouldn't help find her.

Yet the woman in front of me might be able to. Suddenly weary, I opened my eyes. "Let's say I agree to meet you again. How many phone calls could we make in an hour?"

"No one will talk over the phone."

"What? Why not?" Were these people living off the grid or something? Who didn't talk on the phone these days? Granted, most people texted, but this wasn't the sort of thing we could hash out with the swiping of our thumbs.

"They haven't stayed alive and under the radar this long by being stupid. We have to talk to them in person."

My heart sank. "Where are they?"

"The closest contact I have is in Tennessee."

That was no good. I didn't know how far away that was from our current location, but there was no way I could go on a road trip with Carly. There were the logistics to consider like how to get away from Mike, Michelle, and Aidan. But more importantly, I couldn't do that to Michelle. She was barely holding it together as it was.

"There's got to be another way."

"There isn't."

"Coming here today was a huge leap of faith. You realize that, right? I don't trust you."

There was a calculating gleam in her eyes that was reminiscent of the criminal mastermind she must have been. I had to force myself not to shrink away.

"You don't have to trust me. I would think you were a fool if you did. The question is what weighs more—your mistrust of me or your desire to find those girls."

Chapter 4

As I watched Carly walk away, her words echoed in my mind, and I had my answer. Lena would come first. Always. No risk was too great if it meant getting her back.

Aidan walked over and stood beside me. "Are you okay?"

I hadn't been okay for a while except when I'd been with him. Now even that was ruined.

"I'm fine."

"Did she tell you anything useful?"

"Not really. She knows some people we should talk to."

"Who? I'll text Vic and Suze."

I shook my head. "She wouldn't give me their names. She said they wouldn't talk to us anyway. But she could probably get something out of them."

He put his hands on his hips. "So is she going to talk to them?"

Usually, I was the one teasing information out of Aidan. Under different circumstances, our role reversal would amuse me.

"She wants me to go with her."

Aidan cursed. "No. That's not happening."

I walked over to the railing and leaned my elbows on it. A ferry carrying tourists glided along the water of Lake Buena Vista. I moved my hand in a wave motion, and soft ripples slapped against the side of the ferry. Before when I'd wanted to use my powers, I would have to give them time to build. Now they were ready all the time. I could create a tsunami in this lake before Aidan had a chance to snap his fingers.

My little trick was barely noticeable, but it was still stupid to do out in the open in the middle of a crowd. Perhaps a small part of me wanted to get caught. Maybe life would be easier if elementals weren't in hiding.

Aidan leaned on the rail next to me. "You're considering it." His statement was somehow both neutral and accusatory at the same time.

"What would you do?"

Looking away from me, he exhaled. "I don't want to tell you what I'd do."

That was because we both knew he would go to any lengths for Lena and me. Admitting he would go with Carly would give me implicit permission to do the same. I appreciated that while he didn't want me consorting with Carly, he was honest about the fact that he would if our situations were reversed.

"If I don't take this opportunity and something happens to Lena..." My voice grew thick. "I couldn't live with myself."

"I understand that, but what would Lena want you to do?"

I hung my head. Lena wouldn't want me to take any risks, no matter how calculated. But I wouldn't be risking my life—Carly wouldn't hurt me. Working with her would have other ramifications, though. It would hurt Mike and Michelle, which made me sick to my stomach. I could kiss being a guardian goodbye. Heck, the council might even kick me out of the EA for all I knew. But none of those things bothered me as much as never seeing Lena again.

"I wish I knew who her contacts were."

"If we did, then you wouldn't be in this position." Aidan was being extraordinarily calm and reasonable about the whole thing. Seeing Carly in person and observing her interact with me must have calmed some of his fears.

"We're closing in on a week, Aidan. Those girls could be anywhere."

His fist lightly bounced on the railing as he looked out over the water. "I know."

"But what if Carly's lying? What if she's just trying to manipulate me?" That thought set my power abuzz, sending so much activity through my veins, it made my arms itch. I raked my nails around my forearms, trying to ease the unpleasant sensation.

"That's what I'm worried about. She's stayed hidden for fifteen years. How many contacts could she possibly have?"

"I don't know. But maybe there's an entire elemental community that the council isn't aware of. Or maybe they're not telling us about it."

"Maybe." Aidan looked pointedly at my arms. "What are you doing?"

I stopped scratching and looked at my arms. I'd dug so deep with my nails, I'd drawn blood in one place. *Damn.*

"My power. Ever since the fire, it's been... *itchy.*"

Aidan frowned.

"It's fine," I said quickly, tucking my arms out of sight behind me. "Do you want to eat? I saw a taco stand back there."

"Sure." Aidan pulled out his phone and tapped on it. "Let me call Vic. He just texted."

I stood by impatiently while Aidan placed the call. His side of the conversation mostly consisted of "uh-huh" and "really," so I couldn't tell what it was about. But his expression stayed neutral, so I figured the news wasn't super great or utterly horrible.

"Well?" I pounced as soon as he ended the call. "What did he say?"

"They found the group responsible for kidnapping you."

"What?" I hadn't realized they were actively searching. It didn't seem like that should be a high priority right now.

He tucked his phone into his pocket. "They don't have the girls."

"Were they expecting to find them there?"

"No, but they have no other leads. Now at least they can cross them off the list."

"What happens now with that group?"

"Nothing," Aidan said.

"What do you mean *nothing*?" Now that they'd been caught, it angered me they wouldn't be punished. The individuals left in the group might not have participated in my kidnapping, but they were responsible for brainwashing the ones who had. What was to stop them from trying something like that again?

"Think about it, Sophie. What can the guardians do? They're not cops. But now that we're aware, we can keep an eye on them."

That was just another reason secrecy was stupid. If elementals were out in the open, then my kidnapping would have been reported, and those twisted people would have been punished for what they did. They perpetuated hate crimes against elementals, and there wasn't a damn thing we could do about it without becoming criminals ourselves.

I tried to think through my red haze of rage. "How did they find them?"

"They followed the missing persons' reports. Phyllis's sister reported her."

I cringed. Phyllis was missing because I'd killed her in self-defense.

"Anyway," Aidan continued, "they found the group she was involved in. It's small, only about twenty people. But they're passing themselves off as some kind of church or something like that. I didn't get all the details."

"Did they find out who killed the two men?"

Four people had been involved in my kidnapping. Phyllis was one, and another had been shot. The last two were killed when a tree fell on the car the guardians were using to transport them. To say the circumstances were suspicious was an understatement.

"No, I don't think so. Hey, stop it." Aidan grabbed my hands and pulled them off my arms. I looked down to find several deep gouges in my forearms. I hadn't even realized I'd started scratching again.

"Are you sure you're okay?" he asked.

"Yeah, I'm fine," I said. "But maybe I should buy a long-sleeve shirt. I don't want Michelle to freak out."

"Or just stop mauling yourself," Aidan muttered.

I pursed my lips but didn't comment.

We scarfed down some tacos, even though I didn't have much of an appetite. Aidan eyed me the whole time, but even though my skin itched like crazy, I kept my urge to scratch under control. I wondered if I should ask him to take me to a pharmacy to get an antihistamine. Somehow, I didn't think it would help.

We returned to the car and headed home… or back to the hotel anyway. According to Councilwoman West, we wouldn't be going home anytime soon.

I stared out the window during the drive. This situation was so messed up. I wasn't a big believer in divinity, despite my claim that fate had given me the opportunity to call Carly earlier. Praying to a higher power was bullshit. If I wanted something, then I needed to get off my ass and make it happen.

Yet I found myself wishing for a sign to tell me what to do. Should I trust Carly enough to go on a wild-goose chase with her? Would Aidan allow that to happen? I wasn't totally buying his nonchalance. Maybe he was only being calm because he didn't think I would go through with it. And maybe he was right.

I didn't know what danger I would be risking. The only certainty was the trouble I would be in once I returned home. *If* I returned home. Maybe that was Carly's goal—to abduct the daughter that was taken from her. I wasn't a helpless two-year-old anymore, but I had no idea what lengths she was willing to go to to keep me imprisoned. *If* that was her goal.

Or maybe she was being honest. Maybe she did want to get to know me. But where would it end? I doubted she would be content letting me get back to my regularly scheduled life once we spent some time together. But what could she think would possibly happen?

All of those concerns were about after. I needed to focus on during. Would she help me with urgency or take her sweet time so I would be forced to stick around longer? I wished I knew what kind of information she thought we could get from her contacts.

I shifted in my seat. The ride back was taking way longer than the ride out there. We should have been there already. Though I'd been staring out the window, I hadn't focused on the scenery, but now I peered at it. The electronic compass on the dash said we were going west. I wasn't the best with directions, but that didn't seem right.

"Where are we going?" I asked.

"You'll see."

I grumpily crossed my arms. I wasn't in the mood for surprises, but Aidan wasn't likely to spill no matter how much I pestered him.

When I began to recognize landmarks, I shook my head. "No," I said firmly. "Why are you taking me there?" We were nearly to the orchard that was the testing site, the last place I'd seen Lena.

"Relax. No one is out here, and I thought using your powers for a while would be good for you."

I wanted to protest, but the scratches on my arms were evidence that he was correct. I just wished we could go somewhere else. Unfortunately, our options were limited.

When he pulled into the driveway, it looked the same as it had *BLWT*. Only the sight of the neatly organized trees didn't interest me anymore.

We parked in front of the house and got out. Though the abandoned orchard was still undeniably beautiful, darkness loomed over it.

My power seemed to realize why we were there and circulated within me with an intensity that made me dizzy and a little nauseated. I took a step and stumbled.

Aidan caught my elbow, preventing me from crashing to my knees. "Careful." He didn't say anything else and didn't question me further about what was going on or ask if I was okay. Clearly, I wasn't. He wouldn't have brought me there otherwise. I took a few deep breaths to steady myself.

The above-ground pool was sitting in the side yard where Aidan and Vic had constructed it. Not wanting to spend more time there than necessary, I marched over to it. I bent the water to my will, and it swirled faster and faster until there was a dip in the middle of the liquid cyclone and the sides reared up like a Nascar racetrack.

Abruptly, I spun and focused on the closest tree. I pulled air down from the sky, forcing it into the branches. There was a creaking then a loud crack as the tree trunk split down the middle and the two halves crashed to the ground.

Focusing on the ground near another tree, I reached out toward the roots and called on the dirt to expel them. Seconds later, the roots stuck out of the ground like skeleton hands clawing their way out of the grave.

I turned back to the pool. The water was still spinning. I yanked it outward toward the sides of the pool so forcefully that the side panels flew off and the water rushed out onto the ground.

Panting, I stared at it, only coming down from my high when I felt the water soak my toes.

What have I done? We'd only been there a few minutes, yet I'd managed to cause all that destruction. Why was destruction my first inclination? I didn't like it.

My body shook, and my hands twitched with residual power. There was still so much left. But I didn't want to do any more. I'd done enough.

Michelle had warned me about my power controlling me if I didn't learn to harness it. How close was I to the tipping point?

My eyes met Aidan's, and my chin quivered. He opened his arms, and I walked into them as the first tear fell.

THAT NIGHT, MIKE must have convinced Michelle to take another sleeping pill because, while I tossed and turned, she was out cold. My body was exhausted, but my mind refused to rest. The red numbers on the digital clock taunted me. Every minute that ticked by was another minute wasted, another minute the girls had to suffer at the hands of their kidnappers.

I flung off the covers then guiltily looked over at Michelle, hoping the noise hadn't bothered her. She didn't stir. In the dark, I felt around for my laptop and opened it, angling the screen so the light wouldn't shine on my foster mother. I wriggled my fingers and toes as I waited for it to finish booting up. Relief washed over me as I realized my power was at a reasonable level. Though "reasonable" was relative—it was running through me at a faster rate than it had a month ago. Still, I was grateful for the respite. With any luck, it would last a few more hours. I didn't know when I would be able to release it again. Aidan couldn't take me to the orchard every day, and even if he could, I wouldn't want to do any more damage that would provoke questions.

My growing powers were definitely a concern. I wasn't denying that. But I didn't want to burden anyone with my problems when their focus should be elsewhere. Once Lena was safe, I would deal with everything.

When the computer was finally up and running, I opened a browser to search for Holy Mission United Church. My fingers slapped at the letters. The name of the group responsible for my kidnapping irked me. It was their holy mission to kill innocent teenage girls whose only crime was to have been born different than the average person? *Righteous assholes.*

The website was rudimentary and amateur. The home page consisted of a stock photo of a sunset and their mission statement: *We aim to spread holiness and rid the world of impurity.*

Impurity... I supposed that referred to me. Gritting my teeth, I clicked on the next page. I found nothing of note, just the schedule and location for their services. A quick search revealed their "church" was actually a storefront in a run-down shopping plaza in South Carolina. Aidan had told me the group was small, and that confirmed it. It also led me to believe they didn't have a lot of funds, which made me wonder how the hell they had found me in Virginia.

The next and final page showed pictures of all the church had to offer. The pictures were strategically set up to make the congregation seem bigger than it was, but it didn't escape my notice that the same dozen people were in all of the pictures. Suit man—I never had learned his name—and Phyllis were in several of them. I didn't see the other two men. No individuals were identified by name, not even the minister or leader or whatever he called himself.

I spent way too long looking at those pictures, especially the one of Phyllis with two other women. They had their arms around one another, and they looked so normal. *Phyllis* looked normal, not like the deranged and manic woman I'd killed.

Thinking back to that terrible night, I wondered if I could have done things differently. I'd used the bonfire they'd prepared to burn me alive to light Phyllis aflame, not once but twice. Scared and panicked, I would have done anything to survive, and I had—I'd killed.

I closed the page so I wouldn't be tempted to look again. There was no information there anyway. I didn't know what I'd expected. It wasn't as if I were going to find an explanation for why they felt such hatred toward me. It was a chicken or the egg scenario. Did individuals join the church because they were already disgusted by the "impure"? Or did the members lure people in and slowly brainwash them into their way of thinking?

Next, I pulled up the documents about Carly. If I was seriously considering taking her up on her offer, then I needed to know exactly what I was getting myself into. I started with her last known activity because I figured it would provide the clearest picture of who she'd been before she "died." The account of her "death," which I'd already read, didn't tell me anything new—guardians had cornered her in a building and lit it on fire with the hopes of flushing her out. Instead, they'd found a woman's body they had assumed was hers.

Now I wondered who that woman actually was and if the council was wondering that too. Did they realize that Carly's reappearance meant they'd incorrectly identified a dead woman? Her family must be wondering what happened to her. Was she an elemental? Did Carly know who she was? Had she known the woman was there when she'd escaped? Was she dead or alive at that point? Had Carly killed her? There were so many questions I didn't have answers for.

I scrolled to another section of the report, and something dawned on me. Carly's child—*me*—was never mentioned anywhere. Mentions of me could have been removed after the fact, maybe to protect my identity. Or maybe the council had another reason for wiping my existence from the record. Was it possible that whoever had written the reports hadn't even known about me? Patricia West and David Stearns were the only two council members who knew about me. Obviously, the guardians who'd taken me also knew. But since there was no mention of me, there was also no notation of who had abducted me. *Damn.* It seemed important, but West and Stearns probably wouldn't tell me, and there was no way to ask around without outing myself.

I should have been grateful no one knew who I was. It had allowed me to grow up out of the shadow of my mother. The best I could tell, the secret was still mostly under wraps. But I didn't know how long that would last. Once it got out, would my fellow elementals shun me? Other than my immediate family, I wasn't close with any of them. West had orchestrated that when she'd placed me with Lloyd and Belinda, who weren't involved with the EA. Then she'd chosen to place me with her son and the niece of the only other council member who knew about me. I wondered if she had a reason for that other than wanting to keep tabs on me. Again, the only one who had the answers was West, but I doubted she would answer my questions even if I mustered the nerve to ask.

The documents discussed the experiments Carly and her followers had been conducting, but it seemed as though most of the information had been pieced together using notes that were found in the lab. None of the scientists or anyone else in charge was ever questioned. The lead scientist had been killed, but there were other ones. They were referred to in the reports by single initials—*R* did this and *G*

found that. Maybe the council hadn't even figured out who they were.

The report stated that the experiments used live test subjects, but none of their names were listed either. That could have been to protect them, or the council didn't know their identities either.

I already knew the identity of one subject—Suze's sister. She'd left Carly's group and was killed shortly thereafter. But she should have been interviewed in the meantime. I did a quick search for her, but other than her name on the death list, I came up empty.

The more I went through the documents, the more superficial I found them. Either the council was severely lacking knowledge, or there was another, more detailed file somewhere. The latter seemed the most likely. Aidan had found the files with ease. Surely, they would keep the real top-secret files more secure.

In a way, that made me feel better about the council. It showed that perhaps they weren't as inept as I'd come to think of them. But it still didn't make sense why they would keep a watered-down version of the real file... if there even was another version of it.

I banged my forehead lightly against the top of the screen. I'd gone back to those documents with the hopes of getting answers, but I only ended up with more questions.

Like how had Carly killed all the people listed? There were a few accounts of raids and fights between Carly's people and guardians, which probably accounted for some deaths. Carly was given the moniker Cruel Carly because she would supposedly kill her own followers if they turned against her. Yet the list of names was just that—a list. It didn't indicate cause of death, reason for death, or which side the person was on. Short of asking adults who might have known them or researching every individual, I had no way to find out.

Next I focused on the crimes attributed to her. Three whole pages were devoted to the deaths of the guardians who'd been killed while pursuing her that final, fateful day. Many of her crimes were simply breaking EA laws, like using her powers in the open and influencing others to do the same. She'd also hired herself out, which was probably how she had funded her experiments. None of the specifics of those crimes were listed, except for one—she was responsible for the deaths of quite a few gang members. Apparently, a gang had hired her to intercede on their behalf in a turf war with a rival gang. She'd done her job well, and the end result was a slaughter. The El Machote gang had folded after that, and the Cherry Lords became unrivaled. A quick Google search told me they were still in power in Camden, New Jersey.

I wondered if that incident accounted for a lot of the names on the death list. That idea was somewhat comforting. Still, though, good or bad, they were people. Carly was a murderer.

And I was considering going on a road trip with her. I must have been out of my mind. But what if she really was the key to finding Lena?

I'd hoped getting more information would help me figure out what to do, but it had only made me more conflicted. Sighing, I was about to close the document when something caught my eye.

When Carly was a junior in high school, her boyfriend had ended up in the hospital. He'd suffered asphyxiation, but there had been no marks on him. Since he'd ended up with brain damage, he had never been able to explain what had happened. Though Carly was never formally accused of anything, the guardian who'd written up the report suspected she was involved. Heck, that was the first I'd heard of the incident, and I would have been surprised if she *weren't* responsible. Was that the first known instance of Carly using her power for evil?

I did a search for the guy—Cal Peters. He was a baseball star who'd had the potential for getting drafted into the major leagues straight out of high school. So when the tragedy happened, it had been all over the news. I searched the articles for Carly's name but didn't find it, even though a lot of Cal's friends were interviewed. She would have been a minor at the time so maybe her parents hadn't permitted interviews.

Her parents... I hadn't given any thought to them—my *real* grandparents—until now. Were they still living? All that was in this file were their names—Ronnie and Clarice Levitt.

A glance at the clock told me it was nearly five a.m. Though I still doubted my ability to sleep, my brain was on overload. It was time to call it a night. Or heck, a morning.

I stared at the ceiling and counted to one hundred. When I was still awake, I did it again, and again. When I'd reached seventy-eight for the fifth time, I heard the shrill ring of Mike's cell phone through the wall.

Oh, shit. Middle-of-the-night or early-morning calls were never good. I jumped out of bed and flung open the door between our rooms.

Mike nodded to me in acknowledgment but continued listening to whoever was calling with a grave look on his face.

Michelle appeared in the doorway, her expression tense. When Mike finally ended the call—it felt like forever, but in reality was probably only two minutes—his arms dropped to his sides, and he hung his head.

"What is it?" I whispered, scared to know the answer.

"They found Councilman Quigley's daughter, Alexis." Mike paused and took a shaky breath. Finding one of the girls should have been good news, but his expression told me it was anything but. "She's dead."

Chapter 5

MICHELLE LET OUT a whimper that I barely registered. I was numb. Mike called Aidan while I tried to make sense of the news.

Alexis couldn't be dead. She just couldn't. *All* the girls were going to be rescued. I'd believed that in my soul.

But it had all been a lie my psyche had told me to keep me sane and give me hope. *False hope.* Michelle had sunk down on the bed, and her hand covered her mouth. Silent tears trailed down her pale cheeks.

A sob caught in my throat, but I swallowed it. Alexis might have been beyond rescue, but five girls—including Lena—were still out there. I would not give up hope on them.

Aidan quietly opened the door and slipped in. The bed dipped as he sat next to me.

"I'd just gotten off the phone when you called," he told Mike. "All guardians should know by now."

"I can't believe it," I whispered. "She's thirteen." As I spoke her age, I realized my mistake—I'd spoken about her in present tense. I should have said, "she *was* thirteen." She would never age beyond that. *Damn it.* It wasn't fair.

Aidan put his arm around my shoulders and pulled me to him. "I know."

"What happened?" I asked.

Aidan's gaze went to Michelle, who'd been silent except for her whimper. "It's okay," she said in a stronger voice than I'd expected. "I want to know."

He looked at Mike, who nodded. Aidan exhaled before speaking. "Councilman Quigley received an anonymous text with a location for his daughter. A small town in Mississippi. He relayed the information to the nearest guardians, and they were there within three hours. They found her right where the text indicated."

"But they were too late," I said.

"They couldn't have saved her." Aidan's voice was scratchy, as though it pained him to get the words out. "She was already... her body was wrapped in a tarp and hidden in a vacant house."

"How did she die?" Michelle asked.

Aidan shook his head. "They don't know yet. They are no marks on her body. They'll have to do an autopsy."

Oh God. I didn't know Alexis, but I'd memorized the pictures of all the missing girls. I visualized the poor girl wrapped in that tarp, then the image quickly changed to the Y-shaped incision of an autopsy. She was barely a teenager.

"They think she had been... gone for at least a day," Mike said quietly.

Gone... a polite way of saying *dead.* There was no polite way to describe this. A thirteen-year-old-girl had been murdered. She'd been dead for an entire day while her poor family was still hoping to see her again.

Oh God. Was Lena already dead, and we didn't know it yet? Would the next text one of us received be a location where we could retrieve her body?

That inconceivable thought caused my power to surge within me, making me feel as if I were being electrocuted. I gasped and tried to suck in air but only ended up hyperventilating.

"Sophie?" Michelle's voice sounded as if it were miles away and I was only hearing its echoes. "Are you okay? Sophie!"

The surges pulsed through my body in waves, each one greater than the last. I didn't know what hurt more—the pain of thinking Lena might already be dead or the energy trying to burst out of my body.

Aidan yanked me against him so I was forced to look in his eyes. "Let it out," he said through clenched teeth. I realized then that I was gripping his biceps, digging my fingernails deep into his flesh. Despite the agony I was in, it somehow registered that I was probably hurting him, so I uncurled my fingers.

"No, just hang on to me and let it out," he said. "Let it out."

I closed my eyes as nausea slammed into me. My vision made it seem as if there were a strobe light in the room compounding the explosion of pain in my head. My body couldn't handle it. I jerked away from Aidan and fell to the floor on my knees then vomited.

Michelle was by my side, rubbing my back. "Aidan, what's wrong with her?"

"It's her power," Aidan said.

"How long has this been happening?"

"I don't know. It was bothering her earlier today, but it wasn't this bad."

Aidan knelt beside me, and I clung to him as another energy wave hit me. Squeezing my eyes shut, I moaned. If I could have spoken, I would have begged for death. Anything for the agony to end.

"Sophie, you've got to let it out," he said. "Look at me."

"I don't... want to... hurt..." I panted, barely able to vocalize the words. I ground my teeth together and tasted blood as my tongue got caught under my incisor.

Aidan kissed my forehead, and somehow I managed to feel it through the pain.

"I trust you," he said. "You won't hurt us."

It was not the time to argue that I'd ripped apart a pool the previous day or remind him that my powers had killed before, but those were the thoughts that ran through my head as I tried to hold the energy in and tried to calm the vicious surge.

But I couldn't. It was too strong. If I didn't let it out, it would tear its way out of me. I rolled to my back and focused my attention on the ceiling, which was the farthest place from the others in the room. A scream ripped through me as I directed the air near the ceiling to turn into a cyclone. The curtains were pulled from the walls. The ceiling light shattered, raining glass down on us. The art flew off the wall, the canvas shredding as it swirled in the mini tornado. The slam of the bathroom door as it got caught in the wind was deafening.

The power flowed through me, relentless and seemingly never ending.

The mirror mounted on the dresser creaked and was pulled away from the drawers. Slamming into the wall, it seemed to explode, and the shards of glass got caught in the cyclone.

Mike's sudden gasp caught my attention. His fingers covered his forehead, where a sliver of the mirror had sliced his skin.

Horrified, I focused my attention not on the power I was expelling, but on the power still left within me. *Settle, settle, settle. Be calm, calm, calm.* I hissed out a breath. It wasn't listening to me.

"You've got this," Aidan whispered in my ear.

His words gave me the boost I needed to refocus my efforts. It seemed to take forever, but slowly, my power began to recede. Instead of pushing the energy out into the room, I pulled it into myself, burying it.

"Good girl," Aidan said.

I wondered if he realized that I was sucking the energy in rather than letting it out as he'd instructed. But the power within would never fully dissipate. There was simply too much. I secured it in various parts of myself, visualizing an old-fashioned key locking it away. The more keys that turned, the less powerful the buzz became.

As the surges finally ceased, I grew lightheaded.

Aidan has never given me so many compliments.

That was my last thought before I blissfully passed out.

AS I BLINKED crusty tears out of my eyes, sunlight streamed in the curtainless window. A quick glance at the clock told me I'd been out for a few hours.

"How are you?"

I jumped at the sound of Aidan's voice. I was lying on my side, facing the window, and he was sitting behind me on the bed. I really must have been out of it because I hadn't realized he was there.

But of course he was. He hadn't left my side after my kidnapping, so why would he leave it now?

I became one thousand percent aware of him as I rolled to look at him. Concern shone in his blue eyes as he peered at me, and his fingers tapped nervously on his thigh, as though he wanted to touch me to reassure himself I was okay. But I was sure he didn't want to cross any lines, especially ones he'd put in place. I wondered how he would react if I crawled into his lap so he could hold me. Because that was what I wanted to do.

Damn him and his stupid honorable intentions.

He reached out to brush away a strand of hair that had fallen into my face. "Do you feel okay?"

I instinctively leaned toward him, wanting to throw my arms around him and bury my face in his neck. He moved away, and blood rushed to my cheeks.

I took a moment to assess myself. My head dully throbbed, but otherwise, I felt fine physically. My powers were subdued at the moment, and I felt no weaker than I would after a training session.

I nodded. "I think so." I looked around the empty room at the destruction I'd caused. The broken mirror and light fixture had been swept into the corner next to the already full tiny trash can. I thought I'd managed to keep the tornado toward the ceiling, but Mike's battered suitcase lay next to the other rubbish. The front part of it was hanging on by only a few inches of fabric.

Shit. Mike. Before I'd passed out, he was bleeding from a gash in his forehead.

"How's Mike?"

"He's okay. We used butterfly bandages to close the wound," Aidan said. "As long as they hold, he shouldn't need stitches."

Stitches... because of me, because I couldn't keep my shit together. My emotional reaction to the news of Alexis's death had caused my powers to overwhelm me and had nearly sent my foster father to the hospital.

Guilt overwhelmed me, and my powers flared. *No, no, no. Not again.* I needed to stay calm to keep my emotions even. At least this incident had taught me something—my power was tied to my emotions. That had never been the case before.

Trying to settle myself, I breathed in deeply and noticed a slight sour smell permeating the air. I cringed as I realized it was the odor of my own puke. Despite all the other emotions swirling within me, I still managed to feel embarrassed that I'd hurled right at Aidan's feet.

"Where are they?" I asked, surprised Michelle wasn't there.

"My mother called a meeting with all the families. It looks like the accommodations will be ready tomorrow and the families will be moving."

"Even Alexis's family?"

He hesitated. "I'm not sure. But they can't go home without Alexis, so they'll have to go somewhere."

My heart mourned for the girl I'd never met, but it wasn't enough. Because of the secrecy, her family wouldn't be able to mourn her properly. All the friends she'd left behind wouldn't get to grieve her at all because they would never know the truth about what had happened. All they would ever know was that her family abruptly moved away. It wasn't right.

"But there's no other news?" I asked.

Aidan hesitated before he spoke. "No."

"Tell me."

A pained look crossed his face. "I don't want you to get worked up—"

"Is it Lena?" There was a touch of hysteria in my voice.

"No, of course not. I wouldn't keep that from you."

The powers that had stirred to life quieted again. *Thank God.* For days, I'd been desperate for information, but now I was scared of the devastation a text or phone call could bring.

"Just tell me. Don't treat me like I'm a bomb about to explode." Except that was what I felt like.

"There's a lead on some other missing kids," he said. "They weren't taken at the same time like our girls, but we suspect they're elementals."

Hanging my head, I closed my eyes. I should have been grateful for any lead, but I wasn't glad other kids had suffered the same fate.

I swung my legs over the side of the bed and realized I was still in my pajamas. "I should shower and get dressed."

Aidan scooted to the end of the bed and rested his elbows on his knees. "Okay." With furrowed brows, he dug nonexistent dirt out from under his fingernails.

"What is it? What aren't you telling me now?"

As he looked up at me, pain and vulnerability shone in his eyes. "Don't be mad."

Shit. That was what I said when I'd done something that would piss him off. I'd never expected to hear them from him. Energy pooled in my veins, and I was grateful I'd expended so much of it previously. There wasn't a lot left. Still, I exhaled slowly, trying to calm myself.

He reached into his pocket and pulled out his phone. He tossed it on the bed, and I realized it wasn't his phone—it was my direct line to Carly.

"What did you do?"

"I called Carly."

"Yeah, I figured that much. Why?" I wasn't mad exactly, but I was curious.

In less than twenty-four hours, he'd gone from chastising me for calling her to making a call himself. That was a big change for even the most open-minded person, and Aidan was more of what I would call set in his ways.

"I figured if anyone could help you tame your power, it's her."

Glancing away, I considered his choice of words. Despite everything, I wasn't so sure I wanted to *tame* my power. I would rather *wield* it. Though its strength had only recently grown to its current state, it was part of me. Taming it would mean taming me, like cutting out a piece of myself. Was that what he wanted? Was that what Mike and Michelle wanted?

"I haven't had time to practice with my power lately," I said. "There's been too much going on for me to focus on it." Though even if I had, I didn't know if I could have done anything differently. Trial and error would only get me so far before disaster would inevitably strike. I couldn't literally play with fire and not expect to get burned eventually.

"I've felt that your power was stronger lately, but never like this. You were radiating energy."

Wrapping my arms around myself, I wanted to tell him it was no big deal, that I had it under control. But we would both know that was a lie. The increase in my power had worried me, but now that I'd inadvertently hurt Mike and destroyed the hotel room, I was petrified.

I wanted to confide in Aidan and tell him how scared I was, but I didn't want to seem weak. I was given this gift—yes, I still considered my power a gift—and I should have been able to handle it. If I couldn't... well, that simply wasn't an option.

"What did Carly say?"

"That she could help you."

I spun. "Is that all?"

He hesitated. "She wanted reassurance that you were okay."

I could tell admitting that made him uncomfortable because her caring about me meant she didn't fit neatly into the evil box he'd created for her. No, that wasn't entirely right. The box had been created by the council and taught to young elementals in their history lessons. Until recently, I'd shared the same beliefs, but now I wondered if there was more to the history than we'd been taught.

"I think she genuinely cares about me," I said. "She's given me no reason to think otherwise."

Granted, my experience with her was slim, but it wasn't so far out of the realm of possibility that, despite her evil doings, her maternal instincts were intact. Besides that, there was no evidence she'd committed any misdeeds in the past fifteen years. That didn't excuse her previous crimes, but perhaps she'd changed. Or at least maybe she'd learned to keep her urges in check, which was more than I could say for myself.

"I know." He sighed heavily. "You have to go. I hate it. God, I fucking hate it, but I don't know what else to do. I've never heard of anyone being overtaken by their power like that. You can't go through that again."

I smartly didn't point out that no matter how powerful and knowledgeable Carly was, there was no quick fix for my problem. I would likely be overtaken by my power again before I learned to control it.

"I don't want to." My voice shook. "I never felt so fragile. My power was about to rip me in half if I didn't let it out. But I can't do that. Mike got a cut on his forehead this time, but what about next time? What if something worse happens?"

"I know."

Those two words were an acknowledgment of what I already knew—I was a danger to my loved ones. But damn, hearing that from Aidan hurt. *Is he afraid of me?*

"So what now?"

"She's still here in Orlando. I—" He broke off then cursed and stared at the ceiling for a moment before continuing. "I set up a meeting. Tonight. If you're ready to go with her."

I'd already waited too long. Not for me, but for Lena and the four other girls. If I had gone with Carly yesterday, we would have been in Tennessee already, talking to her contact.

"I don't have much of a choice."

"If it was just to get information, I'd still say we could find another way, but you need her. Goddamn it." He rested his head in his hands. "She'd only agree to just you."

I frowned. "What do you mean?"

He looked at me with stormy blue eyes. "I want to go with you. Forget what she says and forget what the council wants—"

I put my hand up to stop him. "What does the council have to do with this? You didn't tell them—"

"Of course not." He sighed. "They want me to investigate the missing kids in West Virginia."

"You have to go."

"Damn it, Sophie. I'm not letting you deal with her alone." Aidan was prepared to push me away emotionally to protect me, but physically pushing me away went against every fiber of his being. Yet it wasn't his decision to *let* me do anything. As much as I cared about him, he wasn't my master.

"If Carly wanted to meet with any other guardian, what would you say?"

"It's not the same."

"It is," I insisted. "We can't pass up this opportunity. I've been training to be a guardian for years. I can do this."

He exhaled and looked upward. "You realize that you're stronger than any elemental you'd be protecting as a guardian, right?"

That thought hadn't really occurred to me, and I didn't see how it was relevant. "You have to trust me."

"I do," he said simply. "I wished to God I didn't, that I had a good excuse to convince you to stay, but you need her help." The air between us stood still as we stared at one another.

"Aidan..." I was on a precipice, prepared to jump, only I didn't know if I had a parachute.

"You scared the shit out of me." His voice was raw.

"I'm sorry." I didn't know what else to say.

"Don't apologize." He closed the distance between us.

"I'm—" I nearly apologized again. "Okay."

He'd seemed so in control during the incident. In fact, he was the one who'd insisted I let my power out. I could see how much that had affected him, and I hated it. I hated that my power had hurt him.

And if he stayed near me, my power might really hurt him.

"Sophie, I..." He trailed off, obviously thinking better of saying what he was going to say. I wanted to urge him to complete the thought, but his strong arms enveloped me and crushed my body to his chest. I wanted to melt into him.

Wrapped in one another's arms, we stood for a few minutes. I pressed my face to his chest, and the steady rhythm of his heartbeat was a calming staccato. But with all the shit going on around us, our stolen moments couldn't last.

"I want you to stay, to keep you out of harm's way. It's irrational, and it's the wrong decision," he said quietly. "This is why we can't be together."

My heart broke a little when he let me go.

Chapter 6

MY HANDS WERE steady as I made the call to Carly.

She answered on the first ring. "Sophie, are you okay?"

"Fine." I didn't want to discuss my health with her, though I would have to soon enough. "Is your offer still good?"

"Which one?"

"Both. I want to talk to your contacts." I took a deep breath and swallowed my pride. "And I need your help with my powers."

Aidan squeezed my hand, and I was grateful for the gesture. Asking for help wasn't easy for me. Lloyd and Belinda hadn't neglected me, but I'd been left to my own devices for most of my childhood. As a result, I preferred to depend on myself.

"Meet me at five," she said without hesitation. "I'll send you the address."

It was nearly noon. That gave me almost five hours to prepare. I didn't have much to pack, but I wouldn't be able to bring everything I had anyway. While I could stash away a bag in Aidan's room and retrieve it when it was time to leave, Michelle might notice if all of my things were mysteriously missing from the room.

Part of me wished I could leave right then so we could start gathering intel as soon as possible. But I was also glad I would get to see Mike and Michelle before I left. I wouldn't be able to tell them goodbye, but perhaps I would be able to do *something*.

"Sophie?" Carly asked.

I'd been so lost in my thoughts I hadn't responded. "I'll be there." I ended the call without saying goodbye. Perhaps it was rude, but I couldn't force myself to care about social niceties at the moment.

Aidan looked at me expectantly.

"Tonight," I said. "Five. She's going to text me the address." Right as I said that, the phone chimed. *Damn.* That was quick. She must already have had a place in mind. But there was no way she could've known I would end up going with her.

That irked me, which was irrational. I should have been glad she was prepared because a delay could've meant the difference between life and death for those girls.

Even as the thought crossed my mind, I realized it was dramatic, like a badly scripted cop show on TV. But it was also the truth.

I showed Aidan the address, which meant nothing to me. It was in Orlando somewhere. He started to type the address into his GPS, but I put my hand on his arm to stop him.

"No. I don't want any evidence of this meeting in your phone."

He stared at me evenly. "There's no way no one's going to figure out I'm involved."

"Maybe not."

"It's no secret I'd lay down my life for you."

My pulse spiked as I processed his words. *I'd lay down my life for you.* He would do the same for Lena, but his voice was so thick with emotion that it seemed as though the sentiment carried a special meaning for me. Or maybe I wanted it to.

"Tell them I slipped away," I suggested. "No one would doubt I'd do something like that." I wasn't a bad kid, but I definitely skirted the rules.

He shook his head. "They know I won't let you out of my sight."

I frowned. "Who's 'they'?"

Stuffing his hands in his pockets, he focused on the wall behind me, not meeting my gaze. "Mike. And probably Michelle." The certainty in his tone was different than his normal confident-of-everything tone.

I narrowed my eyes at him. "What aren't you telling me?"

"Mike had a talk with me," Aidan muttered.

Oh, lord. "What kind of talk?" I cringed as I waited for the answer, hoping it wasn't what I thought it was.

Aidan continued to avoid my gaze. "Sort of a father-to-boyfriend kind."

"What?" All the blood rushed to my cheeks, and mortification filled every cell in my body. "When? What did he say?"

"It was the morning of... the day we... you know."

Oh, I did know. The memory still heated my insides.

I repeated my question. "What did he say?"

Aidan blushed. Actually blushed. "I don't want to talk about it."

Though I was tickled to see how cute he looked while blushing, I felt bad for him. I was mortified, and I'd only heard about the interaction secondhand. Aidan had actually experienced it. I would have killed to be a fly on the wall for that conversation. It had to be both embarrassing and hilarious.

I was all for gender equality, but I was super glad we hadn't evolved to the point of mothers having talks with and threatening their sons' girlfriends. If Suze had tried that with me, I would have never been able to look her in the face again.

But God, I was an idiot. The whole time, I'd been thinking no one but Lena was the wiser when it came to what was happening between Aidan and me.

With an impish grin, I crossed my arms. "Come on. Tell me what he said." I couldn't stop myself from needling Aidan. Not much unnerved him except, apparently, my nerdy and bookish foster father threatening to kick his ass if he didn't treat me right. Or whatever had gone down in that conversation. Aidan wasn't spilling, and unless I asked Mike myself, I would likely never find out.

Aidan gave me a pointed stare. "Can we drop it? It's not important."

He was right. In another time line, it would have been, but not in this one. Not in the one where Lena was missing.

"Okay," I said, getting back to the plan. "You could tell everyone I used my powers on you to get away."

"I'm not doing that."

"Why? Aidan, I'm trying to protect you. Why won't you let me?"

This was so frustrating. I didn't want him getting in trouble for something that was ultimately my decision. True, he'd facilitated it, but I would have come to the same conclusion on my own. There was no need for us both to go down.

"Several reasons," he said. "No one would believe that you'd do that to me. And anyway, I wouldn't want them to. When you come back, you'll be in enough trouble as it is."

"That's my point. You don't have to take the heat for this."

Though Aidan was at odds with his mother and Councilman Stearns, he was somewhat of a guardian golden boy. Many in the EA would be happy to believe I was responsible for the entire ploy, and if that kept Aidan out of trouble, I would let them.

"We don't have time to argue about this." Aidan looked pointedly at the clock on the nightstand. "Mike and Michelle will be back soon, and we need to have our plan worked out before then."

I crossed my arms. "Part of the plan has to be you not getting caught helping me. I can call an Uber to take me to Carly."

He snorted, and it burned my butt that he managed to make it attractive.

"Besides, aren't you supposed to be going to West Virginia?" I reminded him. "When do they want you there?"

"Tonight," he muttered.

"See? You don't have time to take me anyway."

His expression turned dark and menacing, and suddenly I saw him as the skilled guardian he was. "I'm delivering you safely to Carly."

Deciding I could let him at least have that, I stopped arguing. "You can take me, but we need to keep that a secret somehow."

"Fine," he said. "There are other details we need to work out, like you'll have to leave your regular phone behind. You know they're monitoring the tracking app, and if it gets turned off, they'll go looking for you immediately. That could make it difficult for you and Carly to get out of the area."

The discussion made me feel guilty for what I was about to do. I was actively deceiving Mike and Michelle. It was for the good of everyone, but they would have a hard time seeing it that way, especially at first. If Aidan's involvement was discovered—and I hoped it wasn't—he could help them understand why I had to do it.

I held up the phone Carly had given me. "I'll take this one."

"Good. You need to contact me every day."

"What? No. Remember the whole part about not involving you? Don't you think if everyone is aware of—"

I was about to say *how we feel about each other*, but I stopped myself. Aidan had explicitly said he couldn't be with me. Despite our earlier embrace, he was a man of his word.

"You're right that they'll check to see if you've contacted me," Aidan said. "That's why you're going to email me instead of call or text. We'll set up new email addresses specifically for this purpose. You need to let me know where you are in case I need to come for you."

His plan was smart. It would be foolish to run off with Carly and not have a failsafe in place, yet I hesitated to agree. I didn't know what to expect. I might end up in a location with no cell service or Carly might prevent me from contacting him. In that case, I would probably want him to rescue me. But in all other instances, who would decide if a swoop-and-rescue was warranted?

I was so caught up in rescue details that I'd stupidly forgotten my main purpose for going. Of course I had to contact him frequently. I was assuming I would get useful information that I would have to pass on to the guardians somehow.

But I couldn't guarantee they would trust the intel. And if Aidan handed it over, they would wonder where he was getting it. *Damn.* Maybe he was right, and there was no way he could keep his involvement under wraps.

"Sophie, are you getting all this?" Aidan's voice was impatient. When I cleared my mind, I realized he was holding his phone and frowning. "Mike and Michelle are on their way back. We need to wrap this up."

"Shit. How long do we have?"

"Maybe ten minutes."

"Okay, what else do we need to cover?" I gathered a few of my belongings and piled them on the bed. Then I dumped all the homework I'd brought with me out of my backpack and shoved the clothes in there.

Aidan tapped on his phone. "Do you have the credit card Mike gave you?"

"Yes, but if I use it—"

"Right, don't use it. But have it on you just in case. What about cash? How much do you have?"

"Not much. Maybe forty dollars."

"I can give you some. Keep it hidden, though, and use it only for an emergency. Make Carly pay for everything so you don't have to use it."

I was pretty sure I couldn't *make* Carly do anything, but he had a point. She'd invited me on this wild ride, so she could foot the bill.

Everything was coming together really fast. Normally, I was okay with spontaneity—Lena was the planner out of the two of us—but even I would have felt more comfortable with additional preparation. There was no time for that, though.

I felt as though my whole life had been leading up to this. I was finally going to find out where I'd come from, who I was.

As those thoughts flitted through my head, I wanted to bitch-slap myself. Alexis was dead. Lena and the other girls could be next. And I was worried about my identity.

Priorities, Sophie.

I zipped up my bag and looked around the room I'd been sharing with Michelle. With me gone, maybe she would start sleeping with Mike again. I understood her need to be close to me and to be surrounded by Lena's stuff, but I worried about their marriage. Mike might have felt abandoned. He would never say so, but Lena and I were just as much his daughters. He had to be hurting as badly as Michelle, but for her sake—all our sakes—he'd been holding it together.

God, I hoped my leaving wouldn't be the straw that did him in.

It won't. I won't let it. I was going to find Lena and make everything okay again. Failure wasn't an option.

"I set up email accounts," Aidan said and read off the addresses.

"Um... you'd better write those down." Normally, my memory was good, but I didn't trust myself with everything else swirling around in my head.

"I'd prefer not to."

I shot him a sharp look. "Do you want me to email you or not? I don't want to risk forgetting."

Grumbling, he grabbed a hotel-branded notepad off the nightstand and jotted down the addresses. "You need to memorize the password, though. I'm not writing that down."

I blew out a breath. "Fine. What is it?"

Aidan's eye met mine. "Find Lena five twelve. Capital F and L."

I stilled. The password was my mission combined with Lena's birthday. No way was I forgetting that.

MIKE AND MICHELLE returned with the somber news that while the five families who were still hopeful for their loved ones' safe return would be relocating to a community in Jacksonville, the Quigley family was moving to a different location to begin their lives without Alexis. Councilman Quigley had resigned his seat on the council, effective immediately. I couldn't say I blamed him.

People reacted to grief differently. When Aidan's family had been in a similar situation, his mother had thrown herself into her work on the council. His father had turned to alcohol, and Aidan had moved in with Vic and Suze to begin guardian training.

I wondered what would happen to the other five families if the remaining girls met similar fates.

That's not going to happen. But I wasn't able to dismiss the worry as easily as I had before.

Shortly after returning, Mike dipped into the other room to get some work done. It was probably the last thing he wanted to do, but we still had bills to pay, and because we had to keep Lena's disappearance a secret, he had no excuse he could give his clients as to why he couldn't deliver their projects on time. He hadn't worked since we'd been there, so he was horribly behind.

Michelle stared at me suspiciously, as though she expected me to have another episode at any minute. Or maybe I exuded guilt because I was jumping ship in a few hours. My intentions were good, but that wouldn't stop my absence from hurting my foster parents. I hoped once Lena was home safe, they would forgive me and realize the ends had justified the means.

"I'm fine," I reassured her for the tenth time in the ten minutes they'd been back. "I promise." My nerves were on edge, but so far, the energy inside me had been kept at bay. Perhaps it realized I was about to embark on a quest to get Lena back and learn how to harmoniously coexist with it. I tried to convince myself it was part of me, but it seemed like a separate entity when it got out of control. I couldn't explain it.

I wondered if anyone could. I was by no means a science geek, but I wondered what the scientific explanation for our powers was.

"It's my fault," Michelle said. "I'm sorry I've been neglecting you. I was worried something like this might happen."

"Has it happened to anyone else?" I asked. Aidan had said he wasn't aware of anyone reacting to power in that way, but that didn't mean it hadn't happened. Part of me was annoyed. Michelle had expressed her concern about my growing power, but she hadn't given me any specific side effects to watch out for. Granted, she'd been preoccupied lately, as we all had, but she could have told me prior to leaving for testing. But only shortly before then had I realized *I* was who she was worried about. I'd mistakenly assumed Lena was the one with the potential to become super powerful.

She still could, though. At the hands of her captors, her emotions were likely running high, which could spark an increase in power. Or so I'd recently concluded.

"Not exactly," she said. "But I've heard Carly had trouble adjusting to her powers as a teenager."

Nothing was detailed in the file I'd read, but I'd already established that the file was either incomplete or heavily filtered.

"Really? Who'd you hear that from?"

"Patricia," Michelle admitted.

"How would she know?" That was the last name I'd expected her to say. Councilwoman West wasn't big on sharing.

"They knew each other."

Aidan's neck snapped up. I met his gaze, and his eyes were as wide and unbelieving as mine. He'd had no idea either.

"Are you serious?" I tried to picture a teenage Patricia West having a slumber party with a teenage Carly. The image wouldn't solidify in my mind, probably because it was a stupid image. Not counting the nights I'd slept in Lena's room and vice versa, I hadn't been to a proper slumber party since I was twelve. But mostly, I couldn't picture West and Carly having a powwow. Not in a million years.

Michelle shrugged. "They both grew up in Ohio, about an hour apart. They weren't close or anything, but they definitely knew each other."

Damn. I wished Councilwoman West were trustworthy. She was the only person I knew who'd actually known Carly. I couldn't believe Aidan and I hadn't been aware of that. It felt significant, but in what way, I had no idea.

"Now that everything is out in the open," I said, "maybe you could ask Councilwoman West for more information."

"Of course," Michelle said. "I should have done it sooner. I hadn't realized how much trouble you'd been having."

"It's only recently," I assured her, not wanting her to feel guilty.

"Hopefully, Patricia will be able to help. But don't worry, Sophie," Michelle said with a reassuring smile. "One way or another, we'll get you straightened out."

She didn't know how right she was.

Feeling like a deceitful brat, I forced myself to return her smile.

"I'll work with you tonight," Michelle said. "I have to deal with some relocation stuff during business hours, but maybe after dinner. I have papers to grade, but those can wait."

"That sounds great." I nearly choked on the words. "But I understand if you need to work."

Like Mike, Michelle was also behind. It was nearing the end of the semester, which meant she had a lot of grading to do. She'd barely touched her computer since we'd been in Florida.

"Sophie, you're more important than work. I've let you down, and I'm sorry. I promise I'll make it up to you."

"Okay." God, I couldn't even look at her.

Aidan cleared his throat. "Don't forget I'm leaving soon, so I won't be able to go with you."

Michelle's gaze drifted between Aidan and me, and a knowing look came into her eyes. I tried my hardest not to blush and failed miserably. Knowing about Mike's talk with Aidan and that everyone was aware something was going on between us made the situation especially awkward.

"Don't worry," Michelle assured him. "Mike and I won't let anything happen to her." She called Mike into the room so they could both say their goodbyes to Aidan. Then she not-so-discreetly ushered her husband back into their room and closed the door behind them so Aidan and I could have a few more minutes of privacy.

If I wasn't blushing before, I definitely was now.

But we didn't bother saying goodbye because if everything went according to plan, we would be doing that later. He was leaving the hotel supposedly to set out for West Virginia. In reality, he would kill time before picking me up. Hopefully, this would divert suspicion away from him.

"If you're not in the parking lot in three hours, I'm coming back up here for you," Aidan warned.

"I'll be there." I was actually less confident than I sounded because I believed Michelle when she said she wouldn't let anything happen to me, which meant not letting me out of her sight. Somehow, I would have to make it work.

I spent the next few hours observing Michelle as she called my school and did a million other tasks online, like arranging to have our mail forwarded. I had been glad I didn't have to rush off for my rendezvous with Carly, thinking I could spend some quality time with Mike and Michelle, but they were both too busy. There was no way I could initiate it without raising their alarm. Then I wouldn't be able to slip away as I'd planned.

About thirty minutes before I had to meet Aidan, I announced I was tired and wanted to take a nap.

"Good idea," Michelle said. "You must be exhausted. I'll just grade some papers while you rest. Then we'll grab Mike, get some dinner, and find somewhere to practice. Sound good?"

I nodded and made a big show of yawning and climbing into bed. She switched off the lights in the room but remained at the desk, her fingers silently tapping away on the keyboard.

Five minutes went by, then ten. I noisily flipped over. Fifteen minutes. I sat up, punched the pillow, and rearranged the blankets. Twenty minutes. I threw the covers off and let out a loud sigh.

"Am I keeping you awake?" Michelle whispered.

"Yeah, sorry." I tried to sound apologetic. "It's the light from the computer screen."

She closed her laptop, and for a moment, I was worried she wouldn't respond the way I'd anticipated. But it turned out I could predict my foster mother's behavior perfectly.

"I'll work in the other room while you sleep," she said.

"Thanks." I picked up my cell phone from the end table. "I'll set an alarm for two hours. Will you and Mike be okay to wait until then for dinner?" I was the worst daughter in the world. I was acting concerned for my foster parents when in actuality I was using their caring nature to deceive them. Sickness gathered in my stomach, but I ignored it.

Five minutes later, when it was time to go, I closed the hotel room behind me and didn't look back. Well, of course I didn't. The door was solid so it wasn't as if I would be able to see my foster parents anyway. But it was symbolic. I'd made my choice, aware it would hurt them. I wished I could have explained it to them, but I also wished Lena hadn't been taken in the first place.

My wishes didn't matter.

Aidan was waiting for me at the far end of the parking lot in a rental car. I watched him out of the corner of my eye. He gripped the steering wheel harder than was necessary, and I could tell he was grinding his teeth by the throbbing in his temple. I hoped he wasn't having second thoughts.

I was. Not about my decision to go with Carly, but I was second-guessing our minimal plans. While I was glad Carly could help me with controlling my powers, that was the icing on top. My main purpose was to interview her associates for information. I only hoped I would be able to get helpful info to Aidan and that he would be able to pass it along to someone who could do something with it. Though he was a full guardian, he was new, which meant he was on the bottom of the guardian hierarchy.

Aidan pulled into a mall parking lot. I glanced at the GPS on his phone, which directed us to the Crayola Factory. *Huh.* It seemed Carly had taken a page out of my book and chosen a location related to toys. The sign at the fork to the mall entrance said to take a left to get to Crayola, but Aidan took a right.

I pointed. "It was that way."

"I know," he said tightly. "We're a few minutes early anyway, and I want to make sure everything is in place." He pulled to a stop outside JCPenney.

"I've got my bag, the phone, and some money," I said. "What else do I need?"

"I don't know." His hands fisted and unfisted in his lap as he stared at the steering wheel. I realized he was even more uncomfortable than I was with the lack of planning.

It was costing him to let me go because he wouldn't be there to watch over me. His facilitating my going showed how much he believed in me. Though he was worried, he believed I could handle it. Otherwise, he wouldn't let me go.

Once I realized that, the tension left my body. There was no one's opinion I valued more than Aidan's. He'd trained me to the best of his ability, and it was time for me to put those skills to the test while also undertaking another kind of training.

I just hoped Carly would be able to help me get a handle on my powers. But more importantly, I hoped she wasn't mistaken about her contacts being able to help us find Lena.

I put my hands on top of Aidan's. "I'll be fine. You shouldn't worry."

His sidelong glance told me how pointless that comment was. "Promise me you'll ask me for help if you need it. I won't think you're weak." He knew me all too well.

"I promise," I said. "I don't want to mess this up either. There's too much at stake."

"Just don't forget you're at stake too." His blue eyes raked over my face, and my breath caught.

"I won't," I whispered. I wanted to tell him so many things, like how important he was to me and how much his faith in me bolstered my confidence. But before I could put my thoughts into words, he shifted the car into drive and set off toward our meeting point.

Aidan drove toward the Crayola Factory, and I spotted Carly immediately at the back of the lot. She leaned against a white sedan, her ankles crossed. She wore jeans, a fitted shirt, and slip-on canvas shoes. Large sunglasses partially obscured her face. She didn't look old enough to have a teenage daughter, but I was proof that wasn't the case.

Aidan pulled into a space several down from her. Blowing out a breath, he gave me one long last look before getting out of the car and grabbing my bag from the back seat.

Carly was early. I had been hoping to have a few more minutes to prepare, but instead I only allowed myself a few last precious seconds in the car. I hoped her power wouldn't affect me like it had the day before. I'd only been with her for a short time, and I didn't know how I would cope with the effects since I would be spending hours in a confined space with her.

Slowly, I got out of the car. Aidan put his hand on the small of my back as we walked toward Carly. We were a united front, but soon, I would be leaving him behind. The thought of being without him hurt. I'd known it would, but I hadn't realized how much. Half of my heart had been missing since Lena's disappearance, and being separated from Aidan would rip apart the other half. I would be left with nothing.

Carly removed her sunglasses as we approached. I stayed attuned to my powers to see if they were firing up. Much to my relief, they merely sizzled instead of turning into a full-on inferno.

Aidan glared at Carly. "If anything happens to her, I'm holding you responsible."

She sighed, seeming frustrated. "I'm her mother. She's important to me too." She turned to me. "Are you ready?"

Aidan removed his hand from my back, and its absence struck my heart like a bludgeon. Unwelcome tears gathered in my eyes. "Can you give us a minute?"

"Sure." Carly put her sunglasses back on and climbed into the driver's seat of her car.

I turned to Aidan, and he held my backpack out. I slung it over my shoulder and opened my mouth to speak, but my throat choked on the words. Throwing my arms around his neck, I let out a sob. "I'm losing you too." Big displays of emotion like that weren't like me. I hated feeling so exposed, but the swell of emotion within me was too much.

His strong arms wrapped around my body, and he buried his face in my hair for a moment before chuckling. "You're the one leaving."

"I have to go." I wished it weren't true. "It's the only way."

"If I could go in your place, I would."

"I know." Not wanting to break contact with him, I reluctantly pulled back, and my gaze traveled over his face. I'd long since memorized so many things about him, but I was suddenly afraid I would forget.

His hand held mine. "Remember everything we talked about."

I nodded. "I will." Our goodbye was dragging on, and I wasn't sure if it made it easier or harder. It felt like ripping off a Band-Aid agonizingly slowly. "I need to go."

Aidan's eyes bored into mine, but instead of letting go of my hand, he yanked me to him. Cupping my face in his hands, he lowered his mouth to mine. His lips were unbelievably soft and gentle.

I concentrated on the feel and taste of him, knowing I would want to replay that moment in my mind in the days to come. The kiss deepened, taking my breath away and igniting my powers. But they didn't burn under my skin, threatening to consume me. Instead, they were a soothing force, as if they understood the turmoil in my heart and wanted to comfort me.

Aidan broke away first. He'd always been the more responsible one. If it were up to me, we would spend the next hour kissing in the parking lot.

"Go," he said quietly. "Or I might not be able to let you leave."

Mutely, I nodded, still grasping his hand.

He looked directly in my eyes. "Be brave. Stay safe. You can do this." Then he stepped back and shoved his hands into his pockets.

I opened the passenger door and tossed my bag into the back seat. Before getting in, I paused to look at Aidan one last time. "Goodbye, Aidan."

Chapter 7

As I buckled my seat belt, Carly's gaze slyly shifted to where Aidan leaned against the rental car. "So, my daughter and Aidan West."

"Shut up," I said fiercely. I hadn't meant to break out the juvenile language, but it was a knee-jerk reaction. "You don't get to talk to me about Aidan."

What was going on between Aidan and me was everything that was good in my life—or at least it had been—while Carly was everything bad. I wouldn't be with her if Lena weren't gone. And obviously, I wouldn't be with her if she weren't my supposed-to-be-dead evil mother. So no, she didn't get to comment on my relationship with Aidan.

Her eyebrows lifted slightly, and a ghost of a smile tugged at her lips. She put her hands up, palms out. "Fine." She shifted the car into drive and pulled out of the parking lot.

I ignored her and stared out the window at Aidan until I could no longer see him. Only then could I focus on the business at hand. "Where is your first contact?"

Carly glanced in the rearview mirror and switched lanes. "Near Nashville. It will take at least eleven hours to get there."

It was shortly after five, so that meant driving through the night or stopping overnight at a hotel. Neither option was appealing, but I hadn't signed up for the adventure thinking it would be fun.

"Who is it?"

At first I thought she might evade the question as she'd done previously, but she spoke without hesitation. "His name is Jack, and he's one of the most powerful male elementals I've ever met."

"How powerful?"

Carly let out a little laugh. "I'm sure you know as well as I do that him being a powerful male elemental doesn't amount to much."

That was true. The most powerful male elemental on record was only as powerful as a moderately powerful female elemental. Most male elementals, including Aidan and Vic, had little to no power.

"So why do you think he can help us?" I paused. "Why do you think he *will* help us?"

Carly nodded slightly before answering, as though she approved of my questions. "He might not have much information, but he's the closest contact I have, and he's pretty well-connected with other rogues, as you called us."

I'd previously wondered if they had a name for themselves. All I'd ever known non-EA elementals as was rogues. "If you're not rogues, then what are you?"

"Why do we have to be anything?" Carly's tone was bland. "Non EA-affiliated elementals are simply elementals trying to live their lives without the interference of a governing body that has no real power."

Whoa. I barely held in the sarcastic comment for her to tell me how she really felt. I had my own issues with the EA, but Carly seemed to have me beat in that department.

"Will anybody talk to us on the phone?" If her closest contact was eleven hours away, then I hated to think how far the next one might be. Our time—time the girls might not have—would be eaten up by hours on the road.

"Not likely. The people who might be able to help us generally tend to be suspicious and prefer to deal with people face-to-face."

I supposed that was fair, even if it was inconvenient. "And Jack will be willing to help us?"

"Yes," Carly said with certainty. "He owes me."

"Why?"

Carly gave me a wary look.

I shrugged unapologetically. "My being here with you is a huge leap of faith. The least you can do is trust me enough to answer my questions. As you keep telling everyone, I'm your daughter."

She smiled. "By everyone, you mean Aidan."

Touché. Her smartass comment was similar to one I would have made. "You like to remind me of that fact as well."

"I wish I didn't have to."

I ignored her comment. "Why does he owe you?"

Carly sighed, seeming disappointed I didn't want to discuss our lack of a mother-daughter relationship. "It's not what you think. Jack's brother, Jeremy, never intended to father any children because he didn't want to pass on the elemental traits. He wasn't as careful as he should have been and had a daughter. Then he stuck his head in the sand and ignored the inevitability that his daughter would develop powers. His wife is weak, and he didn't have any powers, so I guess he hoped his daughter wouldn't either. Anyway, her powers came on about a year ago. I helped her."

"Couldn't Jack have helped?"

Carly directed the car down an exit ramp. "Those are family dynamics I don't want to get into."

"Why are we stopping?" I frowned as I peered at the gas gauge. It was still above three quarters of a tank.

"Just doing a little switcheroo." Carly pulled into a gas station parking lot and parked next to a green Jeep Grand Cherokee. "Get your stuff. Do you need to use the restroom while we're here?"

"No, I'm good."

Carly got out of the car and went around to the trunk to pull out a suitcase. Then she pulled a key fob out of her pocket, clicked the button, and loaded her luggage into the back of the Cherokee.

We were switching cars.

Slowly, I got out of the white sedan. I stood next to the Jeep, clutching my backpack to my chest.

Carly laughed. "Don't be so suspicious."

Says the woman whose "friends" are so suspicious they won't talk on the phone.

"Why are we switching cars?"

"I would think with your guardian training, that would be obvious."

Of course it was. Aidan had seen the white car, and I would bet he'd memorized the license plate number. *Who's the suspicious one now?*

"This isn't a trap," I told her. "I'm not setting you up."

Carly eyed me over the hood of the car. "Just because I'm ready to trust you doesn't mean I trust Patricia West's son."

I wanted to tell her that Aidan was no more Patricia's son than I was her daughter, but I kept the comment to myself. I wanted Carly to help me, so there was no need to antagonize her. Besides that, I didn't want to air the West family's dirty laundry. However, I was dying to learn about her history with Aidan's mom. Somehow, I didn't think she would be willing to talk about that just yet.

I tossed my bag in the back seat of the Jeep as I'd done earlier when I got in the car. "This isn't stolen, is it?" I joked, hoping to lighten the mood. I knew it wasn't because she'd had the key fob in her pocket.

Grinning, she started the engine. "Nope, but the car was."

My jaw dropped, and my eyes bugged out. "Seriously?"

She shrugged as if it were no big deal. "We didn't hurt it, and I took it from a parking lot a few miles away from here. The owner will get it back, and I even left it with more gas than when I found it."

While that explanation may have rationalized her actions in her mind, it didn't work for me. All the adults who'd had a hand in raising me had instilled in me that stealing was wrong. But I didn't mention my disapproval because again, there was no need to antagonize her. Also, what was done was done. I strapped in, and Carly guided the Jeep onto the interstate.

"We *are* going to Tennessee, right?" I asked.

She smiled. "Yes. I might not tell you everything, but I won't lie about what I do tell you."

I wasn't sure I believed her. Yet the more I thought about it, the more I realized I had no reason not to. In the brief interactions I'd had with her, she had definitely withheld information, but she hadn't lied about it or even tried to hide the fact that she was doing it. In her own way, she was upstanding, and for the first time, I saw a hint of what might have made people follow her.

"How did you find me?" I asked.

"I have contacts in the EA."

"Like who?"

"I don't want to get them in trouble." She looked over at me. "This is a good lesson for you. I have a lot of contacts because people know they can trust me. I don't share their secrets."

Her "lesson" fit in with what I'd just figured out about her, but I hoped she wasn't planning to lecture me on our trip because that would get really old really fast.

I drummed my fingers on the door handle. "People are spying for you." Traitorous EA employees put us all at risk. I realized that statement made it sound as if I was buying into the EA rhetoric, but EA employees should be loyal to the EA. Period. If they had a problem with that, then they should find other jobs. That was why I was struggling with the notion of becoming a guardian—I wasn't sure I could dedicate myself to it wholeheartedly. Though as Aidan had pointed out, I was stronger than anyone I would be guarding, but I didn't see that as a negative.

"I wouldn't go that far," Carly said. "I just have a few contacts employed by the EA who are sympathetic to my cause."

Her cause. The files I'd read about her referenced her cause, but there was no indication of what the cause actually was. "And what is your cause?"

"Choice."

"Choice?" I echoed. It sounded so simple and reasonable. But I would have bet the people she'd killed hadn't chosen to die—she'd chosen to kill them. That was by no means noble or reasonable.

"Yes, choice. You know, our country was founded on freedom."

I rolled my eyes. She was *not* about to compare herself to George Washington. So much for hoping she wouldn't lecture.

She sighed. "If you're not willing to be open-minded, then I'm not going to talk about it."

Her comment annoyed me because it made me sound like a close-minded jerk. But *I* wasn't the one in the wrong. *I* wasn't the one with a list of crimes as long as my arm. *I* wasn't the one who'd been in hiding for the past fifteen years. But whatever. I didn't need to understand her cause. I only needed her to help me find Lena and teach me about my powers.

"So your contact in the EA told you about me," I prompted, wanting to get the conversation back on track.

"I learned you were alive about two years ago, but I didn't find out where you were until you were taken."

Her statement raised so many questions in my mind. "Why did you think I was dead?"

"When guardians were pursuing me and the building collapsed—"

"You mean when you pulled the building down and killed the people in it?"

"That wasn't the only collapsed building in this story," she continued as if I hadn't spoken. "I rarely left you, but the few times I did, I left you in the care of a woman named Nina. She wasn't an elemental, and in fact, no one knew about her. You should have been safer with her than one of my own. Or so I thought. There was a supposed gas leak in the house that led to an explosion. I managed to get to Nina before they took her to the hospital, and she told me you were dead. I had no reason not to believe her."

"But it would have been reported on the news."

"You would think, but you should know better than most that crimes involving elementals—even ones where elementals are the victims—are mysteriously kept out of the public eye."

A month ago, I wouldn't have considered the possibility that the EA would have covered up the death of a child. But the council's response to my kidnapping, the girls' abduction, and Alexis's death had convinced me that if there had actually been the body of an elemental child in that house, they would have done everything in their power to get custody of it before questions could be asked. *Secrecy at all costs.*

"What happened to Nina?"

"She slipped into a coma and died a few days later. Strange considering she'd been recovering from her injuries."

It *was* strange. And it was awfully convenient that the one woman who could've identified my abductors had mysteriously died. Was this the council acting on their *secrecy at all costs* motto?

"Do you think the guardians caused the explosion and killed Nina?" I hated that I felt the need to ask that question and hated even more that I was afraid of the answer. It was one thing for the council to keep things secret, but being responsible for the death of an innocent woman was something else entirely. It was firmly out of the gray area and into reprehensible territory.

"Of course." Carly's tone implied I was stupid if I didn't see that. I definitely saw it, but I didn't want to believe it. I naively wanted to believe there was another reasonable explanation. "You're with the EA, so there's proof they took you at the very least. Everything else is way too much of a coincidence for it to be anything else."

Aidan's mother and Lena's father were the only two council members who knew my history. My stomach roiled. The probability that Carly's theory was true and they were involved horrified me. I tried to calculate how long each of them had been on the council, but I had no clue. There was no reason for me to have ever wondered about that. Even still, their status on the council didn't lend itself to their innocence either way. Surely council members had other elementals do their dirty work. If they hadn't been on the council, Stearns and West easily could have been in that position fifteen years ago.

"So you thought I was dead all this time," I said, putting the mystery of who was responsible for my abduction on the back burner. "Then what?"

"Two years ago, I received a message that a once-prominent EA member wanted to see me."

"Who?" Perhaps I could unravel the mystery after all.

She shook her head. "You should know by now I'm not going to tell you that." *Damn it.* "Anyway, I went to see this individual, and he told me what had happened all those years ago. He'd broken into the house with the intent of kidnapping you, but it wasn't officially authorized by the council. He didn't act alone, and though he didn't tell me who helped him, I have my suspicions. Anyway, to make a long story short, things didn't go exactly according to plan, and the house exploded."

"An explosion sounds like a lot didn't go according to plan," I said dryly. *What sort of plan going awry leads to a house exploding?*

"True enough. But I don't know exactly what the plan was. The man... Let's just say he wasn't in the right state to tell me everything."

What the hell does that mean?

I took a deep breath. "Did you kill him?"

Carly was silent for a moment as she gripped the steering wheel. "No. Maybe I should have, and fifteen years ago, I definitely would have, but he was already living a miserable existence. I figured that was punishment enough. Also, I didn't want to risk being found out when I'd just learned you were alive."

I wondered what weighed more in her decision to let the man live—her assessment that his current life was punishment enough or not wanting to raise any red flags. In the end, she'd done the right thing, but actions meant little without the right intent behind them.

It struck me that I wasn't bothered by the fact that Carly had flat-out admitted she would have killed the man without hesitation when she'd been in her prime. I didn't want to make the comparison between Michelle and Carly, but after witnessing Michelle's mama-bear behavior in the last few weeks, I couldn't fault a mother who would go to any lengths to protect her child.

"So then what?"

"I put feelers out to all my contacts, but I have very few in the EA. No one knew where you were. Most people don't realize I even had a daughter. When you were younger, that was for your protection, but when I was trying to find you, it worked against me. It wasn't until you were kidnapped that my contact came face-to-face with you and figured out that Sophie Hawthorne was actually Cassandra Levitt."

My mouth formed an *O*. "Are you telling me my name is actually Cassandra?"

"Yes."

Oh... my... God. When I'd found out that Carly was my mother, my world had tilted on its axis. Finding out my name wasn't my own sent it into a tailspin. It dawned on me that Sophie Hawthorne was not my legal name.

I'm Cassandra Levitt.

My innermost self, my core, rebelled against that thought. My powers roared to life, flowing through my veins as if they were also protesting.

I'm not Sophie. I'm Cassandra. Those two sentences played through my mind on a loop. The energy beneath my skin made me itch.

I breathed out slowly. *Calm down.* I couldn't afford to have an episode with my powers in the Jeep. It would be dangerous. More than that, I wasn't ready to put on display how out of control I was. Not to Carly. Not right now.

"A rose by any other name," I murmured. When I'd read *Romeo and Juliet* my freshman year, I'd never thought I would find any personal meaning in the lines. Yet they were true. My name was simply a label, a word others used to refer to me. It meant nothing.

"Are you okay?" Carly asked.

I cleared my throat. "Fine." Concentrating on the flow of power, I willed it to slow to a reasonable rate, one I could manage. I wanted to know who had renamed me Sophie, but Carly wouldn't likely have the answer. I also didn't want to dwell on it, not at the moment. I could freak out about it later.

Another thing occurred to me. "When is my birthday?"

"February sixth."

I groaned. That was two months earlier than April eighth, the day I'd celebrated my birthday for fifteen years. I wasn't an Aries, but a... I didn't even know what astrological sign I really was.

That meant I would be a legal adult in three months instead of five *if* I found a way to untangle the mess of my legal identity, and that was a very big *if*. I didn't see any way I could do it, nor was I sure it would be worth it. Anyway, that wasn't important right now.

Carly looked at me with pursed lips. "I know all of this must come as a shock."

It *was*, but I didn't want to admit how much it was getting to me. I didn't want her to think I couldn't handle the truth. She hadn't told me anything I hadn't asked to hear, and I had a feeling we had only scratched the surface.

Chapter 8

AFTER WE STOPPED for dinner, Carly said we could drive through the night if we shared the driving, but I didn't think it was a good idea for me to get behind the wheel of a car when my powers were so unpredictable. So as much as it killed me to add more time until I could get some answers about Lena, I agreed to find a hotel room around eleven that night.

Aidan would have been proud of my responsible, safety-first decision. While Carly was busy checking us in, I quickly emailed him to let him know where we'd stopped.

"Love, Sophie," I tapped out. Then I stopped and stared at the two little words. I erased them and typed, *"I miss you"* instead, but that didn't seem right either. In the end, I simply signed my name and hit send. Unless Aidan indicated otherwise, I would keep my communication with him professional. If he ended up needing to show my emails to the council, I wanted them to be taken seriously. But dang it, I did miss him for both personal and practical reasons. I had a bad habit of acting first and thinking second, which had gotten me into trouble more times than I cared to admit. I'd also been accused of not taking stuff seriously, and I hated to admit I was guilty of that as well. Aidan had always been my safety net,

there to lift me out of the holes I'd dug for myself. Now I was flying without a net, and I was painfully aware of that fact.

Carly came out of the front office and handed me a key card. "We're upstairs in 217." The motel had rooms that opened to the outside and formed a horseshoe around a swimming pool that had seen better days. I mentally took back any complaints I'd made about the small pool at the hotel I'd just left. I also reminded myself that I hadn't offered to pay my share. I didn't know how much money Carly had, so I had no room to complain. I slung my backpack over my shoulder and followed her up the rickety stairs to the second floor.

Carly looked over her shoulder at me but said nothing. Since the great reveal that the basic facts of my life—my name and birthday—were a lie, we hadn't talked much. She seemed to realize I needed time to process everything she'd told me. I also got the impression that she wasn't used to spending so much time talking with another person. She seemed relieved for the quiet. All the descriptions of her had labeled her as charismatic, but I supposed living in hiding for fifteen years changed a person.

Carly easily fell asleep—either that or she stayed so still I couldn't tell the difference. Despite the chill in the room, she lay on top of the covers on her back, straight as a board. Her sleeping style was a little eerie, like a vampire.

Despite my exhaustion after spending hours in the car, I tossed and turned. I couldn't stop staring at Carly in the bed next to me and thinking about Michelle, who'd been in the bed opposite me twenty-four hours ago. God, she must be so worried. I wondered if Aidan had been questioned about my absence. *Probably.* Most importantly, I wondered if anyone suspected he'd helped me. He would want me to focus on my mission and not worry about things that were out of my control, but I couldn't help it. Out of sight didn't mean out of mind, and what kind of person would I be if I didn't care? Mike and Michelle might not have been my biological parents, but they were my family, and it killed me to have to hurt them.

It would all be worth it if it led to Lena.

Since I couldn't sleep anyway, I sat up and tried to gather my thoughts on the meeting with Carly's first contact. Everything had happened so fast that I hadn't come up with a list of questions to ask. Somehow, leading with *"Do you know anyone who kidnapped six elemental girls? Oh yeah, and killed one of them?"* didn't seem like the best course of action. But that was more or less the information I needed.

Plus, I didn't know this person. It was hard to form a plan when the most important variable was unknown. At dinner, Carly had called him to tell him she was stopping by the next day, but she hadn't mentioned me, which was strange considering she'd said Jack didn't like surprises. Showing up with an extra person fell under the umbrella of surprises, but Carly didn't seem to think it would be a problem. I hoped her instincts were right.

The next morning, we packed up early before heading down to the lobby for the complimentary continental breakfast. I shivered as we stowed our stuff in the Jeep. We'd only traveled a few hundred miles north, but it was already so much colder than it had been in Orlando. I hadn't packed appropriately, but I hadn't had a wide selection to choose from.

Carly studied me. "We can stop and get you a coat."

"I'll be okay." I only had about a hundred dollars, and it was my emergency money. I didn't want to waste it on a coat.

Besides, she didn't have one, so it couldn't be that cold where we were going.

Carly was chipper as we surveyed the meager continental breakfast. I would have liked to think it had already been picked over, but I had only seen a handful of other guests, and it was still early—just after seven. Froot Loops with lukewarm milk was the best selection they had. *Yum.* I choked it down because I needed the calories, especially since my amped-up powers burned through my energy.

Carly happily munched on a piece of stale toast. "Tell me about Lena."

It felt like the cereal had lodged in my throat. I didn't want to talk about Lena with Carly any more than I'd wanted to talk about Aidan with her. But since she was helping me find my foster sister, I felt like I owed her. I guessed I had my own code of honor.

"She's sweet," I said. "Much nicer than me."

Carly laughed. "I don't know. You're pretty nice."

I raised an eyebrow. "Seriously?" I'd been giving Carly the cold shoulder, but I must not have been good at that if she couldn't even tell I was doing it. Either that, or Carly had rhino skin.

She shrugged. "Obviously, I don't know you well, but you seem nice, much nicer than me."

I didn't like that she'd used my words. I was about to retort *"Of course I seem nicer because I'm not a murderer,"* but that wasn't true. I'd killed one of my abductors in self-defense, but that most decidedly did not make me like Carly. I'd killed, but I hadn't liked it.

Yet I couldn't confidently say that Carly enjoyed killing. She'd done it many times, but she didn't strike me as bloodthirsty. She struck me as someone who did what needed to be done. *But who decides what that is?*

"Lena's smart," I said. "She'll probably end up with a college scholarship."

"Is she strong?"

I looked around quickly to see if anyone was listening to our conversation. Carly didn't seem to be worried about being overheard. Then again, if we were, no one would know what we were talking about.

"Yes." I realized what Carly wanted to know. She didn't give a damn about who Lena was as a person. Instead, she wanted to know what would make Lena valuable. I couldn't believe I'd missed that. I'd only gotten maybe two hours of sleep, but that was no excuse. If I had any hope of success, I needed to read people better, especially Carly.

"And the other girls?" Carly asked.

I nodded. "All six... *five* of them are strong."

Carly's eyebrows popped up. "Five?"

"Alexis Quigley is dead." I felt heartless stating that fact so coldly, like perhaps I should have used a softer euphemism for death, but the cold, stark reminder of what was at stake was what I needed.

"How old was she?"

"Thirteen."

Carly nodded, not offering condolences, empty words that did nothing to ease the hurt. "We should get going. Grab whatever else you want, and you can eat in the car."

I stood and dumped my cereal in a nearby trash can. "I'm done."

Once we were on the interstate, Carly continued our conversation. "Are any of them stronger with one element over another?"

"I don't know. Lena's great with earth, but she's pretty good with all of them." I couldn't say what strengths the other girls had because I hadn't known any of them personally, and it hadn't occurred to me that I would need to know. The fact that they were strong seemed good enough for me. "Does it matter?"

Carly's shoulders lifted. "Maybe. How old are they?"

"Lena is the oldest. She's seventeen. The youngest is eleven."

"That's just... *wrong*."

Coming from Carly, that meant something.

WHEN WE WERE about fifteen minutes away from Jack's place, Carly called him and told him we would be arriving soon in a green Jeep Cherokee.

At my perplexed look, Carly explained, "Jack is a bit of a prepper. Trust me when I say it's best that we don't surprise him."

I braced myself for a military-type compound surrounded by barbed wire, but when we got to the end of his unmarked long, rambling driveway, we were greeted with a small log cabin with smoke coming out of the chimney. It was downright picturesque and not at all what I'd expected for a prepper's house. Then again, I didn't actually have any experience with preppers, so what did I know?

Jack stood on the front porch, watching our arrival. He wore a green plaid flannel shirt and jeans. He would have looked like any other middle-aged man with thinning hair if not for the gun strapped to his belt and his hawk-like stare. We got out of the Jeep, and Carly waved to him. Instead of returning the gesture, he turned his scrutinizing gaze toward me. "Who's she?"

"Stacey," Carly replied easily. "I'm helping her with her powers, just like I helped your niece."

Somehow, I managed to keep my expression neutral while Carly simultaneously lied to the man and reminded him why he owed her.

"Hi," I said.

Jack grunted then turned and went inside.

"What the hell?" I asked under my breath.

Carly pursed her lips. "Come on. By the way, he thinks my name is Eliza." *Of course he does. Eliza and Stacey coming to visit.*

I followed her onto the porch. Jack had left the door partially ajar, so I supposed that was as much invitation as we were going to get.

Jack stood in the center of the small living room with his arms crossed and his stance wide. Though he hadn't invited us to sit, Carly made herself at home on a threadbare plaid sofa that looked as though it could have been made in the same factory that had made the man's shirt. I lowered myself to the sofa next to Carly. Though she appeared completely relaxed, I sat on the edge of the cushion so I would be ready to jump up if I needed to.

Carly smiled up at him. "How have you been, Jack?"

"Fine," he said grudgingly. "And you?"

"Not bad. How's Hannah doing?"

The man's face softened at the mention of the girl I assumed was his niece. "Good. She made the basketball team at school."

"I'm happy to hear that. You probably know why I'm here."

"No, I don't, actually."

Carly tilted her head. "Have you heard about the EA girls who were abducted?"

His expression turned guarded. "How does that concern you?"

He knows something. My heart started racing. He could give us the tip that would lead us to Lena. I wanted to interject and demand he tell us everything, but aside from asking who I was, he'd ignored my presence. I clamped my lips shut to keep words from flying out.

"I have a connection to one of the girls, so I'd like to find them," Carly said calmly.

"I don't stick my nose in EA business." He shook his head. "I can't help you."

"What have you heard?" Carly asked.

"Nothing." Finality rang in his tone.

"Jack." Carly's voice was somehow soft and sharp at the same time. "The youngest girl is eleven."

"Shit." He rubbed his jaw. "I wish I could help you, but all I know is what you know—six girls were taken. That's it."

Carly looked at him for a moment before sighing. "If that's everything, then I guess we're done here." She stood, and I followed suit. I stared at both of them in disbelief.

"That can't be it," I protested softly. "Please, Jack—Mr..." I realized I didn't know his last name. "Are you sure that's all you know?"

"I said it was." His tone was gruff. It was obvious he didn't appreciate being second-guessed.

"Thanks for your time, Jack." Carly turned to me. "Let's go."

I couldn't believe she wanted to leave after asking him only one question that he'd barely answered. Anger flowed through me, igniting my powers. Ignoring Carly and clenching my fists, I glared at him, trying to determine if he knew more than he was letting on, but his poker face was as good as any I'd seen.

"One of the girls is dead," I said, watching him closely. "She was thirteen."

There was the briefest crack in his fierce expression. "I'm sorry to hear that. It's time for you to go." His right hand went to the gun on his hip, probably an automatic response whenever he was faced with conflict.

I continued to study him, wishing I were as gifted as Aidan when it came to reading people. I had no idea if he was lying to us, but his sympathy seemed genuine.

"*Let's... go,*" Carly hissed in my ear, grabbing my arm.

I yanked my arm out of her grasp. "If you hear anything at all that might help us find those girls, will you promise to call us and tell us what you find out?"

Jack's shoulders slumped ever so slightly, but other than that, he gave no response.

"Please," I pleaded, then I let Carly lead me out of the house.

Once in the car, she unleashed on me. "What the hell were you thinking?"

I whirled on her. "What the hell were *you* thinking? You barely asked him any questions. Do you even care about finding the girls?"

"He doesn't know anything."

"He knew about them, so *that's* something," I retorted. "We should have found out where he got his information from."

Carly laughed bitterly. "He wouldn't tell us that."

"We should have at least asked."

"There was no point."

I raked my nails over the thighs of my jeans, trying to relieve the itching my growing power was causing. "We drove eleven hours for this. For nothing. Is this what it's going to be like with all your contacts?"

Carly's gaze steeled over, and she bared her teeth. "You know nothing."

"*I* know nothing?" I shrieked. Hysteria was taking over. Energy pulsed within me, blurring my vision with each thud. "Your contacts know nothing. This is bullshit."

"No. What's bullshit is you talking to me like that."

"Oh, no. I don't think so. You don't get to drop those motherly lines on me." I gritted my teeth, clenched my fists, and leaned my head back against the headrest as a tsunami of power rolled through my body. I groaned. "Stop the car. I'm getting out."

"No. You need—"

I tuned her out. I was seeing the world in shades of red, and every vein felt as if it were trying to explode. Gripping the door handle, I yanked it open and leaned sideways, prepared to roll out onto the shoulder of the road. But dammit, my seat belt was still hooked. I fumbled with the clasp.

Carly flung her arm around my body, grabbing my shoulder and holding me in place. Moments later, the Jeep skidded to a halt on the side of the road. I finally got the clasp undone and tumbled out. My knee landed hard on the asphalt, and somewhere in my mind, I realized it was going to hurt like hell later, but all I could focus on at that moment was the power trying to tear its way out of me.

I crawled onto the grass and focused on the ground below me. It rumbled, and dirt began shifting in a path, almost as if giant gophers were pushing the soil up from underneath. Gritting my teeth, I tried to keep the disturbance as low-key as possible because I was not cognizant of my surroundings. A bus full of people could have been watching for all I knew.

I registered Carly putting her arm around me and tried to shake her off, but I didn't have the physical energy. My powers were consuming me, and I had little energy for anything else.

My legs shook then gave out, leaving me on my stomach. The gopher path I'd created was so far in front of me that I couldn't even see it. *Screw it.*

I directed all my energy through the path, starting a foot away from me and going out until I felt more resistance, which meant it had reached the end of the tunnel I'd created. Then I sent everything I had at it and blasted the earth into the sky.

A delirious part of me wanted to laugh because it looked like Old Faithful, except the geyser was spouting dirt instead of water. I managed one giggle before I blacked out.

Chapter 9

I AWOKE TO find myself splayed on the back seat of the Jeep. Groaning, I put my hands on my temples, wishing I could blast the pain out of my head like I'd blasted the dirt out of the ground.

Something hard and heavy hit me in the stomach. *What the...* I wrapped my fingers around it—a water bottle.

"Drink up," Carly said from the driver's seat.

I sat up enough to take a few sips. "How long was I out?"

"Almost an hour."

That was an improvement at least. And I hadn't puked, so there was that. But damn it, this sucked. Though part of my reason for being with Carly was for her to teach me about my powers, I hadn't wanted to lose control like that. My powers were strong, but my inability to control them made me feel weak. And I *definitely* did not want to feel weak where Carly was concerned.

I sat up a little farther and looked out the window to see where we were on the interstate. Carly must have been stronger than she looked if she'd been able to get me in the car by herself. I wasn't heavy for my height, but she was smaller than me.

I had mixed feelings about how blasé she was being about my episode. I didn't necessarily want to be coddled, but it didn't escape my notice how different her reaction was from Michelle's. Perhaps that was because Carly had been through a similar experience.

"Where are we going?"

"To see another one of my contacts." Carly paused. "*If you think it's still worth your time.*"

I made a face at her behind her back. Apparently, she was still salty about my reaction to how the interview with Jack had gone. But if our next stop resembled that one, it definitely wouldn't be worth my time.

I blew out a breath and tried to minimize my anger. For one thing, that was what made my powers go haywire, so I needed to keep my emotions under control. Second, if Carly was indeed trying to help, then I should have been grateful she was carrying on in our quest despite my outburst.

Yet what kind of a monster would she have been if she had the ability to save those girls and she looked the other way? I tried not to think too hard about the fact that she was only doing this because I'd asked her. She seemed to subscribe to Jack's mantra of minding his own business.

I put my adult face on and decided to try for a mature conversation. "Do you understand why I'm upset about our meeting with Jack?" My phrasing of the question made me cringe. I sounded like a mother trying to reason with a toddler.

Carly's fingers made a rapid tapping sound on the steering wheel. "He doesn't know anything."

I closed my eyes as a string of expletives ran through my mind. "I think he knew more than he told us. We should have at least asked him more questions to find out. Something could have been useful."

"You don't know these people like I do," Carly said. "Even if he knew something, there's no way to force him to talk. But that's not the case anyway. Jack may be surly, but he doesn't bullshit. If he says he doesn't know anything, then he doesn't."

Carly was missing my point that he might not realize he had useful information. For instance, who had he heard about the girls' abduction from? How had that person heard about it? We could trace the line back until... I didn't know what, but *something*. It seemed like a waste to drive eleven hours then leave five minutes into the interview. I started to worry that my lack of experience and Carly's unknown agenda would doom me to failure.

No negative thinking allowed. I couldn't give up when we'd barely started. I hated to admit that despite the negative outcome so far, Carly's contacts were still my best option for finding information. I tried to think optimistically because that was honestly all I had going for me.

"Okay," I said. "Maybe he'll call if he discovers something."

"Not likely."

"Why not?" Not wanting to have another episode, I struggled to keep my frustration at bay. Though if the weak flow of energy in my body was any indication, an episode right then would have been more like a non-episode. "I can't believe he wouldn't try to help if he had information that could save those girls—girls just like his niece. He seemed to be upset when he heard about Alexis. "

"I'm sure he was, but he avoids involving himself in EA business at all costs. There are a lot of elementals like him. He's not in the minority."

"Is that why you wanted me to see him?" My anger that I had so carefully contained unleashed itself. "You wanted me to see how much he hates the EA?"

She rolled her shoulders. "The EA isn't the force for good you think it is. It's a force for control."

"I can't believe you wasted time trying to show me that."

"Calm down," she said in a tone that annoyed me. "Jack is a good man, even if he does hate the EA. But we're unlikely to hear from him. Jack is all about survival and protecting what's his. He's not particularly close with his brother, but he has a soft spot for his niece. He wouldn't do anything that might make her a target. Think about it—any group that's willing to go up against the EA like that has resources. That's not the kind of group you want to cross."

I let out a frustrated growl. "Nothing you've said has convinced me it was worth driving eleven hours to talk to him. Why did we bother?" *So much for positivity.*

"He knows everything that goes on in the Nashville area, so now we know it's unlikely the elementals we're looking for are in this area, and that's quite a few of them. He also keeps tabs on what happens in Atlanta, where his niece lives, so we can cross that area off the list."

That was something at least, but it did little to make those eleven long hours of driving worth it. I didn't know how many rogue elementals there were, but it didn't seem as if we could cross that many off the list just by eliminating a small area of the country. Besides that, people were transient. There was no way Jack could know every elemental in those areas, especially if he kept to himself as much as Carly said he did. I wasn't even going to try to explain that to her because logic didn't seem to be her strength.

"If he's so averse to involving himself in EA business," I said, "then how can we trust that he didn't lie to us back there? Maybe he does know something."

"Jack is a horrible liar. In case you didn't notice, he's not the most socially adept person. I would have known if he was lying. That's another reason why it's good to talk to people in person. Anyone can lie over the phone, but it's much harder to lie to someone's face."

"True." She had a point. I could attest to that from personal experience.

"Besides, he was on my way to my next contact. And now I know others in his circle are unlikely to have information, so we can plan accordingly." Carly glanced at me in the rearview mirror. "Are you hungry?"

I hadn't paid attention to my stomach, but I realized I was starving. "Yes."

"I figured as much. Expending that much energy burns a lot of calories. Do you have a preference where we stop?"

"No."

I pulled out my phone, wanting to update Aidan, even though all I had was really more of a non-update. Filled with anticipation, I logged into the email account, but my inbox was empty. I frowned and clicked on the spam folder just to be certain Aidan's email hadn't gotten trapped in there. There was nothing. *Well, dang.* The fact that there wasn't any news from him made me fear the worst. Aidan was more than a competent guardian, but he wasn't accustomed to fieldwork. The people we were looking for had already killed a thirteen-year-old girl. They would think nothing of offing a guardian or two.

Aidan trusts me. I need to trust him.

I quickly tapped out a short email, keeping it professional again. Before I hit send, though, I requested a reply. I'd promised to contact him frequently, but I realized that he hadn't made the same promise. We'd been so worried about what I would do that he hadn't even talked about his end of the bargain.

Dang. The temptation to text him was strong, but that would have been a mistake. Patience had never been one of my finer qualities. I hoped the *no news was good news* saying applied in this case.

AFTER LUNCH, I reclined my seat all the way back to take a nap. The silence between Carly and me wasn't comfortable, but I wasn't in the mood to talk either. Besides that, I was exhausted. Not sleeping combined with my powers going haywire had left me struggling to keep my eyes open.

When I woke up, we were parked in a hotel parking lot. It was still light outside. I glanced at the clock on the dash. It wasn't even five o'clock.

"Why are we stopped?" I asked.

"This is our next destination."

I sat up and winced at the pain in my neck from sleeping at a jaunty angle. "Great. Where are we?" Since the first leg of our trip had taken so long, I'd just assumed the next part would take a while as well. That assumption made no sense, but I was exhausted, and my mind was scrambled.

Carly pressed the release latch on her seat belt. "West of Louisville."

That meant nothing to me other than we were in Kentucky. My knowledge of geography was rough at best, but honestly, I didn't care where we were if it put me closer to potentially finding Lena. "When can we meet with your next contact?"

"Tomorrow. Maybe about ten."

Damn. That was not the answer I wanted. There would be a lot of time to twiddle thumbs between now and then. "Can't we do it tonight?"

Carly shook her head. "No. We need to wait until her husband leaves for work."

"Why?"

"Let's just say he wouldn't approve of me stopping by."

I waited for a further explanation and sighed when it was evident one wasn't coming. I hated not being in charge, but more than that, I hated not being informed. I was used to both, but at least with Aidan, I trusted that his goals were the same as mine. I couldn't say the same about Carly. Yet, like Aidan, she wouldn't confide in me until she was ready. How did I get so blessed to be surrounded by the most stubborn people on Earth?

"Is your friend trustworthy?" I asked.

"I wouldn't say she's my friend."

I sighed. "You know what I mean. Can we trust her?"

"That depends."

"That was a yes-or-no question." I wanted to bang my head on the dash in frustration. I'd known going in that Carly's associates were most likely sketchy because, after all, what kind of person would have information on abducted girls and not report it? But I still didn't like it. With Carly, trust was something that happened when Jupiter's fifth moon aligned with Venus, but only if that was on a Tuesday. All of the terms and conditions were maddening.

Carly's gaze slid over to me. "Is the council trustworthy?"

My default answer of *"of course"* was on the tip of my tongue, but I held it back. I may not have always liked the council's rules, but until recently, I'd never had reason to doubt their intentions. I didn't know most of the council members personally, but the two I did know were responsible for the lies I'd been told my entire life. Unfortunately, I also had issues with both Councilwoman West and Councilman Stearns for personal reasons, so I had been hesitant to ask about the lifelong deception. Then everything had gone to hell with the girls being abducted, and my personal issues hadn't mattered anymore.

The EA had been static for as long as I could remember, but I had a feeling that was about to change, one way or another. When the girls had been taken, the EA had been setting up tests for its members to see who qualified for full elemental status. Ones like Vic and Aidan, who had little power, wouldn't qualify, making them second-class citizens. That alone was a hot-button issue for me. The reason for the testing in the first place was another problem.

For years, we'd adhered to the Langston Agreement, which prohibited all elementals worldwide from using their powers to influence politics or cause harm. Recent events had caused the council to question whether the EA should leave the agreement, which was why testing was needed—to see who would be permitted to vote. Since testing had been disrupted, the vote was postponed, but surely it would be rescheduled eventually.

And of course the abduction of six girls—three of whom where council members' daughters—right out from under everyone's noses was a wake-up call. What we were waking up to, though, I had no clue. Frankly, I didn't care. I couldn't care about anything until Lena was safe.

But I didn't want to admit my doubts to Carly. Everyone I loved was part of the EA. Some of them, like Aidan, were EA employees. While I had no problem voicing my concerns about the council's actions to Aidan or my foster parents, talking negatively about the council to Carly was something else entirely.

Once again, I let Carly check us into the hotel. It was slightly nicer than the one we'd stayed in the previous night, but that wasn't saying much. I didn't complain, though. Carly had paid for everything thus far and hadn't asked me to contribute. In the room, I dropped my stuff on the floor and flopped on the bed, thinking we had an hour or two before we needed to scrounge up dinner.

"Get up," Carly said. "We need to work on your skills."

Considering I'd had an episode earlier, a lesson was exactly what I needed, but it was also the last thing I wanted to do. While I could feel the soft tingle of my power flowing through my veins, it was a gentle, warm sensation. In other words, my power was playing nice, and I didn't want to piss it off.

"My energy is still pretty low," I said. "Wouldn't it be better to wait until it's stronger?"

Carly gave me an assessing stare, and I could tell she knew I was trying to weasel my way out of whatever she had in store for me, which was stupid—working with my power was one of the reasons I was there.

"It'll be fine," she said.

I stood and shook my limbs to loosen my body. I would mentally prepare myself on the way to wherever we were going to work. Normally, I would've loved to have been given the opportunity to flex my elemental muscles, but I was gun-shy. And that was exactly why I needed to put on my big-girl panties and suck it up. Living in fear of my powers was not an option.

I grabbed my jacket. "Okay, let's go."

Carly shook her head. "We're not going anywhere. In fact, you can lie back down."

"Seriously?" I hated to break it to her, but the last time I'd used my powers in a hotel room, I'd trashed it.

"Yes. Just do it." Carly's voice was laced with irritation. She obviously wasn't used to having someone question her directives. Then again, Aidan was used to it, and he still got annoyed.

Aidan... I was dying to check my email to see if he'd responded to my second message. It had only been twenty-four hours since I'd seen him last, but that felt like so long ago.

I'd never been apart from my family like this. It wasn't something I'd dwelled on or even realized until now. Poor Michelle must be frantic with both Lena and me MIA. I hoped she could forgive me when I returned. My gut told me that as long as I came back with Lena in tow, all would be forgiven.

I sat on the edge of the bed and looked at Carly with a questioning stare. She sighed and motioned that I should stretch out. I lay on my back and crossed my ankles. My weakened powers sensed my unease and sparked to life. *No, no, not now. No more using my power in confined spaces.*

"Are you sure—"

"Close your eyes," she commanded, cutting me off. "Have you ever meditated?"

"Nope." Trying to be a good student, I let my eyelids fall, but I really wanted to roll my eyes.

"That's what I figured." Her voice had a note of derision that was insulting. I didn't know why it bothered me, but it did.

I opened my eyes to glare at her. "Hey, what's that supposed to mean?"

"You're wound tighter than a banjo string. Now close your eyes."

I shot her one last fierce look before complying. "No, I'm not," I muttered. *Not normally. Sorry if my foster sister being kidnapped has gotten me a little stressed out.* "What's that even mean anyway?"

"I don't know. It's just something my daddy used to say."

Hearing Carly mention her father was unexpected. Hearing her refer to him as *daddy* was even more unexpected. I opened my eyes and sat up. "My grandfather?"

"Yes," she said slowly. "He was."

"Oh." I couldn't keep the disappointment out of my voice. "So he's dead?"

"Yes," Carly said tersely. "Can we focus on the task at hand?"

All I knew was the man's name—Ronald Levitt—but I was overcome with sadness. Family was being yanked away from me at every turn, whether it was learning my family wasn't actually my family or this, that my biological relatives were dead. I wondered what kind of a man Ronald Levitt was to have raised a woman like Carly.

Obviously, her father was a sore subject, so I let it go for the moment and didn't inquire about her mother, my grandmother. Or about my own father for that matter. I assumed he hadn't been in the picture long. Anyway, it was all I could do to manage quality time with one deranged parent. I certainly wasn't ready to add another one in the mix.

Carly narrowed her eyes at me and huffed, obviously having lost her patience. But she still hadn't given me clear instructions, so I didn't know what I was supposed to be focusing on.

"What do I do?"

"Meditation is simple. Close your eyes. Focus on your breathing."

I did as she asked and waited for further instruction. When none came, I asked, "Okay, now what?"

"That's it," she said.

"That's it?"

She couldn't be serious. Meditation was supposed to be some mystical art of connecting with a higher power or something. But according to her, all I had to do was breathe with my eyes closed. Apparently, I'd been doing meditation my whole life without realizing it. I held back a snort but just barely.

I heard Carly stretch out on the other bed, presumably to do some meditation of her own.

"Clear your mind of all thoughts and focus only on your breathing. Pay attention to the movements your body makes as you inhale and exhale. Concentrate on how the air feels as it moves in and out of your body."

I reached under my head to fluff my pillow and punched it a few times to try to give life to the flattened lump. Then I slipped my shoes off and kicked them to the floor.

"What are you doing?" Carly's voice was exasperated.

"Making myself comfortable." I closed my eyes again and tried to remember exactly what she'd said to do—something about feeling the air in my lungs and other woo-woo nonsense.

Stop. How do you know this won't help?

I was never one to buy into New Age stuff, but Carly struck me as a no-nonsense person. If she found value in it, then I should give it an honest effort. It couldn't hurt. *I can't believe I'm doing this—lying here breathing while Lena is going through God knows what.*

Settling back onto the pillow, I closed my eyes and exhaled. As I took a breath, I focused on the feeling of the air as it traveled through my lips.

The last time I'd focused so much on the sensation of my lips was when I was kissing Aidan. God, I wished I were doing that instead of trying to feel myself breathe. I'd much rather feel him and his soft, full lips any day. Heck, *every* day.

Focus, Sophie.

I didn't *want* to focus, though. Lying there and literally doing nothing went against everything I knew about accomplishing something. If I wanted to get better at something, I trained and practiced it. I didn't do the exact opposite and do nothing.

Okay, so it wasn't *exactly* nothing. After all, I was breathing. But that was a basic function of staying alive. I wouldn't consider it an activity.

If Michelle were there—in some strange, not-going-to-happen scenario in which she and Carly were working together—she would've had her hands on her hips and her lips pursed while giving me the mom stare. She would've wanted me to try. And she would've been angry that I wasn't taking this seriously when Carly was trying to help.

I sighed. Thinking it might help to feel my breathing, I put my hands on my belly and concentrated on it rising and falling.

One... two... three...

No, that wasn't right. Was I supposed to count my breaths? I wasn't counting sheep in an attempt to fall asleep.

I tried again but found I was so focused on the feeling of inhaling that I forgot to exhale. Meditation was making me forget how to breathe. *What in the ever-loving heck?*

Peeking at the nightstand, I stifled a groan. *Three minutes.* That was how long I'd been attempting to meditate. I sure hoped Carly had another trick up her sleeve because this one wasn't working.

I turned my head to look at Carly. She lay flat on her back with her hands folded on her stomach. *Peaceful. She looks peaceful.*

I took the opportunity to study her. Objectively, she was an attractive woman—smooth skin, full lips, shapely brows. She wore minimal makeup, and her hair was in a messy bun on top of her head. Her body appeared toned, as though she exercised regularly and took care of herself. Lying there with her eyes closed, she had an air of innocence about her.

Fifteen years had passed since she'd "died." I wondered what she had done with herself that whole time. I'd told myself that I didn't care, but I couldn't help but wonder.

I hated that I did, but I wanted to know. The woman had given birth to me, and she cared about me in some way. However, I hadn't completely put to rest the notion that she might have ulterior motives, that she might want to use me for something.

Kind of like I'm using her?

That truth made me cringe, but at least I was up front about it. Carly claimed she wanted to get to know me, but I didn't buy it completely. The past twenty-four hours hadn't exactly been quality mother-daughter bonding time, and we hadn't really talked much about me. Then again, my countenance hadn't exactly been inviting, but I wasn't going to apologize for being on my guard with Cruel Carly. Spending time with her was a means to an end—the end being finding Lena.

If I got to know Carly a bit along the way and got some questions answered, then great. If not, I would be disappointed. But Lena's disappearance had made me understand my priorities, and while solving the mystery of my past was high on the list, it wasn't number one. My family—the adopted one, not my blood one—came first. And they always would.

Chapter 10

THAT NIGHT, I slept better than I had in weeks. After dinner, we'd meditated twice more, so perhaps there was some benefit to it. I still had doubts that it would help me control my powers, but I would take a restful night. Maybe I would even press my luck and meditate before bed again that evening.

While I waited for Carly to finish getting ready, I checked my email again.

Finally. There was a message from Aidan. I opened it, and disappointment immediately struck me at how short it was.

Made it to West Virginia, but our contact has gone missing. So now instead of looking for lost kids, we're looking for her.

Stearns questioned me. He doesn't believe I don't know what happened to you. Now they're watching me very closely, hoping to intercept a call from you, so I probably won't be able to email often.

They? Who the heck was *they?* Damn Aidan's ambiguous pronoun usage. How were Mike and Michelle? He didn't mention anything about them. I couldn't fathom what they must have been thinking.

Apparently his idea to set up the new email accounts had been the right one, though. He'd correctly anticipated we wouldn't be able to call or text without the council finding out.

There was just one more line in his email.

Stay safe.

That was all I got, and it wasn't enough. I stared at the small screen, wishing I could will more words into existence. Aidan had told me basically nothing. If *they*—whoever *they* were—were watching him that closely, he might have been lucky to send me an email at all. But seriously, how closely could they be watching him? Aidan was a trained guardian. Surely he could manage a few solo minutes with his phone to send me a proper email. It didn't even have to be *his* phone. He could access email from any device with an internet connection.

I was pissed. Aidan's email was supposed to set my mind at ease, not make things worse. He'd told me just enough to make me worry more. I'd never been a worrier, but I'd never been away from my loved ones like this either. And of course one of my loved ones had never been abducted by psychopaths. I didn't know if the kidnappers were psychopaths in the technical sense, but there had to be some kind of crazy going on for them to kidnap six elemental girls. And now Aidan's contact was missing. That couldn't be good.

I hit the reply button and furiously tapped out a response, even though I had nothing new to tell him. I mentally cursed him again. I wanted to know who was watching him and exactly how much trouble he was in. That was precisely what I'd wanted to avoid. Though if I was honest with myself, if everyone knew about our relationship like he seemed to think they did, he would've been under surveillance whether he'd helped me or not. Heck, he was supposed to be keeping an eye on me, so there was no way he would've been off the hook.

Carly finished getting ready, so I hauled myself off the bed.

Kentucky was freezing, especially in the morning and especially since I'd come from the warmth of Florida. I missed it already. My meager clothing selection and lack of a proper coat made the weather even more unbearable. I briskly rubbed my arms as we walked to the Jeep.

Carly eyed my behavior but said nothing about it. "What does Aidan have to say?" she asked instead.

My eyes widened. "Nothing. What do you mean?" God, my voice sounded squeaky... and guilty.

Carly rolled her eyes, and the action made her seem too young to have a seventeen-year-old daughter. "I know you're communicating with him."

"No, you don't," I said automatically. *What a stupid response. I basically just admitted I was.*

"What kind of a fool do you take me for? For starters, I know you're not stupid, so I know you didn't run off with me without creating some kind of plan." She had me there. "And secondly, I saw the way that boy looked at you. He's going to keep the leash as tight as he can."

Whoa. There were several things wrong with her statement. Aidan could never be described as a boy, but more importantly, I wasn't on his leash. That was positively insulting.

"He's not my master," I said with disgust.

"Bad choice of words. But I know his type."

"You should be so lucky," I snapped. She'd better not talk trash about Aidan to me, or I would be the one in danger of flying into a homicidal rage.

Carly cocked her head. "Perhaps."

I crossed my arms and stared out the window so she would make no mistake that the conversation was over.

She drove us to an empty parking lot.

"Let's see what your powers can do when you're in control," she said.

The notion of being in control made me snort. I was beginning to think I would never be in control again. Before getting out of the Jeep, I took a moment to assess my power level. It buzzed through my veins at an annoying but not yet uncomfortable level. Since I was about to expend energy, I called to it, urging it to increase, something I hadn't done since my powers had gone supersonic. They heeded my call, and I was pleased to find I could still dial them up if I wanted to.

I got out of the Jeep and walked a few yards away from it.

Seeming amused, Carly leaned on the hood. "Where are you going?"

"The last few times I tried something like this, it got really destructive really fast. I don't want to damage your Jeep."

She shrugged as though she weren't concerned. "You're not as powerful as you think you are."

I put my hands on my hips and narrowed my eyes at her. "Why don't you demonstrate your power, then?" It galled me that one of the reasons I was with her was to get help with my extreme power level, but she didn't seem to think it was a problem. I'd nearly sent Mike to the hospital—that wasn't something to dismiss.

She laughed. "No, thank you."

I tried to stare her down, but it was hard to look fierce while shivering. She walked toward me, and when she got within two yards, the air warmed significantly, as if I'd stepped into a room with a blazing fireplace.

"Is that you?" I asked. *Duh, obviously it is.* I'd pulled that little trick a time or two.

"Of course. I wear a coat when it would attract notice not to, but I'm happier not wearing one. They're too bulky and hard to move in."

Now that sounded more like the Cruel Carly of legend, the one who would need to strike down an enemy at a second's notice.

"Doesn't it wear you out?" I asked.

"Not really. I'm sure you've figured out by now that the more energy you generate, the more it will continue to generate."

"Use it or lose it," I whispered.

"Kind of."

One of the controversies surrounding the testing was that the bar to achieve full elemental status was set too high. But I'd been astonished to learn how low the bar actually was and even more astonished that Michelle had anticipated many in our ranks would have a hard time passing. The council banned displays of power and put so many restrictions on using it in general that most elementals rarely—if ever—did. Obviously, the council members and guardians couldn't be everywhere to police every elemental's actions, but it seemed as though most of them followed the rules. Me? Not so much. If given the opportunity to use my power and get away with it, I gladly took it. Truth be told, I sometimes used it in situations that were neither advisable nor discreet. What good was having the powers if I never used them? Anyway, I'd had a theory that elementals were a dying breed—lack of use was making us lose our powers.

Though at times I longed to be normal, the thought of losing my powers petrified me. They were part of me, and I didn't know who I would be without them. I didn't want to examine too closely what that said about me.

"What do you want me to do?" I asked, feeling like I was having a déjà vu moment from both my pre-testing with Aidan's mother and my practice session with Michelle.

"Do you see that line there?" Carly pointed to a faint white line on the aged asphalt. "Crack it."

I frowned. "My powers don't work on pavement." She should know that. We were elementals. Asphalt was man-made.

She stared at me for a moment, appearing as though she wanted to say something but had second thoughts. I was definitely having second thoughts about whether she would be able to help me. She might have been powerful—though I'd yet to see evidence of that—but she was a sucky teacher.

"There's earth under the parking lot," she said finally.

I studied the vacant lot, eying the cracks where grass had climbed its way up toward the sunlight. But there were no splits along the line she wanted me to crack.

I wasn't one to back away from a challenge, but I didn't think I could do it. The white line stretched the length of the parking lot, running straight down the center and forming the top of thirty or more parking spaces.

As I studied my target, Carly studied me, making my hackles rise. Though she'd witnessed my powers when I'd thrown a temper tantrum, she didn't seem convinced that my powers were of concern. I guessed my geyser of dirt hadn't impressed her. Obviously, I hadn't been trying to impress her, but her reaction annoyed me. My power level demanded her respect at the very least.

I stretched my arms out, as if that would make more room in my body for my power. Willing it to get stronger, I closed my eyes and reveled in the sensation of it flowing through my body like a current. It made me light-headed and dizzy. *More. I want more.*

When I was nearly drunk on the intensity of it, I returned my attention to the asphalt. *No, look below it.* I visualized the red-tinged dirt that must reside beneath the lot. Extending my power to it, I let the vibes caress it and intermingle with it until it accepted my authority. Then I commanded it to push together in a thin line under the faded white paint, similar to what I'd done the day before. Except this required much more control because I needed the pressure to be strong enough to crack several inches of asphalt.

A line of sweat beaded up on my forehead as another one ran down my spine. Yet despite my exertion, there was no visible movement. *Damn it.* I would not fail Carly's test.

I pushed myself further than I thought possible and dug deep down to pull every lingering ounce of energy out of my body. As I did that, I felt the sensation of falling, as if my psyche were free falling down a black hole. Dizziness—and not the good kind—overtook me. My knees shook as I struggled to stay on my feet. Then suddenly, I felt a zing, and my power resources were refilled. They were more than refilled. They were greater than they were when I'd started. *Level up.*

It took me a few seconds to get a handle on my increased strength. But as soon as I bent it to my will, a crack formed in the center of the white line at my feet. I grinned and commanded the earth to force its way up through the concrete.

Mere seconds later, a ripple extended from the small crack at my feet.

Breathing hard, I stared at the ground. *I did it.* Triumphantly, I beamed at Carly.

She gave me a small approving smile. "Good job. Let's go." She turned her back to me and walked to the Jeep.

My face fell. I'd worked my butt off to form the long crack in the concrete like she'd asked. Surely she could give me a better response than *"good job."* I deserved more than that.

And now that I took a second to think about it, I wondered why she'd asked me to do that in the first place. The parking lot was abandoned, but someone owned it, and they would have to pay to have the damage fixed. Given the list of crimes Carly was accused of, I shouldn't have been surprised that she would think nothing of a little destruction of private property. But damn it, I wasn't okay with it. I'd been so eager to please Carly, I hadn't even considered the fact that I was committing a misdemeanor.

I stalked to the Jeep, slid into the passenger seat, and slammed the door.

"What?" Carly asked. "Why are you sulking?"

"I'm not sulking." Though with my crossed arms and sour expression, my declaration didn't hold much weight. I yanked the seat belt across my body. Everyone else who'd witnessed my power had been concerned and at least partially terrified of it. So yeah, maybe I was hoping Carly would have a bigger reaction than a simple *"good job."*

God, I wanted her to be proud of me. The thought sickened me. Carly may have given birth to me, but for all intents and purposes, she was not my mother. I shouldn't give a damn what she thought.

Michelle would not have approved of my action. While she was willing to violate EA rules to train Lena and me, she generally followed them, and that meant she did not use her powers in the open. Plus, she would have considered the owner of the property and not wanted to cause a hardship for another person.

"Just say what you're thinking," Carly said. "I'm not going to try to read your mind."

"I did exactly what you asked—" I stopped myself before I asked her for praise. *Pathetic.* I felt small, like a child yelling *"Look at me!"* to her parents.

"You did. Good job."

Ugh. Again with the *good job* bit. My power rippled through me as my irritation rose. I exhaled slowly, using the effort to get myself in check. "I guess I don't understand why you wanted me to do that. What was the point?"

"Your powers are strong, but they're not as strong as they could be." She paused. "As they *should* be."

"You just met me." That wasn't exactly true, but whatever. "How the hell would you know how strong I *should* be?" I was one of—if not *the*—strongest elemental I knew. Staring out the window, I gaped at that fact—it hadn't occurred to me until that very moment, but it was true. *I'm the most powerful. So just how strong does she think I should be? And why does she want me to be stronger?*

A conversation regarding the experiments Carly had done surfaced in my mind. When I'd been kidnapped, I'd been injected with a form of Infirmi, a drug that Carly's followers had created. It suppressed elemental powers. However, her followers had also been working on another one that was supposed to create or increase powers. *Holy mother of all things...*

I almost didn't want to ask, but I had to know. "Did you experiment on me?"

"What?" Carly looked over at me with indignation. "No. Hell no."

Relief washed over me. "So how strong do you think I should be?"

"At least as strong as me, but most likely much stronger."

"Why? Was..." I took a deep breath. "Was my father strong?" In the previous story of my life in which Amanda Hawthorne, Lloyd and Belinda's late daughter, was my mother, my father hadn't been a factor. I'd long ago accepted that I would never know anything about him. But now that could change. Yet I'd put off asking about him. I already felt disloyal to Mike and Michelle by wanting to get to know my birth mother, but that was natural. Adopted children searched for their birth families all the time. My wanting to know about my father and how powerful he was was the same as adopted children wanting to know their family medical history. Still, I couldn't shake the guilt.

Carly looked as though she were warring with herself. "It's complicated," she said finally.

Her answer should have been *yes* or *no*. I could think of only one thing that would make it complicated. "Did you experiment on him?"

She pulled to a stop at a red light. "No."

"So how powerful was he?" I asked again.

"He was strong in his own way." She was putting me off, and I had no idea why or what her cryptic response was alluding to.

"What's his name?"

"Jason."

Just Jason? Considering how my reunion with my birth mother was going, I wasn't sure I would ever want to find my father, but it seemed as though I wouldn't be able to anyway. Still, a large part of me was curious about a man who would enter into a relationship with Carly.

"Is he still alive?"

"I don't know. We lost touch." Carly had a faraway look in her eyes, as though she were lost in the past. The light turned green, and the car behind us honked, snapping her back into the present. "It was better that way." Her tone indicated the subject was closed. "I can't believe you'd think I'd experiment on my own baby."

"You experimented on other people, so it's not that far-fetched."

"They were adults, able to make the decision for themselves." Carly didn't deny the fact that she had indeed experimented on elementals. Well, not her personally, but scientists had under her direction. But her candor didn't earn my respect. I was too filled with disgust at her actions.

A tiny, molecular-sized part of me argued that adults agreeing to participate in her experiment were no different than adults participating in experimental medical treatments. I was still too irritated with her to give that justification any consideration.

"What were you hoping to achieve?"

"Choice," she said. "Everything is about choice. Some people view their powers as a burden, almost like an affliction or an illness. Infirmi could have given them the option to suppress their powers and essentially be normal."

"Why would anyone want that?" The words were out of my mouth before I realized I was saying them. For a time, I'd longed to live a normal life, but that was the difference—I wanted to *live* normally. I didn't necessarily want to *be* normal. The thought of losing my powers horrified me. But I thought of Lena, who'd never been comfortable with hers. I wondered if she would choose to suppress them if she could. Much of her misgiving toward her powers was a result of her parents being killed by witch hunters. If that hadn't happened, maybe she wouldn't have such a hard time accepting the elemental part of herself.

Carly grinned. "I didn't say *I* wanted that, but some elementals do. It's something most of them won't admit to because it's a taboo subject."

If anything, I would think most EA elementals would want *more* power to ensure they would qualify as voting elementals. I could see why some of them wouldn't want to admit they wanted *no* powers.

"If there are elementals who really do want that, they could get their wish. A more powerful version of Infirmi is out there."

Carly's expression darkened. "I know."

"What do you know about it?"

"Not much." I could tell it troubled her to admit that. "It was only after you were kidnapped that there was talk about it. Whoever is behind it managed to keep it a secret."

"All of my kidnappers were killed," I said, conveniently not mentioning I'd killed one of them. I still tried not to think about it. "So guardians weren't able to question them and find out where they got the drug from."

"Yes, that was a misjudgment on my part."

My eyebrows shot up, and my stomach clenched. "What do you mean?" I asked slowly, watching her intently.

She flipped on her turn signal, not seeming to notice my scrutiny. "Oh, I thought you'd figured it out already. I killed them."

Chapter 11

"*WHAT?*" I MUST have heard her wrong. Did she just casually admit to cold-blooded murder?

She shot me a surprised look. "Obviously, I wasn't going to let them live. They tried to *kill* you."

I was well aware. After all, I was the one they'd attempted to burn alive to cleanse my impure soul or some such nonsense. But our country had a justice system for criminals. Granted, that crime wasn't reported because the council kept elemental issues under wraps, but still.

The matter-of-fact way she talked about dealing justice to my kidnappers was scary. She was eerily unimpassioned about the whole thing. While she'd purposely committed murder, I'd only accidentally killed someone in self-defense, but the fact that I'd taken a life tormented me.

Also, the method of murder—dropping a huge tree on top of a moving vehicle—displayed how powerful Carly was. I couldn't imagine wielding enough air power to lob an entire tree. And not only that, but she'd managed to hit a car that was going at least fifty miles per hour in the exact perfect spot to kill the backseat passengers but not the driver. That took an insane amount of control.

I could only hope that Carly's actions were partially a result of her distress in learning that the daughter she'd thought to be dead all these years had nearly been killed. Somehow, though, I knew I was looking into a window at the Carly of old, the one who'd caused devastation without a second thought.

That was a good reminder for me. Although Carly was my birth mother, she was first and foremost a force to be reckoned with. I remained strong in my conviction that she wouldn't hurt me, but I was concerned about my loved ones.

Irrational fear gripped my heart, and I pulled my phone out to check for an email from Aidan, even though I'd just gotten one. Obviously, there was nothing new. I was being ridiculous. There was no way Carly could have hurt him because she'd been with me the whole time, but she might have had associates to carry out her bidding.

My rational brain kicked in. *Unlikely.* She was not in a position of influence like she had been. If she had followers, she risked being found out by the EA, which she obviously didn't want. She was smarter than that.

Yet if she were that smart, she had to realize that since I'd run off with her, the truth about her non-death would soon come out. So perhaps she no longer cared about staying off the EA's radar.

I clutched my phone tighter, wishing I could call Aidan. Being with Carly was screwing with me. I hated to admit it, but I was too emotionally wrapped up in the situation to be one hundred percent objective.

Aidan wasn't completely objective either, though. He loathed Carly.

I wished she hadn't dropped that bombshell on me right before we were going to interview another source. And damn it, I also wished I hadn't used my powers earlier. My brain was fuzzy, and my emotions were all over the place. *As if these circumstances aren't already less than ideal.*

Carly parallel parked in front of a light-blue house with a big porch. Children's playthings, like plastic slides and tricycles, littered the front yard. A small wooden sign near the mailbox read, "Shari's Childcare."

"We're visiting a daycare?" I asked. This was about the last place I'd expected us to go. Jack was more in line with the type of person I expected Carly to associate with.

"Yes." Carly didn't get out of the car right away and instead stared at the house for a few moments. *What is she waiting for?* She seemed to be having some kind of moment, and I wondered if she was having second thoughts about seeing this person—Shari, I assumed.

"Well," I said slowly. "What are we waiting for?"

"Nothing." Carly opened her door. "Let's go."

I followed her down the front walk. Despite my initial surprise at stopping at a daycare, I felt more comfortable there than I had at Jack's. At least I could be reasonably certain Shari wouldn't be armed, not with little kids running around.

Carly ignored the doorbell, choosing to knock softly on the door instead. The tall windows on both sides of the door were masked with curtains, and there was no peephole, but there was a glaringly obvious camera directed right at us.

I pointed to it. "Look."

"Yeah, I saw it."

It was smart, and if I were a parent, I would have felt much better about leaving my kid there with that camera in place.

A woman with wild curly hair and dark skin opened the door. Her pleasant expression vanished, and her eyes widened when she realized who was standing on her porch. She pushed the door closed, but her split second of shock provided Carly enough time to put her arm out and stop the door from closing.

"I don't want to talk to you," Shari said angrily. "You're supposed to be dead."

"Surprise," Carly said wryly.

"Not a good one." Shari pushed on the door again, but Carly's foot was now firmly planted. "Go away."

"This will only take a minute," Carly said. "Did you know a group of EA girls was kidnapped?"

Shari's momentum against the door stopped for a beat before she resumed pushing. "That has nothing to do with me."

"I wanted you to be aware, all the same."

"So why come here? You could have just called. My number's listed."

Carly glanced at me before speaking. "I don't have many regrets, but you're one of them. I wanted to tell you in person that I'm sorry. I feel like I owe you that."

Shari's eyes softened for a moment before returning to a hateful glare. "Words. That's all those are. They're worth nothing." Somewhere behind her, a child started wailing. "I'm busy. You need to leave now."

I expected Carly to press for more information, but instead, she removed her foot from the door. Shari firmly closed it in Carly's face.

"Okay." Carly let out a breath. "We're done here."

I followed her off the porch. "That's it?"

Two interviews down. Two sets of worthless results.

"Yes." She didn't look at me as she finished the walk to the Jeep and got in the driver's seat. Before I got in on the passenger's side, I eyed the house one last time. I thought I saw Shari watching us from behind the curtains, but I couldn't be sure. As Carly pulled away from the house, I seethed. She knew Shari wouldn't help us—it was obvious they hadn't been on good terms the last time they'd seen one another. We'd wasted our time there so Carly could have a shot at redemption with an old friend.

"What were you apologizing for?" I asked.

"I'd rather not discuss it," she replied. "It's Shari's business."

"Oh no, I don't think so. You're supposed to be helping me find Lena, not seeking forgiveness for whatever horrible thing you did."

"I didn't ask for forgiveness."

"Yeah, probably because you knew she wasn't going to give it to you."

"That's not why. She's responsible for her own decisions. That doesn't mean I can't be sorry for the outcome."

"You said she was a regret. What does that mean?"

Carly shook her head. "No. I don't want to talk about it."

"You promised to help me," I said quietly, "but your first two contacts have been a waste of time. Are you planning to actually help me?"

I understood why she'd wanted me to meet Jack, but witnessing Shari's cold reception served no purpose. If Carly wasn't actually intending to honor her promise to help me, I wanted to find out what her true intentions were.

"Yes," she said. "I keep my promises. Shari's husband is a professor of psychology. He studies human development, so naturally he studies the development of elemental children as well. He's connected to a lot of them, so he would know if any other kids were taken. And if he didn't know, then he needs to know."

That made me wonder if the kids in Shari's care were elementals and her husband's subjects. Though Carly had said she had contacts in the EA, I assumed Shari wasn't one of those. That meant that if the kids were elementals, they most likely weren't associated with the EA. That might not matter, though. At first, I'd thought Lena's kidnappers had targeted EA young adults specifically. But the kids Aidan was looking for in West Virginia weren't part of the EA. It seemed as though any young elementals might be fair game, so I was glad we'd warned Shari.

"Why wouldn't they already know about it?" I asked. "Jack did."

"They run in different circles. Like I told you, there are more non-EA elementals than you realize."

I didn't want to admit it to her because it made me sound ignorant, but I hadn't known there were so many. I'd thought rogues were very rare.

"We should have talked to her husband. What if he knows something and didn't share it with her?"

"Unlikely." Carly's know-it-all attitude pissed me off.

"You don't know that. It's been fifteen years since you've seen them."

"Darius is the only person who's tried to kill me and was allowed to live," Carly said in a monotone. "Talking to him was not an option."

I stared at her. "What the hell did you do to them?"

She sighed. "Shari took part in the trials for the drugs we were developing. She got pregnant during the process but didn't realize it. She miscarried and was never able to get pregnant again. Something about her taking the drug while pregnant made her permanently infertile."

"Which drug did she take?"

Carly's gaze slid over to me. "An early version of Infirmi."

Shit. That was what I'd been injected with—or a new version of it anyway. I was only seventeen, so having kids was nowhere close to being on my radar, but it hadn't even occurred to me to worry about whether I would suffer from permanent side effects that weren't related to my powers.

Poor Shari. She made her living watching children, so I assumed she must love them.

"Did she know that was a risk?"

"No one knew. While our scientists were brilliant, sometimes they could be reckless."

"But you were in charge." My words were accusatory.

"Yes. So it all comes back to me. I was young and naive. I didn't know any better."

Fifteen years had passed, so Carly was definitely older, but that didn't necessarily make her wiser. "You weren't young and naive when you killed my kidnappers just last month."

"What does that have to do with this? Are you sorry they're dead?"

"No... yes... I don't know," I muttered. "Murder is wrong."

"Not if it makes the world a better place."

I kind of hated myself for it, but I couldn't argue with her logic.

CARLY WANTED ME to work with my powers for a while, but when I insisted on not damaging any more personal property, she rolled her eyes and called me a Goody Two-shoes. I laughed. No one had ever called me that before, but I supposed it was all relative.

While she looked for a suitable location, I asked about something that had been nagging me. "You were supposedly burned alive. How did you survive?"

That was the official story, and in fact, a charred body was found in the burnt house. Yet the more I thought about it, the more things didn't make sense. If Carly was as powerful as everyone said she was, then how had they managed to beat her? They obviously hadn't, but I was still curious to hear the story from Carly. I was also curious to see for myself how powerful she was and, if I were honest, what I might one day be capable of. Other than warming the air around us, she'd yet to show any of her abilities.

Carly's expression darkened as she recalled the unpleasant experience. "They had several of their most powerful guardians, and from the best I could tell, they switched them out whenever one got tired."

"Did you have anyone there to help you?" I asked.

Carly stared straight ahead, not answering. She might not have wanted to talk about the dead body that everyone had assumed was hers, but I wanted to know.

"Whose body did they find?"

"Her name was Grace." Carly's voice was soft.

I couldn't bring myself to outright ask if Carly had killed her. "How did she die?"

Carly didn't hesitate in answering. "In the fire. She was caught, the same as me. But her control of fire was never good. She miscalculated."

I studied her, wondering how much of her explanation I could believe. I didn't want to think she had killed that woman, knowing the EA would most likely identify the body as her. Carly was a killer—I had no disillusion about that—but there was a big difference between killing my kidnappers and killing an innocent woman to aid her escape.

I didn't ask who Grace was, but I made a mental note to find out her full name. Her relatives deserved to know how she'd met her end. I'd purposefully avoided directly asking Carly about all of the people she'd killed. But I couldn't continue on the path with her blindly any longer. I would have to bite the bullet and initiate that conversation eventually.

She pulled off on the side of the rural road we'd been driving on. "Is this good?"

I surveyed the open field. It didn't look as though it belonged to anyone, and there wasn't much I could destroy. For the next hour, I worked on my fine control. I commanded single blades of grass to bend, pulled a single drop of moisture from the air, and dug a hole so narrow that only ants could fit through it.

It was pointless. I could do all of those things on my own, and I was already aware that I needed to practice if I wanted to get better. But being able to bend a blade of grass wouldn't help me when my powers got out of control. I told Carly that.

She seemed annoyed. "Learning control with all levels of power is important. Then when your powers are ramped up, you'll be used to controlling them."

"It seems like it would be easier to figure out how to keep them at a lower, more manageable level."

"I wouldn't teach you that even if I could." Her tone was cold, as though the idea disgusted her. It pissed me off. There was nothing wrong with not wanting my powers to get out of control. Besides that, part of our arrangement was her teaching me to control them.

I glared at her. "You promised you could help me."

"I will help you." She pinched the bridge of her nose. "Just not in the way you think."

I threw my hands up. "What the hell, Carly?" I put the emphasis on her name because I knew it was a slap in her face every time I used her name instead of calling her "mom." She hadn't said as much, but her slight flinching was a dead giveaway. It was odd, though. Carly didn't look like anyone's mother, and she definitely didn't act like it. She hadn't had to act like a mother for fifteen years. Maybe she would have been different now if I hadn't been taken from her.

She put her hands on her hips. "The only reason you can't control your power is because you've never been allowed to use it."

"That doesn't mean I haven't." I was definitely no Goody Two-shoes when it came to following EA rules, or any rules for that matter. However, unlike Carly, I was more discriminate in the ones I broke. All rules were not created equal.

"Just barely," Carly retorted. "If you'd been using it your whole life the way you should have been, you'd be much stronger by now. They stunted your development by making you ignore your powers all these years."

I wouldn't say I'd ignored my powers. It would be impossible not to notice the energy that buzzed within and called to me. But she was correct that I'd been taught not to use my powers. So had everyone else in the EA. *Use them or lose them.*

"What would you have us do? Use our powers in the open and expose everyone?" Though I didn't agree with EA rules, I was still an EA member, and Carly's negative comments made me defensive.

Carly's eyes burned. "Yes. Exactly that."

My question had been facetious. I hadn't expected her to answer in the affirmative. "Why?"

"Why not? Why should we have to hide? We were born with these talents the same as someone who is extremely intelligent or very athletic. A star athlete or a genius is allowed to benefit from the abilities they're born with. So why shouldn't we?"

I opened my mouth to argue with her out of principle, but I closed it quickly. She had a valid point, but it went against everything I'd been taught, that we shouldn't use our gifts for personal gain. However, it wasn't any different from a super-tall person using their height as an advantage in basketball. No one claimed it wasn't fair when shorter players didn't make the cut.

"What about witch hunters?" I asked instead.

"If elementals were taught to use their powers properly, no one would ever be able to touch them."

Properly. That meant defensively, possibly even lethally.

I turned away. I shared her opinion that elementals should be allowed to use their power for self-defense, but I was in the minority. Of course, I didn't know how many elementals actually agreed or disagreed with that sentiment because no one talked about it. EA doctrine said we weren't supposed to use our powers. End of story. But I would have bet that those who'd made that rule hadn't stared down death with only their powers to save them.

"Not everyone is comfortable using their powers like that," I said. My thoughts went to Lena. If it came down to her using her power to save herself, I didn't know if she would do it. I hoped she wouldn't have to find out. It would break her.

"Not everyone is a witch hunter," Carly retorted. "Not everyone will be against us. And sure, once we're out in the open, we'll face prejudice, but we'll be able to fight for equal rights, just like any other group of people."

I zeroed in on her wording—*Once we're out in the open.* She seemed certain that was something that would come to pass. "The council will never go for something like that."

"We've already established that they don't rule over all elementals." Carly looked at me sadly. "When are you going to learn that there's more to being an elemental than blindly obeying the council?"

"I don't blindly obey them."

"Keep telling yourself that."

Enough. Carly needed to get off her high horse. She claimed she wanted to get to know me, but so far when I'd expressed my opinions, all she'd done was take jabs at me. "Disobeying the council didn't work so well for you, did it?"

Hurt flashed in her eyes, and for a second, I felt guilty, but only for a second, especially since the hurt was gone as quickly as it had appeared.

Her mouth firmed. "Obeying the council didn't work so well for those girls either, now, did it?"

I gasped. My blow had been low, but hers went beyond that. One girl was dead, and another was only eleven years old. *How dare she?* My powers raged within me, and I wanted to lash out at her, to command the air to slam her against the hood of the Jeep. I clenched my hands at my sides instead. "You're a monster," I said through clenched teeth.

She shot me a disgusted look. "There's that blind obedience again. Do you believe everything you hear?"

I didn't, but after the last few minutes, I was starting to believe more of it. "How many people have you killed?"

She shrugged. "I didn't bother keeping count."

I didn't think she could still shock me, but I was wrong. "If that doesn't make you a monster, then what does? Do you have any respect for human life?"

"Just because someone is alive doesn't mean they deserve respect."

This was Cruel Carly. I'd begun to think the stories of her ruthlessness were exaggerated, but I could definitely see they weren't. Hurt and disappointment leached from my pores. I was afraid my desperation for her not to be one hundred percent despicable had clouded my judgment. Maybe I had imagined the positive traits I'd identified in the last two days. I'd sympathized with her and had even begun to like her a little.

"Simone Arcand deserved your respect."

Carly's expression softened slightly at the mention of Suze's sister. "You shouldn't talk about things you have no knowledge of."

"You killed her." My voice shook. "What else do I need to know?"

"She died as a result of the experiments, but I didn't kill her."

"It's the same thing."

"She wanted to be there. She came to me."

"She was from a respected elemental family. Why would she do that?"

"Choice. I keep telling you that. She didn't ask to be born an elemental any more than you asked to be born my daughter." She sighed. "Look, I don't know how many deaths you think I'm responsible for—"

"Hundreds."

Carly laughed. Actually laughed. "You've got to be kidding me. That's absurd."

Her genuine reaction made me doubt what I'd heard, what I'd *seen*. There were hundreds of names on the list in her file. The council wouldn't have made those up. Those people were dead, and their blood was on my mother's hands.

"You killed some of your own followers."

She leveled her gaze at me and threw her shoulders back. "If they deserved it."

My whole body shook. My nightmare was coming to life. I was the daughter of a cold-blooded killer who had no remorse for what she'd done.

I walked farther out into the field to put some distance between us. I didn't want to breathe the same air as her. I stretched my hand out and watched the grass ripple like spectators doing the wave at a baseball game. When I could no longer see the motion, I did it in reverse. The action used up a minuscule amount of energy.

With my emotions running high, my power pulsed beneath my skin, but I wasn't in the mood to do more frivolous tricks. I stalked to the Jeep and threw open the door. I wanted to abandon Carly, but I couldn't, not when she was the only avenue to getting the information I needed.

Carly returned to the Jeep as well. When she got into the driver's seat, I shifted so that I was closer to my door. She disgusted me.

"You didn't even ask to hear my side of the story." Carly's voice was quiet and laced with hurt.

I had no patience for her bruised feelings. I still wasn't convinced she had any. "You killed hundreds of people. How can you possibly think that's a story I want to hear?"

"The number is not that high," Carly said, contradicting her earlier statement that she hadn't kept track. "Anyway, most of them were gang members." She said it as if that excused her actions.

"You hired yourself out. You killed for the highest bidder."

"That's one way of looking at it. But innocent people in their territories were getting caught in the middle of their turf wars. One way or another, blood would continue to be shed until one of the gangs eradicated the other one. I merely sped up the process and got paid to do it. For years following that, not a single innocent person was killed in gang warfare. Is that such a bad thing?"

No, it wasn't. Her actions had definitely been in a gray area *if* she were telling the truth. Though I didn't know why she would lie—the facts were verifiable.

"They were still people," I said. "It wasn't up to you to make that decision."

"They made their choices, and I made mine."

Choice, choice, choice. I was sick of hearing about her beloved *choice.* "I don't want to talk about it anymore."

Carly also seemed content to let the matter rest. *Thank God.* For the remainder of our time together, I would have to make a point not to bring up that kind of stuff, which would be hard considering we would probably visit more of her former associates. But that was the only way to keep the peace between us. It only had to last long enough for me to get the information I needed. Then Carly could climb back into the hole she'd been living in.

I couldn't help but wonder if she regretted spending time with me. If I hadn't needed her resources to find Lena, maybe we both would have been better off never meeting face-to-face. She could have kept her dream of a mini-me daughter, and I could have continued pretending she wasn't as bad as everyone made her out to be.

We stopped for lunch, and I ordered twice the amount of food I normally would have, but my power burned through calories like nobody's business. Carly only ordered a normal person's amount of food, though. Granted, she hadn't been using her powers like I had.

"Who are we seeing next?" I asked in between bites of double-bacon cheeseburger.

"Greta Mueller." Carly's nose wrinkled as she watched me unwrap my second burger.

Whatever. She could judge me all she wanted.

"Is she like Jack or Shari?" In other words, did she know Carly as Eliza, or was she from Carly's past?

"She's from before."

"I assume she doesn't know you're alive?"

"Nope," Carly said. "Honestly, I'd prefer to keep it that way, but if she's still like she was when I knew her, then she'll be useful."

"Why?"

"She's ambitious, calculating, and ruthless."

I stared at Carly, but she didn't seem to notice the irony. Still, if Carly was describing her old friend that way, then I would definitely be on my guard.

Chapter 12

GRETA LIVED ABOUT two hours north of Shari in a small town in Ohio.

"We're almost there." Carly looked around as we passed through a downtown area lined with mom-and-pop shops and local restaurants. It was quaint, the kind of place from a Hallmark movie, except for the boarded-up storefronts interspersed between the others.

"Is this where you grew up?" I asked.

Carly seemed surprised by the question. "No. I lived on the other side of the state. Why do you ask?"

"Just curious."

"What else was in my file?"

The truth was the file was lacking, but I didn't want to tell Carly that because I didn't want her to think the EA was weak. While I didn't trust the council, I trusted Carly even less. Of course, I suspected the file wasn't complete.

So I shrugged. Since Carly was in the habit of giving me incomplete answers, I would return the favor. Unfortunately, while it bothered me, it didn't seem to bother Carly one bit.

"You can ask me anything you want," she said. "My life wasn't that interesting. My mom died when I was young, and my daddy raised me. My mom was EA, but my dad wasn't. When he realized how powerful I was, he reached out to them."

"Is that how you know Patricia West?"

"Yes. Her family was the closest elemental family to ours." She didn't elaborate.

My obstinate side didn't want to let her know I was interested, but my curiosity won out. "Were you friends?"

Carly grinned, but there was something dark behind it. "You could say we were frenemies. Patty always was a little bitch."

I blinked at that last part. *Patty?* I had little love for Aidan's mother. Probably the only thing I liked about her was the fact that she had given birth to the guy I loved. Carly's description was pretty accurate, but out of respect for Aidan, I stayed silent, though he would probably agree with Carly too.

I wished I had known Councilwoman West before her daughter—Aidan's sister—had been killed by witch hunters. I desperately wanted to believe that had broken something in her, like my supposed death had broken something in Carly. But if this was a broken Carly, I didn't want to think about what a whole Carly would've been like.

"Just a few more minutes," Carly said. "Greta is dangerous. It would be best if you take the Jeep and come back for me later."

I snorted. "You can't be serious."

"If she figures out you're my daughter—"

"Then we'll deal with it."

"It won't be a momentary problem," she said quietly. "Being my daughter puts a target on your back."

"I'm not worried," I said sweetly. "If anyone tries to hurt me, you'll kill them, right?"

Carly's neck jerked as she looked at me with narrowed eyes. "I can't bring you back from the dead."

Good point. One brush with death had been enough to last me a lifetime. But I'd been naive and unprepared then. I was smarter now and more powerful... if I could manage to control my powers.

One belief that Carly and I shared was that using our powers was fair game for self-defense. I didn't like the idea of harming someone with my gifts, but if it came down to a choice between me and them, I would choose me every time.

"If you think I'm staying in the car, then you haven't gotten to know me at all in the last forty-eight hours."

Carly's expression was a mix of pride and anger. She would have thought less of me if I were content to run away and hide, but at the same time, she didn't like being disobeyed. If she spent much more time with me, she would have to get used to it. Despite her accusations that I unquestioningly followed the EA, I'd never been good at blindly taking orders.

"Follow my lead and do as I say." Carly's tone dared me to challenge her.

"Fine." While I wasn't willing to be left behind, I was more than willing to be the second-in-command. Though I'd been trained as a guardian, I had no practical experience. But I was an asset, and it would've been foolish for me to wait in the car. Plus, the visit with Greta sounded promising, and I wanted to hear exactly what she said to make sure I relayed the information to Aidan correctly.

Carly parked in front of a large white house with a full wraparound porch. Though it wasn't dark yet, the Christmas lights on the gutters and railings were already lit. A bright-red-and-green quilted wreath hung on the front door, and fake candles with light bulbs sat in every window. It was so cheerful and in juxtaposition with the dangerous individual who supposedly resided within.

"Won't she be at work?" I asked. There was no car in the driveway.

"She should be home by now. She teaches second grade."

"I thought you said she was dangerous."

"She is. But she's got to make a living somehow."

"As a teacher?" *Good God.*

Carly smiled wryly. "Haven't you heard there's a teacher shortage? They're desperate."

"But—"

"Relax," Carly said. "I'm sure she separates her professional life from her... extracurricular activities." She got out of the car, and I reluctantly followed.

Halfway up the sidewalk, I put a hand on Carly's arm to stop her. "Wait. If she really is dangerous, we can't let her keep teaching kids. That's just... It's not right."

"What do you want me to do?" Carly asked. "Write a letter to her principal?"

"I'm serious, Carly," I snapped. "I was kidnapped from my school. If Greta is shady, she might help with something like that."

"I don't think she'll put her job at risk."

I shook my head. "Think about what you're saying. Is she more concerned about the kids or keeping her job? Because they're not the same thing. And it matters."

The youngest girl who'd been kidnapped was eleven, which meant she was either in the fifth or sixth grade. It made me sick to my stomach to think of other kids being taken advantage of by their teacher, who also happened to be a dangerous elemental. As far as we knew, they'd only taken elemental kids. But we knew next to nothing. They could easily be using regular kids for something too. I didn't know a lot about scientific experiments, but I knew enough to know a control group was needed.

"Okay," Carly said slowly. "If we discover she's a threat to her students, we'll do something about it."

I wondered if it pained her to agree to do something because it was the right thing to do instead of because it benefitted her.

I followed Carly up to the porch. She pressed the doorbell, and I heard the faint strains of "Rudolph the Red-Nosed Reindeer." *You've got to be kidding me.* I recognized this kind of house. On Halloween, it would be the house in the neighborhood that gave out full-size candy bars. However, in my twisted reality, it was more likely that the house would be featured on the news, with neighbors saying they'd never suspected a thing about the nice lady who lived there and how shocking it had been to discover the stack of bodies in her basement.

Okay, so I was probably being overdramatic, but it didn't sit right with me that Carly's former follower, who Carly had described as calculating and ruthless, was an elementary school teacher. For goodness' sake, the woman was shaping the young minds of America, but she'd experimented on people in her past, or she'd at least condoned it.

Greta swung open the door without taking the time to peek through the windows first. Or maybe she was incredibly stealthy. She looked exactly like my first-grade teacher—she had platinum-blond hair styled in a bob and perfectly manicured nails. She wore what could have only been described as a teacher's Christmas sweater. She must have had a thing for Rudolph because the poor guy was appliquéd on the front, complete with 3-D felt antlers.

"Carly?" Greta's expression was bewildered, then she laughed. "Sorry. You remind me of someone."

Carly smiled. "It's me, Greta."

"Omigod!" Greta somehow managed to make the phrase sound as if it were all one syllable. She yanked Carly to her chest and wrapped her arms around her. "How is this possible?"

With a grimace that only I could see, Carly slowly disengaged herself from Greta's embrace. If not for the reason we were there, it would have been funny. Carly wasn't a touchy-feely kind of person. "It's a long story." In other words, she wasn't telling.

"Well, come in. Don't stand out here in the cold." She looked at me. "Who's this?" she asked kindly.

"Sorry," Carly said. "This is Stacey."

Hearing myself introduced as Stacey a second time was no less jolting than it had been the first time. If we were going to continue interviewing people, I needed to get used to it. At least she hadn't referred to me as Cassandra. That would have been way too weird. I wondered if she still thought of me as that name in her mind.

Lines formed on Greta's forehead as she scrutinized me. I could see the dots connecting in her head, and an unspoken question appeared on her face.

"I'm Carly's cousin." As the words left my mouth, I could practically feel a wave of irritation waft off of Carly.

She smiled tightly. "A very distant cousin."

Once Greta turned, Carly shot me a look. I shrugged. If she didn't want me to improvise, then she should have come up with a solid game plan.

Inside the house, there were Christmas decorations everywhere—figurines on the mantel, cross-stitched doilies on the tables, even framed pictures on the wall. At the center of it all was the biggest Christmas tree I'd ever seen, and it was real. The scent of pine was overwhelming, but that might have had more to do with the scented candles than the tree.

Greta gestured to the couch. "Have a seat."

I shifted aside some polar bear stuffed animals so there was room for Carly and me to sit. Greta sat across from us in an armchair, leaning against a stuffed Santa Claus toy and making it look as though the stuffed, bearded man had his arms around her.

"Not that I'm not happy to see you, of course, but what the heck?" She laughed, and it was a bright, cheery sound, although there was a touch of fakeness to it, or maybe I was reading into it since I'd already decided I didn't like her. Even if she weren't one of Carly's former cronies and what Carly deemed a "dangerous elemental," I still wouldn't have liked her. She was too sugary sweet, and no one could be like that all the time. We'd only been there a few minutes, but something told me that was the normal façade she presented to the world.

However, her question was fair. It wasn't every day that a supposed-to-be-dead person from the past showed up at the door.

"We were in the area," Carly said, not bothering to explain how she was still alive. "My cousin and I are taking a girls' trip to visit some colleges."

Greta pursed her lips as though she wanted to press Carly for more information, but instead, she pasted a smile on her face. "Which ones?" She must have realized it was pointless to ask Carly about things she obviously didn't want to talk about.

I coughed, hoping it didn't sound like the fake ploy for time that it was. "University of Ohio?" *Dear God, please let there be a University of Ohio.* Every state had one of those, right? I should have said Ohio State. I knew that existed because of their football team.

"You mean Ohio University?" Greta asked.

"Yeah. That's the one." I felt like an idiot, not that it mattered. This was a fake college trip, and I wasn't bothering to apply to schools anyway. I had to graduate high school first, which wasn't a current priority. *Poor Lena.* That stuff mattered to her. She was going to be so behind.

"I went to Kent State," Greta said. "If you have time, you should go there. It's a great little town."

I wondered when Greta had gone to college—before or after she'd been in Carly's posse. I'd never thought of Carly's followers as educated individuals, instead picturing them as hell-raising heathens. But there were scientists in the mix, plus Shari's husband was a child psychologist, so obviously my perception was incorrect.

"How have you been?" Carly asked, taking the attention off me. "How are your parents?"

Greta smiled sadly, and genuine grief filled her eyes. "My parents passed away a few years ago. As you can see, I inherited the house."

"I'm sorry to hear that," Carly said. "They were nice people. Are you married? Do you have kids?"

"No. It's just me rambling alone in this big old house." She laughed. "But enough about me. My life isn't anything special. I want to know about you. You're the one who must have an interesting story to tell."

"I've just been laying low. Living here and there and working here and there. I guess you could say I'm a nomad, which is why Stacey's parents asked me to take her on this trip. They don't like driving, but I don't mind it."

"Well, I wish you'd stuck around back then. Everything went to hell when you left." Greta put her hand in front of her mouth and giggled. "Sorry for the language."

Seriously? It was taking an extreme amount of effort to keep my eyes from rolling.

"That's a shame." Carly shook her head. "I haven't seen anyone from the old days, so I don't know exactly what happened."

"It was a mess. No one could decide who should take your place, so there was a lot of fighting. Without you to rally behind, no one got along." There was a bite to Greta's words, as though she knew they were the correct ones to say, but they ate at her. I wondered if she had tried to take control and failed.

I wouldn't have envisioned Carly as a peacekeeper, but I supposed if she were the leader of a group of volatile individuals, that came with the territory. She was definitely better equipped to do it than Greta. Something was off about the woman, and that wouldn't inspire confidence.

"I guess our cause wasn't strong enough," Carly said sadly. "If it was, it should have been able to survive without me."

Greta let out a nervous laugh.

I saw exactly what Carly was doing, laying on a guilt trip. I wondered how she felt about the whole thing, if she really felt as if they should have been able to carry on without her. How dedicated was she to her cause? She claimed it was "choice," but that was so broad. I still wasn't one hundred percent clear what she hoped to accomplish.

"That makes me sad," Carly continued. "Because the more I think about it, the more I understand how important it was. Still is."

Greta nodded so quickly, I was afraid her jaw was going to crush her tongue. "Definitely."

"I've been spending a bit of time with my younger cousin here." Carly looked at me affectionately, and I tried to return the gaze. "It's made me realize that what we were doing is more important than ever. If we'd been successful, Stacey wouldn't be in the situation she's in."

Holy heck. I hoped I wasn't going to have to come up with a situation. I was fine with thinking on my feet, but it seemed as though Carly had a plan, and I didn't know what that was. Greta had taken to her right away, and I didn't want to ruin the vibe flowing between them. We really should have planned things out better, but I was coming to realize that Carly was spontaneous. She didn't like to be boxed in and would rather go with the flow. The same could be said for me, and I didn't like the comparison. Anything that put Carly and me in the same section of a Venn diagram was bad news.

Greta put her hand on my knee. "You poor dear." I looked down at my toes, trying to look sad or disappointed or something. I didn't know what the appropriate response was. *Shit. Maybe I should act angry.*

"Anyway, you're the first person I've reached out to, for obvious reasons." Carly smiled and nodded at Greta, who beamed from the praise. Or at least, I guessed she considered it praise. I didn't. "Have you kept in touch with anyone else? I'm horribly out of the loop."

Greta clapped her hands gleefully. "Are you saying what I think you're saying?"

Carly chuckled modestly and tossed her hair over her shoulder. "Don't get too excited yet. It all depends on putting the right team together. I think that's where we went wrong last time."

I didn't think Greta could perk up any more, but she looked like a Labrador who'd caught a whiff of something. "Oh, really? Who were the weak links from before?" Gossip and trash talk—that was what she scented in the air. It was the universal weakness of petty females everywhere.

Carly waved her hand, dismissing the question. "The past is in the past. There's no sense getting into it now. But we'll definitely have to be more careful this time around. No weak links allowed."

"I never told you at the time, but I always kind of thought some in our group were soft."

"We won't make that mistake again." An orange cat walked into the room and twirled itself around Carly's legs. She picked it up and stroked its head. "I think our priority needs to be the enhancement drugs."

Greta frowned. "Really? Why not Infirmi?"

"If our people are stronger than everyone else, then weakening their powers won't matter. They'll bow to our will anyway." Carly leaned her face close to the cat's and made kissy noises. She was freaking me out. I'd come to somewhat trust her in the last two days, but the ease with which she was sliding back into her old role was frightening. Besides that, the new rhetoric of forcing others to bow to their will did *not* sound like "choice" to me.

Greta tapped her fingers together. "There are some people you need to meet."

With a thoughtful expression on her face, Carly continued to pet the cat. "Who?"

"I don't want to say too much without talking to them first, but trust me. You *need* to meet them."

Carly laughed. "That's what people told me about our 'weak links' too."

Greta shook her head so emphatically that her platinum bob swooshed from side to side. "Not these people. Trust me. They've already made great strides with Infirmi."

Carly pursed her lips. "Infirmi doesn't impress me."

"What they've done with it will. One drop of it can mess up an elemental's power for months. They're close to making the result permanent." Greta smiled sadistically. "I know you said Infirmi isn't important, but tell me there aren't a few elementals you'd like to see stripped of their powers."

Carly laughed. "I can think of a few."

"Great." Greta stood. "If you'll excuse me, I'll make a few phone calls."

"Stacey and I really can't stay long, though," Carly said. "I told her parents I'd have her back in a few days."

"Don't worry," Greta assured her. "Something tells me they'll make meeting you a priority."

Another cat wandered in. This one was all black except for its paws, which were white. It jumped up on my lap, unbidden, and rubbed against my chest. When I did nothing, it glared at me. *Okay, I guess I'll pet you.*

I listened to the tapping of Greta's feet on the stairs and the closing of an upstairs door before turning to Carly. "What the hell?" I hissed.

Carly scratched behind the orange cat's ears. Her entire front was covered in cat hair, but she didn't seem to mind. "What?"

"Something about Greta is off. I don't trust her."

"I don't either. She's a two-faced bitch." Well, that summed it up succinctly. I was relieved we were on the same page at least. "That's what makes her useful to us."

Absentmindedly, I continued to pet the black cat. We were looking for shady people who kidnapped children, so it made sense that we would have the most luck finding them through another shady person. Still, it made me uneasy. Despite how I'd spent the first two years of my life—I was making an assumption since I didn't actually remember them—I had spent the last fifteen surrounded by upstanding individuals. With my lack of respect for rules, I was probably the shadiest one in my family. And I wasn't all that shady, not in the grand scheme of things.

Suddenly, the cat hissed at me and jumped off my lap. On the floor, it arched its back and glared at me. *What the hell?*

Greta returned to the room, looking like a completely different person. Gone were the Christmas sweater and orthopedic shoes. Now she wore all black, complete with a badass black-leather moto jacket. Her features also looked sharper somehow, as if she'd contoured her face in the five minutes she had been upstairs. She was as bipolar as her black cat. The orange one was purring in its sleep, curled up in a contented ball on Carly's lap.

"Let's go." Greta's tone was all business, much different from the saccharine one from before.

"Where are we going?" I asked.

"You're going nowhere," Carly said. "I'm sure Greta won't mind if you hang out here for a while." She looked at Greta for confirmation, but the other woman's expression remained impassive.

"I don't think so." I smiled sweetly. "I'm the future, remember? I want to be part of this movement."

"Great," Greta said. "We always welcome young people into the mix. I'll drive. Let me pull the car around." She turned on her heel, and a few moments later, a back door slammed.

Carly glared at me as she peeled the cat off her lap. "Sophie, you shouldn't—"

"Don't pull that crap with me," I snapped. "If she's leading us to the people who have Lena, then I'm going. That's the whole reason I'm here."

Carly seethed as she looked at me, and I could tell she was fighting to hold back harsh words. Nothing she said would make a difference, though. Besides that, I couldn't take her seriously when she was covered in cat hair.

"I'll never forgive myself if something happens to you," she said finally.

I wanted to tell her that forgiving herself for my getting hurt because of a decision I made was the last thing she needed forgiveness for, but I could think of a laundry list of other things that should have been on her list.

Obviously, I still didn't know Carly very well, but one thing was certain. She wasn't one hundred percent evil like the council would have everyone believe. There were definitely aspects of her that were shady, like killing my kidnappers on an apparent whim, but a woman who loved her child couldn't be all bad.

Or perhaps I just thought that because I was the child in question.

"We should drive ourselves," I said. "I don't want to be stuck wherever we're going."

Picking cat hair off her shirt, Carly shook her head. "She won't let us drive. I wouldn't be surprised if she made us wear blindfolds."

I laughed. It sounded ridiculous, like something out of a movie. But Carly wasn't laughing, and she seemed annoyed by my response. I bit back my laughter. "Why do you think that?"

"Because it's something I would have done. Assuming this is the group of people we're looking for, they've managed to stay under the radar. They're not going to risk giving up their location, not even for me."

Greta honked the horn, so we filed out the front door. Carly pulled the door closed behind her, first making sure it was locked. *How considerate.*

Carly took the front seat of Greta's Jetta, leaving me the back. The radio was tuned to a Christmas station, though the volume was turned down low. Before I could get my seat belt buckled, Greta tore down the driveway.

I gripped the door handle. "In a hurry?" *Jeez Louise.*

Greta grinned at me in the rearview mirror. I wished she would keep her eyes on the road.

"Tell me about these people," Carly said.

Greta shook her finger at Carly. "Uh-uh. You'll meet them soon."

"How did you meet them?"

"Nope. Not talking about that either." Greta giggled. "You know the drill, Carly."

Carly sighed. "Indeed I do."

But I didn't. I didn't know what the heck they were talking about. Greta turned up the radio to a volume that prohibited talking. Surprisingly, not hearing her chatter made me more anxious. Electricity sizzled under my skin, and I tried to focus on my breathing the way I had in meditation, but it was impossible with the way the car was whizzing along the back roads. God, the last thing I needed was to lose control in the back seat of a car. I was far from it, but it wouldn't take long for my powers to ratchet up to uncontrollable levels.

I pulled out my phone to check for an email from Aidan and almost dropped it in my haste to open his reply.

He jumped in without preamble:

Alexis's death was caused by complications from her asthma. There was an unknown drug in her system.

My initial reaction was relief, then guilt for feeling relieved. *I'm a horrible person.* But if her death was at least partially due to a preexisting condition, then that made me feel more confident they didn't intend to kill the girls. The drug in her system was alarming but not unexpected. I'd made a full recovery after being injected with Infirmi, but who knew what they'd used on the girls. Apparently, Aidan didn't know, or at least he hadn't said.

I returned my attention to the email.

No other news about the girls. Or the West Virginia kids. We have a lead on our contact.

Thinking there must be more, I scrolled down, but that was it. *Damn it, Aidan.* His debriefing was way too brief. I didn't have time to respond, and I didn't have anything new to share anyway. Hopefully, that would change in the next few hours.

The good news was unspoken—even though they hadn't found the girls, there had been no texts with the locations of where to claim their dead bodies. They were alive.

A lot can be done to someone without killing her. I squeezed my eyes to ward off the unpleasant thought. Lena was alive, and that was what mattered.

Greta took a hard turn way too fast, and I slid across the seat. My anxiety increased, and the energy in my veins throbbed. *Shit, shit, shit. Pull yourself together, Sophie.* Closing my eyes, I imagined a bubble around myself and filled that bubble with warm air in an attempt to expend some of the energy. The trouble was that trick took little effort these days, so it didn't do much good.

I leaned forward so I could see the clock on the dashboard. We'd only been in the car about twenty minutes. The sun was rapidly setting, shrouding the inside of the car in darkness. I wasn't afraid of the dark, but the lack of light made our current situation seem more ominous.

When we stopped at a traffic light, Greta clipped her phone into the holder on the dash and pulled up GPS directions. I peered at it, trying to figure out where she was taking us. Then it dawned on me—she shouldn't have needed directions. If she were heavily involved in this group, then she should have already known how to get there. Also, she wouldn't have displayed the address on her phone like that for Carly and me to see.

I wondered if Carly realized the same thing. Her posture remained relaxed, and her fingers tapped on the edge of the door to the beat of the music. I wished I were an empath so I could channel some of her calmness. While I was normally okay with being spontaneous, this situation freaked me out. My guardian training was all about preparation. Guardians didn't walk into situations blind, which was exactly what we were doing. Caution was the name of their game.

But I could handle it. I *would* handle it. This wasn't like when I'd been kidnapped—I knew I was about to enter into a dangerous situation, and I wasn't alone. Carly was on my side, which was oddly comforting.

We reached the end of the town we'd been cruising through, and Greta turned the car onto a rural state road lined with dense trees. As the car zoomed around the curves, its headlights illuminated white snow on the ground beneath the trees. There was no snow anywhere else, so the trees must have kept the ground shaded so that the sun couldn't melt it.

The car jerked to the left and into the opposing lane. Greta had taken her hands off the wheel and was clutching at her throat. Carly grabbed the wheel and guided the car back into the correct lane. "Step on the brakes!" She had to yell to be heard over "White Christmas."

Instead, Greta did the exact opposite, and we sped up. Though she was still making choking sounds, she was no longer grasping her throat. She reached into her jacket and pulled out a syringe. Before I could shout a warning, she jabbed Carly in the neck and pushed down on the plunger. Then I heard a sharp intake of breath as Greta's airway opened up.

Either the shock of getting stuck caused Carly to lose her grip on the power she'd been using to suffocate Greta, or whatever was in that syringe was ridiculously fast acting.

"Bitch!" Greta reached into her jacket and pulled out a small black gun.

"Gun!" I yelled.

Carly went for the gun, and Greta took her hands off the steering wheel in an attempt to keep possession of it. A shot fired through the windshield. Instinctively, I ducked and covered my head. Despite the struggle between the two women, the car continued to speed down the road, veering left and right as the steering wheel got bumped before finally careening off into the grass. We were going to end up wrapped around a tree if Carly didn't get control of the car soon. But her powers had at least temporarily been incapacitated. And if she'd been given the same Infirmi that I had, she might pass out soon.

My powers were already flowing, so I sucked the air out of Greta's lungs. She made gasping and choking sounds, but she still didn't let go of the gun. *Damn it!*

A branch scraped the edge of the car. We were inches from the tree line. I could reach the steering wheel between the seats, but they were fighting over the gun there. So instead, I reached my arm between the window and the driver's seat. I almost got a hold of the wheel when we ran over a large stump or something and Greta's body slammed into my arm, knocking my elbow hard against the window.

Carly saw what I was doing and yanked Greta forward. *Why wouldn't she just pass out already?* Unfortunately, Greta noticed me as well and slammed the back of her head into my forehead. For a brief second, I saw stars. I shook it off and finally grasped the steering wheel then yanked it to the left, veering us away from the trees.

Another shot fired, this time into the passenger door. Carly yelped.

"Are you hit?" I shrieked. Carly didn't respond.

Greta's arms went limp, and Carly yanked the gun out of her hands. A moment later, Greta's head slumped forward and knocked my hand off the steering wheel.

I grabbed for the steering wheel. "You've got to get her foot off the gas."

Carly yanked on Greta's leg then shifted the car into neutral. "I've got the wheel."

I let go and extricated my arm from between the window and the seat. Then I flexed my elbow and winced at the pain.

It took forever for the car to slow, but it never stopped because we were on a slight decline. Carly guided it toward a tree. The car hit it lightly then stopped. She shifted the car into park and turned to look at me. "Are you okay?"

My adrenaline was at a near-lethal level, and my heart felt as if it were going to pound its way out of my chest. But other than my hurt arm and the dull throb in my forehead from Greta's headbutt, I was fine.

I nodded. "You?"

She yanked the needle out of her neck and threw it on the floor with a disgusted look. "Fine."

I gestured to the syringe. "How is that affecting you? Do you feel light-headed?"

"No. It zapped my powers, but it's already fading. What a sucker-punch move." She rolled her neck and rubbed at the injection site. Blood was smeared on her fingertips.

"Where's the blood from?"

Carly looked at her fingers as though she hadn't noticed it was there. She probably hadn't. "Oh. The bullet got me."

My eyes widened, and my heart beat faster. "Shit. What do we do?"

"Relax. It just grazed my calf. But since my blood is in the car, we'll have to torch it."

I didn't even blink. That was messed up. *Arson after getting shot... just another day in the life of Carly Levitt.*

Chapter 13

CARLY'S LEG BLED all over the place, but she didn't seem affected by it, not even when we pulled Greta out of the front seat.

"Should we tie her up?" I was totally out of my element.

"No. She'll be awake soon." Carly grabbed Greta's left arm. "Help me pull her into the woods."

I wanted to know what her plan was, but I did as she asked. It wasn't the time to argue. As we dragged Greta along the ground, she moaned. *Shit.* Carly wasn't lying about her being awake soon.

"What about the car?" I asked.

"We'll deal with that later."

We stopped about twenty yards into the trees. Greta's black jacket had gotten a huge scrape on the sleeve from a branch on the way there. I felt more regret over that than what we'd done to her. It was a damn nice jacket.

Carly nudged Greta with her foot. "Wake up."

I thought Greta's eyes fluttered, but she didn't open them. Wondering if she was faking, I peered at her, but I couldn't tell. It was so dark, I could barely see.

"Her car was a push-button start," I said. "We should check her pockets for the keys."

Carly flashed an approving smile. "Good point." She knelt next to her old comrade and frisked her, coming up with a key ring. She tossed it to me. "Go see if there's a flashlight in the car. Little Miss Girl Scout here probably has an emergency kit."

Damn. I wish we had thought of that before we dragged her all the way out there. Maybe then her jacket wouldn't have gotten ruined. *Why am I so fixated on that?* Maybe because the whole situation was surreal.

I trudged back to the car, and sure enough, there was a AAA-approved emergency roadside kit in the trunk. Before I returned to Carly, I searched the car for something to hang out the window so anyone who drove by wouldn't think the car was abandoned. I didn't know what Carly had in mind, but I was pretty sure we didn't want any witnesses. Hopefully, passersby wouldn't notice the bullet hole in the windshield.

It was so much easier walking through the woods with the flashlight. With any luck, the trees would be dense enough that no one from the road would be able to see the weak light.

I shone the flashlight on Greta's face, and her eyes squeezed tighter. "She's awake," I said.

"I know. I was waiting to see how long she would try faking, but we don't have time for that." Carly stepped over to Greta and kicked her in the gut so hard I winced.

Greta's eyes popped open. "Bitch." Her speech was slurred.

"Where were you taking us?" Carly asked.

"Where I said."

"No," Carly said calmly. "You never said where. You didn't say who either. It's time you gave me some answers. Then I'll decide if I still want to go."

"That's not how it works."

Carly chuckled. "I'm pretty sure you have no say in this."

"They'll kill you."

"They can try." Carly knelt next to Greta. "Tell me why you're carrying a gun." Greta's mouth clamped shut, and she turned her head away. "Your friends must not have gotten very far with the enhancement drug if you need a gun. Or perhaps they refused to give it to you. Which is it?" When Greta refused to even look in Carly's direction, my birth mother sighed. "Why do you have to make this difficult?"

Difficult wasn't how I would have described Greta—she was still lying on her back exactly where we'd dumped her. Uncooperative was a more appropriate term.

Carly rose. As she stepped back, Greta sat up suddenly and reached for Carly's ankles, but she was still disoriented, and Carly easily sidestepped.

The ground beneath Greta's legs rumbled and shifted, parting to take her in. She clawed at the ground, but it only opened wider. She fell into the hole. I gaped as the ground continued to shift and dirt rolled over her. The end result left her trapped beneath the surface, as though she'd been buried standing up. She reminded me of someone who'd been buried in the sand at the beach. Only her head was free.

Holy crap. The beam of light on Greta's face danced as my hand shook. Carly had trapped her in the ground in a matter of seconds.

"Where were you taking us?" Carly asked.

"Screw you," Greta spat. Then she inhaled sharply and shrieked. I couldn't tell what Carly had done to her. "Okay, okay," she yelled. The ground around her rippled slightly, and I realized Carly must be using the dirt to squeeze her underground.

It was both freaky and fascinating.

"A neutral location."

Duh. I'd figured that much out already, though I doubted the location was entirely neutral. Most likely, it would have been deserted, and we would be sorely outnumbered. The odds would be stacked against us.

"Tell me more," Carly said.

"I don't know. When I told them you were at my house, they said they wanted to meet you. That's it."

"Who are they?"

Greta's head moved slightly as though she were trying to shake it, but the ground held it in place. "I can't tell you."

"You're going to have to do better than that," Carly said.

"They'll kill me."

Carly waited a beat. "What makes you think I won't?" The ground shifted again, only this time, it slowly closed in around Greta's neck, inching up to her face.

I wanted to stop Carly. Greta might not think she would go through with it, but I did. And though I knew the extent of what Carly was capable of, I didn't want to witness it firsthand.

But damn it, Greta had information that might lead us to Lena, and at the end of the day, I cared more about Lena than anything else. One girl had already died. *Can I live with myself if we don't do everything in our power to make sure the remaining five stay alive? Am I willing to trade Greta's life for theirs?*

Killing Greta, especially if she didn't give us any concrete information, wouldn't put us any closer to finding the girls.

"Give us names," I said.

Greta refused to speak, even though the dirt kept inching up her face. "Stop," I said when it was nearly to her eyes.

Carly stopped but looked disappointed to do so. "You're lucky she's nicer than me," she said to Greta.

"She's no good to us if she's dead," I said.

Carly arched one eyebrow with a slight grin on her face. "My way is a lot more fun."

"Knock it off, Carly."

She shrugged, but the grin remained in place. Good Lord, we were doing a good-cop-bad-cop routine without even meaning to. What would it take to get Greta to tell us what we wanted to know? I didn't know if what Carly was doing qualified as torture, but if it didn't, it was close enough.

I knelt next to Greta so I could look her in the eyes. "What are you afraid of? Will they really kill you?" It was kind of stupid to ask her a question when her mouth was covered, but her wide eyes gave me the answer I needed. "If you help us, we might be able to help you."

Behind me, Carly made a disapproving sound, but I didn't care. I valued the girls' lives more than Greta's, but there was no need to shed blood if it wasn't necessary. Although technically, we weren't the ones shedding blood. Carly was the only one bleeding, courtesy of Greta's gun.

"Let her talk," I said to Carly. The dirt rolled off Greta's face, kind of like pantyhose rolls down a leg.

"I'll die before I help her." Greta looked at Carly with such hatred that I wondered what had happened between them all those years ago.

I stood. "That was your last chance." I placed the flashlight at my feet and turned to walk away.

"So you're just going to let her kill me?"

I paused and looked over my shoulder. "You probably know better than I do that Carly doesn't need anyone's permission to do anything." I looked at Carly. "I'll be in the car."

God, I hoped I wasn't making a mistake. Greta seemed to be under the impression that I was holding Carly back, and maybe I was. Maybe by walking away, I was sentencing Greta to death. But one thing was clear—Greta was scared of these people, even though she was supposedly in league with them.

On the tree in front of me, there was a bouncing, round circle of light. I looked back, but it wasn't Carly shining the flashlight my way. Besides, our wimpy flashlight wasn't that strong.

"Shit." Carly's voice came through clearly in the darkness. I heard a rustle of dirt, then our flashlight started to bob in my direction. "Someone's coming. Get to the car."

She didn't have to tell me twice. We jogged side by side, our meager light barely providing enough illumination for us not to trip on fallen branches. When the car was in sight, I pulled the clicker out of my pocket and fumbled to find the right button. Carly slid into the driver's seat, and I climbed into the passenger's seat. My foot came down on something hard on the floorboard, and I reached down and wrapped my fingers around the gun. Though I didn't have a lot of experience with guns, I had enough that I easily found the safety.

Carly pulled off onto the road, and I looked behind us regretfully, not because we'd left someone back there buried alive, but because it had all been for nothing.

"Where are we going?" Perhaps I should have inquired about Greta, but I wasn't sure I wanted to know. I was a hypocrite, willing to walk away so Carly could do the dirty work but not willing to condone it.

Carly adjusted the mirrors. "Back to Greta's house to get the Jeep."

"What about this car?" It was in rough shape—scrapes on the side and bullet holes in the windshield and passenger's door. Miraculously, it still purred like the orange cat that had fallen asleep on Carly's lap.

"We'll take it somewhere to dump it."

"Could you tell who was coming?" Whoever it was had been coming from the other direction, so I assumed there was a road on the other side of the woods, but I didn't know for sure.

"No clue, but they had huge flashlights." Carly paused. "Greta got lucky."

I closed my eyes and hung my head, knowing I was going to regret asking this question. "Would you have killed her if you had longer?"

Carly took a moment to consider. "Do you really want to know the answer to that?"

I took that as a yes. *Damn it.* "Why did you attack Greta in the car?" That should have been my first question. In fact, I should have asked it back in the woods, but by then, the damage had already been done.

"I don't trust her. She could have been leading us into an ambush. If they figured out how powerful you are, and especially if they found out you're my daughter, they'd want you." *Just like they wanted the other six girls.* The words went unspoken, but they didn't need to be said aloud.

"Is there anyone you *do* trust?" I asked.

"Yes, but because they're trustworthy, they probably aren't wrapped up in this. They wouldn't condone kidnapping children."

She had a point, but instead of putting us closer to finding Lena, the events of the evening merely complicated everything. I hadn't thought that was possible. Being so horribly mistaken sucked.

"This is a disaster. We should have met them," I said. "They can't have that many facilities. I could have agreed to be a test subject, and then they'd take me to where the girls are."

Carly looked over at me as if I were crazy. "And then what?"

"I don't know." I was so frustrated. I'd insisted on coming along, but if I hadn't, maybe Carly would have gone through with meeting them. For better or worse, I was her Achilles' heel. Just like I was Aidan's, though he wouldn't appreciate my pointing out that he had something in common with Carly.

"I should have killed her," Carly said with a chuckle. "Then we wouldn't have to worry about her corrupting young minds."

Oh my God, I'd totally forgotten my concerns about Greta being an elementary school teacher. "We still need to do something about that."

"I don't think we'll have to. If the police get involved in this incident, her... *friends* will be pissed. If that wasn't the police in the woods back there, whoever it was will probably call them." Carly tapped on the steering wheel. "Unless those were her friends, which I don't know how they'd have found us. Either way, she's screwed."

"Well, that's something at least." Getting her out of the classroom was a small comfort. "She's not right in the head."

"She's definitely got a touch of crazy. That's nothing new, but it's gotten worse. She didn't realize that I knew, but she was trying to turn everyone against me at the end."

"Why didn't you take her out?" I wasn't an evil mastermind, but it was common sense to neutralize threats. Also, that seemed to be Carly's MO.

"Keep your friends close and keep your enemies closer. It's cliché but true."

"Do you think her... I really hate not knowing what to call these people. Should we call them... I don't know... the bad guys?" That sounded so lame and made the situation sound less serious than it was.

She laughed. "I'd probably go with something more... *ahem*... colorful."

I could think of a few four-letter words that would be appropriate. "What will they do to Greta when they find her? Should we be worried she'll tell them about us?"

"No, because even if she does, we're going to find them." The way she said it, all matter-of-fact, should have made me feel better, but it didn't. They were just words at this point. We had no intel.

Suddenly exhausted, I rubbed my hands over my face. I laid my head back against the headrest and closed my eyes. Forty-eight hours—that was how long I'd been with Carly. They'd been the longest forty-eight hours of my life.

Although I had an insane amount of power flowing through me, I didn't feel anywhere close to losing control. Perhaps my threshold had increased. The fact that my power wasn't spiraling out of control was a relief. I wished I knew why, but I couldn't think about that at the moment. There were other, more pressing matters to attend to.

The radio was still tuned to Christmas music, and Carly hummed along to "The Little Drummer Boy." *What in the heck?* She appeared to be in a good mood, as if she hadn't been shot, as if we weren't driving what was technically a stolen car we planned to torch, as if we hadn't left her former friend buried up to her neck. That might not have been exactly true—for all I knew, Carly had buried Greta completely before she'd run away. I would actually have been more surprised if she hadn't.

Carly pulled into Greta's driveway and drove around back. She used the button on the car's console to open the detached garage before putting the car in park and turning it off. "Go inside and wipe down anything we touched, just to be safe. And grab me a snack."

"Sure," I muttered as I got out of the car. "A snack. I'll just steal some food while I destroy evidence."

I let myself in the back door, using a key on the ring we'd pulled from Greta's pocket. At least we didn't have to add breaking and entering to our list of crimes that evening. Just entering.

The door opened into a mudroom, and I knew right away without looking that it was where the cats' litter box was. I covered my nose with one hand while I searched for a light switch with the other. Once I flipped it, I remembered I was supposed to be erasing our prints, not leaving more. *Ugh.* I was not meant for the criminal lifestyle. I grabbed a towel from a laundry basket and wiped down the light switch and the doorknob, then I hurried through the kitchen to the front room and tried to remember everything we'd touched. I didn't think anyone would look for prints in Greta's house, but I was happy to play it safe.

Back in the kitchen, I opened the pantry door in search of snacks and hit the mother lode. Seeing all the food made me realize how hungry I was, so I grabbed a bag of Doritos, a box of Cheez-Its, a package of Oreos, and a box of Nutter Butters.

It seemed Greta had the same taste buds as her second-grade students.

I nearly jumped out of my skin when I felt something rub against my ankles. The black cat looked up at me and let out a pitiful meow.

Shit. I didn't know how long Greta would be gone. We couldn't leave the cats there without someone to take care of them, and we definitely couldn't take them with us. But I had to do something.

I piled my snacks on the counter, and a magazine caught my eye. Adam First, a rock star, and his girlfriend, actress Missy Storm, were pictured on the cover, posing on the red carpet at her most recent movie premiere. They'd died recently in a yacht accident, and the council suspected an elemental was responsible. Vic and Suze had gone out to California to investigate, but the only thing they'd found was that a suspicious woman had been involved. With Lena's abduction taking up most of my mental and emotional capacity, I'd forgotten all about it. But now that I was traipsing around with a suspicious woman, I had to wonder.

I would wonder later.

"Cat food," I muttered, using the towel to open various cabinets. I found a big bag of cat chow under the sink and filled their food bowls to overflowing. But I didn't know how much cats ate since I'd never had one. I shrugged then set the bag on the floor and ripped a hole in the front. That should last them at least a week. If I were feeling really charitable, I would clean the litter box before I left, but I wasn't quite that generous. The cats could pee on the floor if it was too dirty for them, and Greta could deal with that cleanup.

Finally, I scooped up my snacks and exited the way I'd come in, pausing to wipe my fingerprints from the door handle.

Carly was leaning against the side of the Jetta. "What took you so long?"

"I had to feed the cats," I muttered.

Carly looked at me as if I'd lost my mind. "You take the Jeep and follow me. We need to find somewhere to dump the car." She plucked the Cheez-Its out of my hand and replaced the box with the keys to the Jeep.

I trotted around to the front of the house and barely had time to start the Jeep before Carly was coming down the driveway. With one hand on the steering wheel and the other shoved deep into the bag of Doritos, I followed her west toward Indianapolis. After about an hour, she turned off on some back roads. They were deserted and reminded me of where we'd left Greta. I wondered if Carly knew where she was going or if she had made a lucky guess.

She guided the car off the road into a field but stuck her hand out of the window and indicated that I should stop. I shifted into park and waited, wondering if I should get out of the car to help her. I decided against it and watched from afar.

She continued driving until it appeared the car got stuck, then she got out and started pouring something all over the outside and inside of the car. I was too far away to see what it was, but undoubtedly, it was something flammable.

A bolt of light flashed across the sky, catching me by surprise. We had been fortunate so far and hadn't run into any snow or bad weather, but it appeared we'd run out of luck. I hoped it didn't rain until the car was done burning, whenever that would be.

Truthfully, I thought torching the car was overkill. We could've wiped our prints off the car and poured bleach on the spots of Carly's blood. I realized then that I should have been looking for first-aid supplies instead of spending so much time on the cats. I doubted Carly had done anything to take care of her wound, which I hadn't even seen yet, so I had no idea how bad it really was. I hoped Carly was careful and didn't catch herself on fire in her endeavor to burn the car because she poured a ridiculous amount of fluid on it. We didn't need to add burns to her list of injuries.

She stepped away from the car and leaned down to pick up something she must have put down earlier. I gaped as I realized what it was—a blowtorch. I didn't even want to know why the heck Greta would have one of those. I supposed it was good for us that she did, but it bewildered me all the same.

Carly moved around the car, and it almost seemed as though she were dancing. She had a lightness to her step. When the car was engulfed in flames, she put her hands in the air and whooped. She was definitely enjoying this. It made me a little sick to my stomach. I understood why she thought it was necessary, but I didn't get why she had to be so exuberant about it.

She ran to the Jeep, and when she got into the passenger's seat, she was out of breath. I pulled onto the road, not waiting for instructions on where to go. Though the area appeared deserted, I didn't want to stick around long enough to see if that perception was true.

"Keep going toward Indianapolis," she said. She reached into the back seat for the Oreos and ripped open the package. "A storm's coming." She sounded awfully gleeful about it.

"Let's just hope it holds off until we can find somewhere to stop." I wasn't the most experienced driver, and I didn't want to be stuck behind the wheel at night on unfamiliar roads in the middle of a storm—and while my power was surging like an electrical storm.

Carly didn't comment. Instead, she plowed her way through half of the Oreos before she bothered to offer me one. She was giddy, and I could almost feel the energy rolling off her in waves.

"Did you have time to take care of your wound?" I asked.

"No, but it barely hurts."

I'd never been shot, but I doubted it barely hurt. *Whatever.* She was an adult, and I wasn't in charge of her.

As she turned her attention to the Nutter Butter bars, I remembered the magazine I had seen at Greta's house. My gaze slid over to Carly. "Have you ever been to the West Coast? Like California, maybe?"

"Sure. I've been there."

"Recently?"

"Not in the last few years. Why do you ask?" Before I could answer, a streak of lightning crackled across the sky. "Pull over."

It was my turn to look at Carly as though she were crazy, and let's face it, the jury was still out. "What? Here? Why?" It would make the third time we'd stopped on the side of the road, and nothing good had come from either of the first two stops.

Carly already had her hand on the door handle. "Just do it." Afraid she would open the door while we were still moving, I did as she asked. She hopped out of the car before I even put it in park. "Come on."

Now what?

With her arms in the air, Carly ran from the Jeep. I cautiously followed her. She stopped in the middle of the field, closed her eyes, and breathed deeply. "Do you feel that?"

Feel what? The cold? Because it was freaking freezing, and my hoodie wasn't cutting it. I warmed the air around me and felt instant relief from the bitter chill.

There was a flash, and a bolt of light hit the ground only yards in front of Carly, which sent dirt flying up. I screamed, grabbed Carly, and pulled her toward the car, but she dug in her heels.

"Are you crazy?" I yelled.

She smiled. "I've got it under control."

The realization that she'd caused the lightning to hit the ground struck me as violently as the bolt had slammed into the ground. I released my hold on her. "Why would you do that?"

"It's fun. You try."

"You want me to play with lightning?"

The wind picked up and blew Carly's hair around her face. In that instant, I could relate to sixteenth-century New Englanders who'd mistaken elementals for witches because Carly surely looked like one.

"It's not playing with it." She giggled. "Okay, maybe it is. But try it. There's nothing like the feeling of the raw energy." She turned away from me, and moments later, a tree in the distance was cleaved in half with a loud cracking sound. The two sides fell to the ground with a thud.

My power jumped to attention, like a dog straining on its leash. I tried to rein it in, but the more Carly used her power, the more mine called to me. Still, I stepped back, prepared to wait in the Jeep until Carly was done playing. Then a familiar itch returned, and the skin on my arms was on fire. I raked my nails down my sleeves, but it did little to quell the uncomfortable sensation, and my sleeves were too tight for me to push them more than a few inches past my wrists.

Damn it. I hated that my power and my body worked against me. I hadn't lost control in the sense that I had previously, but I also wasn't in command. My power had a will of its own, and it didn't match with mine.

Carly looked over her shoulder at me. "Come on. This is a perfect time to practice. It's much easier to call the lightning when it's already there."

Her comment implied she could bid lightning to strike when it wasn't storming. *Oh boy.* What was even more frightening than her seemingly unlimited power was her nonchalance about it.

My foster mother's words rang in my mind—*she could be stronger than her mother ever was.* Would I eventually be capable of controlling lightning? Hell, perhaps I was already capable.

I took a deep breath. Carly was right. It was the time to test my limits. There was a flash in the clouds, indicating a gathering of electricity—or so I assumed. I didn't actually know much about lightning. Closing my eyes, I focused on it, trying to forge a connection with it.

"Let it happen naturally," Carly whispered over my shoulder. I hadn't even heard her move behind me. "Embrace Mother Nature's power. Respect it. Don't command it, but ask it to do your will."

I wanted to snort and roll my eyes. *Ask it?* Like "*excuse me, Mother Nature, can your lightning come out to play?*" It was the stupidest thing I'd ever heard.

I refocused my effort on forcing my bidding upon it. The power in my body circulated restlessly, growing more and more out of control, yet the lightning failed to heed my call.

"You're trying too hard," Carly said. "The secret to wielding the elements to their full potential is to give up control."

Your power could control you. Michelle had warned me about that.

I shook my head and stepped away from Carly. "No. I can't."

"You can. You can't influence the elements without opening yourself up to them."

Her choice of words wasn't lost on me. I'd been taught to control my powers my whole life, and in the last month, I'd desperately fought losing control. Even Carly had used that term. Everything was always about *control, control, control*. But that was an arrogant and foolish notion. For whatever reason, we'd been blessed with the gift of having a connection to the natural world, and we shouldn't treat it as a power struggle— we would never win. But we could definitely *influence* the world around us.

It was a subtle but important shift in thinking.

And scary as hell.

But I realized the more I resisted working with my power, the more I tried to control it, the more out of control it became. It made no sense and perfect sense at the same time.

I exhaled, and with the breath that left my body, I released my already tenuous grip on my control. Every muscle in my body relaxed, and the power that had been fighting to get out calmed, turning into a soothing and pleasant sensation, as if my insides were wrapped in an embrace. I let out a contented sigh.

"That's it," Carly said quietly. "Now connect with the natural world around you."

The air in my lungs felt more vibrant than it ever had. Under my feet, I felt slight shifts in the earth. Deep beneath the surface, I could feel the ebb and flow of water. My senses were more attuned to the elements than they ever had been. It felt magical.

I extended my reach toward the sky and felt the currents of energy from the storm. I let them wrap around my consciousness, giving myself over to them. It felt natural, much more so than fighting the urge as I'd done my entire life.

I coaxed the lightning to do my bidding. It cooperated because the natural world and I were of the same mind—we were connected.

A smile graced my lips as a vibrant streak of lightning crashed to the ground in front of me.

Chapter 14

AT THE FIRST sign of rain, we decided to pack it in. Once I calmed down a bit from the exhilaration of my experience with the lightning, exhaustion set in. It was well after midnight, and we still needed to find a place to stay.

Carly was still hyped up, so I kept possession of the Jeep keys. She didn't protest, but she also didn't offer any advice as to where we should go. I decided to drive for another hour in the same direction we'd been going and stop at the first hotel I found. Luckily, we were closing in on the outskirts of Indianapolis, which gave us options. I selected a nicer hotel than the ones we'd stayed in previously and stuck my hand out for cash after parking in the lot. Carly readily handed over her wallet. As I walked into the lobby, I couldn't help but peek at her license. *Eliza Cartwright.* That action made me remember that respectable hotels asked for ID upon check-in. *Damn it.* I spun on my heel and retrieved Carly from the car.

After we got settled into a room with one king-sized bed— the only room they'd had available—Carly passed out almost immediately. I wondered if the drug Greta had given her was giving her more trouble than she was letting on. Considering how she'd used her powers, it couldn't have affected her that much. Or maybe it had, and she was normally even more ridiculously powerful than what she'd shown. One person possessing so much raw power was scary, especially when that person was Carly.

I had so much to discuss with Aidan, and damn it, an email didn't cut it. But it was all I had. I opened my email, and even though I'd just heard from him earlier that evening, I was disappointed that the only message in my inbox was from an African prince who needed my help to claim ten million dollars. I opened up the compose email screen and quickly summarized everything that had happened that evening. It was the middle of the night, so he probably wouldn't get it until tomorrow, but regardless, I was in a hurry to get it sent so he would see it at the earliest possible opportunity. As I stared as my completed email, I realized just how surreal all this was. Only a month ago, my biggest concern was how to sneak out of the house for a date with my then-boyfriend. Now I was worried about how to stop my evil birth mother from killing people, all while trying to search for my kidnapped foster sister.

I plugged my phone into the charger and flopped back onto the bed. Carly snored softly next to me, but I had trouble finding sleep. While my body was exhausted, my mind buzzed, trying to process everything that had happened. Yet I also couldn't form a coherent thought. Today had been the single longest day of my life.

THE NEXT MORNING when I woke up, Carly was already out of bed. I dozed while I waited for her to get out of the bathroom.

After about twenty minutes, I got up and tapped on the bathroom door. She wasn't in there.

Shit. Where the heck was she? There was no note, and I couldn't see where I'd parked the Jeep from our window, so I had no idea if she'd left the hotel. I hated to admit how unnerved I was by her absence. Over the last three days, we'd become sort of a team—a dysfunctional team, but a team nonetheless.

I grabbed my phone and was surprised to see that it was nearly eleven. *Shit.* I didn't know when checkout was or what our next step was. *Where the heck is Carly?*

Quickly, I scanned my inbox, hoping for a message from Aidan, but it was empty. *Damn it.* Surely he'd read my email by now. Worry nagged at me. The last I'd heard, his contact was still missing. Aidan could take care of himself, but he wasn't invincible. *What if he's missing too?* I refreshed my inbox, but nothing magically appeared. After staring at the screen for another few seconds, I put the phone down. I would have to trust that Aidan was handling his side of things, because I had my own things to handle.

I rooted around in my bag for a semi-clean change of clothes. I could only get by another few days before the clothes became too dirty and rank to wear. I was already out of clean underwear. It looked as though I would have to spend some of my limited cash on that.

The door swung open, and Carly walked in, carrying two plates full of breakfast food that also had coffee cups balanced on them. I didn't know how she had managed to get the door open. I jumped up to help her.

"I snagged us some food as they were cleaning it up." Carly's hair was wet, telling me she'd already showered. She looked tired, though.

"Thanks," I said. "When is checkout?"

"In about ten minutes."

So much for showering. "Let me grab my stuff." I knelt down next to my bag.

"No rush. I got us the room for another night."

I stopped shoving my clothes into my bag and looked up at her. "Why?"

"We need a day to regroup."

Shaking my head, I got to my feet. "No. We don't have time for that." Especially now that Aidan could be MIA. We needed to get to the bottom of things. I wasn't losing anyone else to this tragedy.

"Greta's gone underground," Carly said, ignoring my protest.

"How do you know?" I asked. "Who was it in the woods last night?"

"The police. It was on the news." She took the lid off her coffee and dumped in three packets of sugar. "It was also on the news that Greta slipped away, so they're looking for her."

"Damn." I didn't know what that meant for us. Had she run to her friends to tell them about us? Or had she run away from them because they were a threat to her too? Or maybe she was just plain hiding.

"Yeah." Carly ran her hands through her hair. "I'm going to reach out to Jack again—"

"We're not driving back there, are we?"

She shook her head. "I'll call him. I want to make sure he hasn't heard anything else. *If* I can get him to talk on the phone.

He's a surly bastard. But this thing with Greta has me even more convinced that we need to look into people from my past."

"Do you suspect any of them are involved?" I picked up a pastry and tore off a piece.

"My suspicion about Greta was correct. But it's been fifteen years. So who knows?" She crossed the room to a drawer and opened it. "Plus, I want to find someone who can analyze this." She pulled out the syringe. I hadn't realized she'd retrieved it from Greta's car before burning it.

"It didn't affect you very much," I commented. "I wonder how it compares to what I was stuck with."

It was alarming that Greta had just happened to have some of the drug. Did they pass it out like breath mints after a dinner party? *Thanks for coming! Here's your Infirmi.* But more than just their members had it—so did Holy Mission United Church and who knew how many other twisted organizations. The group we were looking for couldn't be as secretive as they once were if they were selling it.

Damn it. Now I really wished Carly hadn't killed my kidnappers. If she hadn't, then the guardians might have been able to figure out who had given them the Infirmi. The girls' abduction could have been prevented.

I considered telling Carly about Holy Mission and proposing we go question them, but she might want to kill the entire congregation. While I didn't agree with their beliefs and practices, we had no proof any of the other people were involved. As far as I knew, they were just bigoted assholes, which was not a justifiable reason for unleashing Carly on a homicidal rampage. *Unfortunately.*

But if we didn't make progress on any of the other avenues Carly was looking into, we might have no choice but to pay them a visit. Asking questions about my four kidnappers without raising suspicion would be next to impossible, though. Hopefully, it wouldn't come down to that, especially because it would probably be a dead end, anyway. I was doubtful this group would allow the idiots at Holy Mission to be able to identify them.

"That's what I want to know too," Carly said. "Did you look at the lab report on that drug?"

"No." I hesitated for a moment. "I might be able to get my hands on a copy of it. But I doubt it." Aidan had been able to swipe Carly's file, but if they were watching him as closely as it seemed from his cryptic email, then he wouldn't be able to help. And that was assuming he was merely incommunicado rather than missing like his contact. *God, why hasn't he emailed me?*

Carly drained the last of her coffee. "I might know someone who can help. It's just going to take time to find him."

Carly began tapping away on her phone, so I let her be. The more I pestered her, the longer it would take. She'd said she wanted the day to regroup, but I was still hopeful we could get moving later that day.

I ate, showered, and twiddled my thumbs while Carly did whatever she needed to on her phone. At one point, I asked her if I could help, and her response was a look that would make someone think I'd asked her to shave a honey badger. *Whatever.* It wasn't totally crazy that I could be useful. Instead, I took the Jeep and set out in search of underwear and lunch. I was successful on both accounts. What struck me as odd, though, was the fact that Carly hadn't batted an eye when I told her what I was doing—going out into the world unsupervised. I was so used to having a guardian or Lena with me that it felt strange to be out by myself. I considered myself independent, but how independent was I really if being out alone felt weird? Not crippling, just... *weird*.

When I got back to the hotel, Carly hadn't made any progress finding the person she was looking for. And an email from Aidan hadn't arrived in my inbox no matter how obsessive I was about refreshing it.

"What's the backup plan?" I asked.

"Working on it," she muttered.

"What about Jack? Did you get in touch with him?"

"No." Carly was snippy and obviously agitated, so I let it go. But every hour that passed with us stuck in the hotel room made me antsy.

While I was out, I'd figured out how to set up my email account with the app on the phone and had set it to ping if I got a message. When it buzzed, I pulled the phone out of my pocket so fast, I fumbled like it was a hot potato.

It contained one line—*Guardians are coming your way.*

That was it. Still, relief overwhelmed me, and my heart felt lighter. *He isn't missing.* Of course he wasn't. This was Aidan. He could handle himself.

Once my relief passed, I tossed the phone onto the bed with a frustrated growl. Why hadn't he given me more information? Learning if they'd found his contact or the missing kids would have been helpful.

Actually, it wouldn't have done Carly and me any good, but I still wanted to know. At least he'd warned me about the guardians. Running into them could be problematic.

"What?" Carly asked without looking up. "What did Aidan say?"

I swallowed my annoyance at her question. I didn't know why it bothered me so much when she mentioned him. It was probably in part due to our not being stealthy with our communication.

"Guardians are coming."

Blinking, Carly looked up. "What? Here?"

"I don't think so." I hadn't actually told Aidan where we'd ended up, so he might still think we were near Greta's house. *Damn it, why wasn't he more specific?* "They must have found out about Greta."

"It was only a matter of time."

"We should go," I said. "We're too close to there. They could find us." I hated feeling as though I needed to run from guardians. They were the good guys. But they would capture Carly if they could, and I couldn't let them take her. I would have liked to say that was solely because I needed her, but it was more complicated than that.

Carly's mouth stretched into a cocky smile. "Evading guardians is nothing new for me."

I rubbed my temples, which had suddenly started throbbing. Her comment reminded me that though we were temporarily on the same team, we were on very different sides overall. "You will not kill them. Promise me that if we run into guardians, you will *not* kill them."

She glowered at me. "Fine," she said primly.

My hands balled into fists. "What the hell, Carly? Asking you not to commit murder isn't an unreasonable request."

"I said I wouldn't." She sounded like a petulant child.

I tried to decide if I could believe her. "I'm serious. I know these people. They're my friends and family. I'll be one of them soon." The jury was still out on that little fact, especially after running away. I doubted the council would allow me to join the ranks of guardians after this stunt. But Carly didn't know that, and she needed to know how closely I was tied to the guardian network.

"They took you from me! I thought you were dead!" Her outburst caught me off guard since she usually kept her emotions on a low simmer, but her anguish was genuine. A pang of guilt hit me, even though it wasn't my fault she'd thought I was dead all those years. I stood by my assertion that if she hadn't been doing evil things, the council wouldn't have taken me. As far as I knew, they weren't in the practice of abducting random children, only the offspring of evil masterminds. But I wasn't naive enough to think I knew everything about the council.

"That was fifteen years ago," I said quietly. "Today's guardians didn't do it."

Carly laughed bitterly. "Why don't you ask Greg West about that?"

I frowned, and it took a minute for me to register who she was referring to. "Aidan's father?"

"Forget it." As if that were possible.

"No. You brought it up. What are you saying?" The information Carly had given me so far had been carefully curated, but that tidbit fell outside that realm. It seemed more like a slip of the tongue. It was obvious from Carly's closed-off expression that she wasn't going to follow it up with another one.

Carly stood and started gathering her things and stuffing them in her bag. "You're right. We should get going. We have a drive ahead of us."

Chapter 15

CARLY AND I didn't speak the entire five-hour drive to a Podunk town outside of Pittsburgh, nor did we speak over dinner in our new hotel room. Her comment about Aidan's dad plagued me. I had no idea what she was alluding to, and I knew she wouldn't tell me more. It made no sense. She had no problems slandering council members, so the husband of one shouldn't have been any different, especially since she'd already established that she didn't care for Patricia West. *Why is she holding back?*

I had to decide if I should tell Aidan about what Carly had said. I'd told him everything else so far, but nothing had been personal. His relationship with his parents was shaky at best. Did I want to risk making it even worse by telling him something I wasn't even sure had merit? However, even though Carly might omit things, she'd never flat-out lied.

As had become our routine, Carly slept peacefully while I tossed and turned. I stared at her in the darkness, feeling resentful not only because she was sleeping when I couldn't, but because she'd complicated my life in ways I hadn't anticipated. I'd known spending time with her wouldn't be easy, but now I wondered if I'd made the situation worse. The incident with Greta hadn't put us any closer to finding the girls. If she told her friends we were looking for them, they could retaliate in some way. The girls could suffer. Greta's friends could move them to another location, making it even harder to find them. *As if that's possible.*

In the morning, Carly and I barely spoke. So when it was time to go, I mutely packed my things and followed her to the Jeep. Once on the road, I checked my inbox and was pleased to see Aidan had responded. I was even more pleased to see it was longer than his previous one-liner.

We found my contact. Unfortunately, we were too late. She's dead. We suspect whoever took those kids found out she was talking to us. Now we have no more leads, and those kids are still missing.

Sophie, be careful. I don't want to tell you what they did to that poor woman. It was bad... really bad. Promise me you won't take any risks. I want to see you again.

I ran my fingers over the screen, touching Aidan's words and wishing I were touching him instead. It was too late to avoid risks, and in fact, we needed to take every chance we got if it could bring us closer to the girls. These people weren't afraid to kill—they had killed Aidan's contact, and Greta was petrified she would be next. *I* was petrified they would decide their test subjects weren't worth the effort and would dispose of them.

For Aidan to say what they'd done to that woman was bad spoke volumes. Cold, hard fear took root in my heart and inched through my veins until I broke out into a cold sweat.

I couldn't afford to be at odds with Carly, no matter how much she pissed me off, so I sucked it up and asked her who we were meeting. It would not do either one of us any good to be unprepared for the meeting.

"Wanda was with me from the beginning," Carly said. "She's a year younger than me, and she sort of... *attached* herself to me when we were teenagers."

I could read between the lines. Carly was the dominant one, and Wanda had followed her around like a needy puppy. Still, Carly's tone was affectionate, and I could tell she was fond of Wanda.

"Was she ever part of the EA?"

"No, though she desperately wanted to be. Her family was poor, and their abilities low. If they were part of the EA, I doubt they'd qualify as full elementals."

"If she wanted to be part of the EA, then why would she join you?" Although Carly maintained that the main purpose in her crusade was "choice," it was no secret she was anti-EA, which made sense. The council was about control—choice didn't factor into their decisions, decisions that affected all of us.

Carly took a moment to formulate her response. "It wasn't so much that she wanted to be part of the EA. She just wanted to belong somewhere."

I understood the feeling. Fortunately, I had my adopted family now, but when I'd lived with Lloyd and Belinda, I had felt isolated. Keeping my elemental abilities a secret had been drilled into me my entire life. They'd been petrified I would show off and expose us, so I hadn't been allowed to do things normal girls did, like have sleepovers. I was independent by nature, but I would have been lying if I said it hadn't sucked.

I wondered if Wanda's childhood had been as isolating as mine. Since her powers were weak, she probably didn't have the nagging about keeping her powers a secret. But had her parents kept her separated from other children for another reason? Or maybe Wanda had done that to herself.

Even though Carly was anti-EA, she had to admit it served a purpose—community. Maybe instead of setting herself up as its enemy, she should have tried to bring change from within.

Yeah, because council members like West and Stearns are so amenable to change.

"Here we are." Carly guided the Jeep into a diner parking lot. The front right tire hit a huge pothole, causing me to almost bang my head against the window. Carly maneuvered around another pothole before pulling into a space.

The diner didn't look to be in any better shape than the parking lot. It was one of those rectangular-shaped ones that was supposed to resemble a railcar. Pieces of the metal siding were missing, and other parts were hanging off.

Carly opened her door. "Come on. Let me do the talking."

"I'll try," I said as we walked toward the front door. When Carly gave me a look, I shrugged. "Would you rather I make a promise I can't keep?"

Carly rolled her eyes.

Two bells tied to the diner door jingled loudly as we walked in. I was relieved to see the interior was maintained better than the exterior. It was currently decorated with garland and poinsettias, and there was a big plastic glowing Santa Claus near the cash register. A sign instructing us to seat ourselves was posted. There was only a handful of customers, which wasn't surprising considering the odd hour. It was 10:45, too late for breakfast and too early for lunch. But when we slid into a vinyl booth, I eagerly studied the plastic menu. The quick breakfast we'd grabbed at the hotel hadn't cut it.

A waitress holding a thick paper pad appeared. She barely looked at us. "Can I get you something to drink?"

"I'll take a Coke," I said.

"Hello, Wanda," Carly said casually.

The use of her name caused the woman to actually look at Carly, and she did a double take, clutching the paper pad to her chest. "Oh my God. I know you're not... Are you... Is it really you?"

She was not what I was expecting at all. For starters, I hadn't realized Wanda worked there—I'd thought this was simply a meeting place.

Wanda was slightly pudgy with unremarkable eyes and mousy hair pulled up into a thin ponytail. She was the type of person who faded into the background. She would always be a sidekick and never the star of her own story.

Carly smiled, reminding me of a queen smiling down on her subject, which was odd considering she was actually looking up at Wanda. "It is."

"Oh my God." Wanda used the pad to fan herself, as though she were feeling vapors or something. "Some people said you might be around, but I said no way because there's no way you'd be alive and not let me know." Her words were slightly accusatory, which surprised me considering how in awe of Carly she was. I wouldn't have thought she would do anything that might offend her.

Carly folded her hands in front of her and donned a guise of regret. "After Cassandra died... I just couldn't. You understand, right?"

Wanda patted Carly on the shoulder. "Oh, honey, I know." Though she spoke the words, she didn't successfully mask the hurt in her expression. "It was so sad. No one was more heartbroken than me to hear about it."

"Miss!" A man on the other side of the restaurant called to Wanda.

Wanda spared him an annoyed glance. "I'm coming." She turned back to us. "That's Roy. He's in here every other day, and he's a pain in my ass. He knows my name, but he calls me "Miss" to annoy me. So, Carly, can I get you something to drink?"

"Water, please."

Wanda tucked the notepad into her apron. "I'll be right back with that water."

I wasn't Carly's clone or anything, but there was a definite resemblance so I'd waited for Wanda to look at me and put the pieces together like Greta had. But once she'd learned Carly was sitting in front of her, I had apparently ceased to exist. Wanda was Carly's biggest fan.

I hoped she remembered my drink.

Carly hadn't bothered looking at the menu.

"Are you eating?" I asked.

"I'll get something, just to make it worth Wanda's time to have us at her table."

That was actually really thoughtful of Carly. Sometimes I had a hard time reconciling this side of her with the side that had tortured Greta and killed my kidnappers in cold blood.

And okay, she'd killed those two men for my sake. I never would have asked her to do it, but I hadn't lost any sleep over their deaths either. Did that make me as bad as Carly?

I would say one thing for my twisted mother—she had her own sense of loyalty.

I decided what to order and tucked the menu behind the condiments. "Is there anything else I need to know about

Wanda?" I asked in a low voice. "Is she secretly a psycho like our friend, Greta?" My initial impression was that Wanda was bored with her job and phoning it in, not that I blamed her. But that didn't help me get a read on her character. She'd seemed thrilled—though slightly put out—to see Carly, which could only work in our favor.

A smile graced Carly's lips. "Wanda's a good woman. I didn't want to involve her in this, but I couldn't track down anyone else I trusted."

"If you trust her, then maybe we should have started here," I said.

Carly shook her head. "No. Wanda has made a life for herself. I didn't want to mess it up for her."

"And now?"

She leveled her gaze at me. "Now I'm putting your interests in front of hers."

Ouch. Talk about a punch to the gut. Though none of this was my doing. Carly had made herself a dangerous person to associate with long before I was born. To use her own words, everyone had made their own choices, and Wanda had chosen to align herself with Carly long before I came into the picture.

Wanda returned and placed a glass of water in front of Carly, who gestured to me. "This is Stacey, by the way."

"Oh, right," Wanda said. "You wanted lemonade?"

"Coke," I corrected.

"Be right back, hon."

I hoped she was a better waitress when she wasn't surprised by her long-lost BFF. *Jeez Louise.* She returned quickly with my soda and set the glass in front of me so hastily that it splashed over the top. If I hadn't grabbed a napkin, the stream of liquid would have ended up in my lap. I took a sip and wrinkled my nose. *Ugh. Diet.*

"I get off in about half an hour," Wanda said. "Do you want to grab a cup of coffee? I know somewhere that serves much better stuff than the crap we have here."

"I'd like that." Carly smiled, and I tried to determine if it was real or just for show.

"Great." Wanda started to walk away, but I called her back. "Oh, did you want to order something?" Wanda really was the worst waitress ever. If I weren't so freaking hungry, I would have just told her to forget it.

We placed our order, and sure enough, when the food came out fifteen minutes later, mine was not even close to what I'd ordered. Carly's, of course, was perfect. I choked it down anyway. After Wanda clocked out, we followed her to a coffee shop that was indeed an upgrade from the diner. They even got my order right. We sat at a table in the corner, as far away from the other patrons as we could.

Wanda patted Carly's arm. "So where have you been?" Though she smiled, I could tell she was bothered by having to ask the question. For a moment, I felt sorry for her. She had obviously considered Carly to be her BFF at one time. It seemed while fond of Wanda, Carly didn't return the sentiment. Otherwise, she wouldn't have waited fifteen years to at least let Wanda know she was still alive.

"Nowhere special. Here and there." *Nice non-answer, Carly.* "It's been hard. Losing Cassandra broke me."

Wanda nodded. "We all loved Cassandra."

That was news to me. When I'd thought about the first two years of my life when I was with Carly, I had never considered the other people that were around. And Greta hadn't mentioned me at all. But some of her followers must've known me or at least known about me. It would've been nearly impossible to hide a pregnancy.

"I realize now it was wrong of me to disappear the way I did," Carly said. "But my mind wasn't in the right place, and the EA had it out for me. The fact that they killed my child was proof of that, and I didn't want anyone else to get in their crosshairs."

I shifted uncomfortably. Carly knew the EA hadn't killed her child—after all, I was sitting right there—and I didn't like that she was continuing to use that story. I understood she couldn't set the record straight without giving away my identity, but if there really were discord between EA elementals and rogues, her continuing to perpetuate the myth that the council killed children wouldn't help matters. Of course, they had kidnapped at least one. But I firmly believed they thought that was in my best interests.

Yet doubt nagged at me. When I'd learned the truth about my past, my foster parents had told me the council's plan to use me as leverage against Carly. However, they hadn't had any specifics, and since Carly had "died," the plan never came to fruition anyway. Lloyd and Belinda might not have been the most loving guardians, but I'd always been taken care of. More than that, the council had kept me off everyone's radar, which I'd come to believe was a good thing. Had people known where Carly's daughter was, they could have tried to hurt—or kill— me as retribution for their own dead loved ones. I'd like to think the other elementals in the EA wouldn't have wanted my toddler-sized head on a platter, but grief did weird things to people.

I wished I knew what the heck Aidan's dad had to do with any of it.

"I understand," Wanda commiserated. "You know, something about the way they said you died never felt right to me. I guess that's because you didn't actually die."

Carly laughed. "You know me too well."

Wanda couldn't know her that well anymore. After all, it had been fifteen years.

Wanda gazed adoringly at Carly. "Everything fell apart once you were gone. It just wasn't the same without you. No one could fill your shoes." Her words echoed Greta's so closely, it was eerie.

Though Carly had said Wanda *attached* herself to her, I wondered if it hadn't been more of a symbiotic relationship. Carly seemed perfectly self-assured as an adult, but it couldn't have hurt for her to have such an adoring follower when she was a teen.

Carly smiled. "We did have some good times, didn't we?"

They talked as if they had belonged to a social club instead of what was supposed to have been a revolutionary movement. Though from what Carly had said and what I'd observed about Wanda, it probably had been more of a club to her.

"We sure did." Wanda laughed. "Do you remember those two fools from the rest stop?"

Carly chuckled as if it were a fond memory. "How could I forget?"

"I bet they thought twice before trying to put their hands on a woman again."

If I were reading between the lines correctly, it sounded as though maybe men had assaulted them and Carly had taught them a lesson. That was an odd memory to smile and chuckle over. Then again, torturing Greta had kicked Carly's endorphins into high gear.

The two women continued their conversation, reminiscing and talking about Wanda's twelve-year-old son. I finished the rest of my coffee and sat silently, wishing Carly would get to the point. We were closing in on being there an hour, but so far, we'd learned nothing helpful. It was making me rethink the value of the conversation with Jack. At least that had been short, sweet, and to the point. Even the interview with Greta had progressed quicker.

"So what are you going to do now?" Wanda asked. "Now that you're back, do you have any plans?"

Basically, Wanda was asking if Carly wanted to get the band back together. *Lovely.* I hoped to God the conversation wouldn't take the same turn as it had with Greta. That hadn't ended well.

Carly lightly tapped her fingertips on the table. "I wouldn't say I'm back." *Thank God.*

Wanda's face fell. "Oh."

"Don't be so sad." Carly laughed softly. "You have more important things to worry about now, like your son."

Her comment made me pause. If she'd felt that way fifteen years ago, perhaps her own child wouldn't have been taken from her.

Wanda pressed a button on her phone and checked the time. "I'm actually late picking him up. His daddy ran off on us the first year, so it's just the two of us."

"Before you go," Carly said, "I actually need your help. I need to find Jared Hammond."

Wanda shifted, suddenly seeming cagey. "Why?"

"It's probably better you don't know," Carly said. "But it's important."

Wanda cringed. "I hate to be the one to tell you this, but Jared was killed a few years ago."

Carly put her hand over her mouth. "Oh no. Poor Jared."

"It was really sad. They broke into his house and killed him in his sleep. He probably didn't even hear them come in over his sleep apnea mask."

Fire flashed in Carly's eyes, and for a moment, I wondered if Jared's killers would face the same fate as my kidnappers if Carly found them. Despite Carly's many character flaws, I couldn't fault her loyalty. Though she had let all her followers think she was dead. Although now that I thought about it, Wanda had been surprised to see Carly, but she hadn't been shocked she was alive—more like surprised to see Carly at her table. Greta had similarly quickly recovered from the shock of seeing Carly alive. How many people suspected or knew Carly was alive? Perhaps she hadn't been as stealthy as she thought she was.

"Poor Jared," Carly said again.

"No one thought much of it at the time because he had a stash of pain meds from his back surgery that he was selling on the side. He might have even been making other stuff and selling it. I don't know for sure. But anyway, at the time, people figured addicts were the ones who broke in."

Carly leaned back. "Why would Jared do that? He was brilliant."

Wanda shrugged. "After you left, he got busted buying supplies off the black market for the experiments. No lab would hire him after that."

Carly stared off into space, seeming disturbed by that information. I was surprised she hadn't already known. It seemed as though she would have kept tabs on him like she'd apparently done with Wanda, Shari, and Greta. Though I supposed it would have been impossible to keep up with everyone, especially if they didn't want to be found.

Wanda put her hand on Carly's arm. "Don't blame yourself. He made his own choices."

Choice, choice, choice. Always choice.

"They weren't looking for drugs," Carly said quietly. "Or at least, not the narcotic kind."

"What do you mean?" Wanda asked.

"A group started manufacturing Infirmi. Probably other stuff too. And I bet they stole our research from Jared. The time line makes sense."

Wanda's eyes widened. "I'd heard about that, but I didn't put two and two together."

"What did you hear?" I asked. *Finally.* Maybe we would get some information we could use.

Wanda looked at me in surprise, as though she'd forgotten I was there. "Just whispers about a group working on it, but I didn't think anything of it. There's always talk, you know?"

Wanda left shortly after that to collect her son, and Carly and I remained at the table. Carly's expression was murderous, making her appear formidable. A busboy cleared all the other tables but gave ours a wide berth.

I swallowed. "What now?" As much as I didn't want to talk to Carly while rage burned in her eyes, I didn't have the luxury of steering clear or even giving her time to cool down.

"We go see someone else. Nikki Blanchard," Carly said in a monotone. "I didn't know her well because she joined us near the end. Greta brought her in, but she was idealistic and driven.”

“Idealistic how?”

“She wanted to ramp up her powers so she could use them for good. She had the idea she could prevent natural disasters like tornadoes or at least make them less severe.”

Her idea wasn’t a bad one, actually. A strong elemental might be able to divert a tornado away from populated areas. But the woman being friends with Greta made me immediately wary. “Do you know where she is?”

“No. Like I said, I didn’t know her well and haven’t thought about her in years. But she’s the director of a women’s shelter, and that number is listed online.” She stood and pushed her chair in. “Let’s go.”

Once in the Jeep, Carly called the shelter, but Nikki wasn’t scheduled to be in until later that afternoon. The shelter was almost two hours away, so we decided to start driving there. Though Carly was willing to call Nikki, she still preferred trying to speak to her in person. Plus, we didn’t have anything else to do.

When we arrived at the address listed on the website, we discovered the address was actually for a central office rather than the shelter. It made sense that they would want to keep the location of the shelter secret for the protection of the women seeking refuge.

The receptionist smiled at us when we came in. “Can I help you?”

“We’d like to see Nikki Blanchard,” Carly said.

“Ms. Blanchard is still at the shelter this morning, but we expect her in any minute. You’re welcome to wait.” She gestured to a pair of rickety chairs whose integrity was questionable.

"We'll come back," Carly said smoothly. We returned to the Jeep to twiddle our thumbs. Carly stayed engrossed in her phone, and I downloaded a stupid game to pass the time. When an hour went by and Nikki still hadn't shown up, we went back in.

The receptionist looked at the clock and frowned. "That's odd. Ms. Blanchard is normally here by now. I hate for you to wait around if she's been held up. Let me call her."

She got no answer on Nikki's cell phone, so she called someone at the shelter. As she murmured into the phone, her frown deepened. "She wasn't at the shelter this morning," she said once she hung up. "That's so odd. I didn't think she was scheduled off today. Can I leave her a message for you?"

"No, thank you," Carly said, and we hastily retreated to the Jeep. Carly immediately called Wanda and asked her to hunt up Nikki's address. Since Wanda didn't have it, we were left to wait again while she tried to find someone who did.

"Is Nikki part of the EA?" If she were, then her information would have been in the EA database. Not that it would've helped us, I remembered with a pang. Even if a call to Aidan could have been made undetected, there was no way he would have been able to get the information we needed.

"No," Carly said. "She left. She didn't agree with the secrecy policy. She wanted us to use our powers to help people."

That's right. Carly had already said something to that effect. "Is there someone else we can talk to while we wait on Nikki?" All this waiting was maddening.

"No." Carly's voice was hoarse.

I remembered then that Nikki wasn't originally who Carly had wanted to see. "I'm sorry about Jared."

"He was a nice guy," Carly said quietly. "So smart. He got his degree at Cal Tech and could've gone on to do anything. Instead, he chose to help me. Because I asked him."

I didn't say what I was thinking because it was judgmental, and I wasn't perfect either. But perhaps Carly should have considered some of those things before she started on her crusade and before she abandoned everyone she'd sucked into her endeavor. That last part might not have been fair since she'd been grieving the loss of her child, but still. Her obligations and responsibilities didn't go away just because I'd "died." From what Greta and Wanda had said, Carly was integral to the operation. Surely she'd realized that. Why wouldn't she have put contingency plans in place in case of her absence? Maybe her ego had been too big to consider that.

It took Wanda almost an hour to come up with the address, which was about twenty miles away. By the time we got there, the sun had gone down.

Nikki lived in a townhouse community, which meant lots of people were around. The complex was the kind that had parking spaces rather than driveways for the residents, so we couldn't be sure if the car parked in front of her unit was hers. It was actually kind of comforting for me that the house wasn't quite so isolated. I couldn't forget that Greta and Nikki had once been linked, even if only in a loose way. Considering Greta was a second-grade teacher, the fact that Nikki ran a women's shelter didn't necessarily vouch for her character. If Nikki did turn out to be like Greta, I would feel much better being in a more populated area.

We walked up to the front stoop, and strains of music came through the door. Someone was home. Carly rang the doorbell and pounded her knuckles on the door, but there was no answer, even though she did it several times. The music was loud, but it wasn't that loud. Whoever was inside should have been able to hear us. The blinds on the front windows were drawn, but one of the slats was damaged. I hopped off the stoop and went over to it to try to see inside. However, when I leaned against the storm window, it fell off, as though it had just been placed there and not installed correctly. Either that, or it had been tampered with.

"Carly." I pointed at the window. Her face darkened, and I knew she was thinking the same thing I was. *That's not good.* She motioned for me to back away from the window. I followed her to the car, and she started fishing through her purse.

"I didn't try the window," I said. "It might be unlocked. If it is, you can boost me up."

She pulled out her wallet. "I don't think so."

"Okay. Whatever. *I'll* boost *you* up."

"People will notice if we try to climb in the window," Carly said. *Damn.* I was just thinking I was glad we were in a populated area, and it figured that in this case it worked against us. "But if the deadbolt isn't locked, I can probably get the front door open with this." She held up her credit card. *That's a handy skill. Why aren't guardians trained to do that?*

I followed her back up to the front door, and we knocked one last time. Then I shielded her while she worked on the lock. When I heard the front door open, I turned and cringed, half-expecting to find an angry person staring at us.

Instead, the person inside didn't stare at us at all. She couldn't.

She was dead.

Chapter 16

CARLY DROPPED TO her knees beside the body of a petite dark-haired woman. She checked for a pulse, but I already knew that it was a lost cause—the bullet hole in the woman's temple was evidence of that.

Her eyes were open and unfocused, yet it seemed as if she were staring at me. I squeezed my eyes shut, but the image was burned into my mind. Bile rose in my throat, and I swallowed.

"Is this Nikki?" I asked.

"Yes." Carly stood. "I don't think she's been dead long. Goddamn it." Power rolled off her in waves, and mine surged as well, making me antsier. I exhaled, forcing myself to relax and not fight the power. I'd learned my lesson.

My guardian training kicked in. "We should check the rest of the house," I said quietly.

Carly nodded. "You're right."

"You take upstairs, and I'll take down."

Before I could move into the other room, Carly put her hand on my arm. "Let's stick together."

"It'll be faster to split up." Even as I said that, I could hear Aidan's disapproval in my head. He would have wanted me to stay with Carly.

Carly's response was to tighten her grip on my arm, and I realized it would actually be faster to stay with her rather than spend the time convincing her I was right.

The music still blared, so it masked our steps as we made our way upstairs. There were only two rooms, so it didn't take long to figure out there was no one there. Neither the bedroom nor the office looked as if they had been disturbed, but of course, we couldn't be sure since we'd never been there before. There was a laptop and some other electronics in the office, which led me to believe the incident hadn't been a robbery.

"Let's finish checking downstairs," I said. "Just to be sure."

I led the way downstairs, and there happened to be a break in the music just when we reached the first level. That was the only reason I heard the doorknob on the front door turning. I didn't have enough time to warn Carly before the front door swung open.

Carly rushed in front of me, knocking me into the wall. The man who had walked in didn't even have time to register our presence before an end table flew across the floor and clipped him behind the knees. He stumbled, but it only took him a moment to recover and reach into his jacket. He pulled out a gun and pointed it at us.

Instinctively, I put my hands in the air. When Carly didn't follow suit, I slowly lowered them. *This is bad. What's she going to do?*

"What are you doing here?" he growled.

Beside me, Carly closed her eyes and began breathing deeply. I stared at her in disbelief. *She chooses now to meditate?* Not at all the response I'd expected.

"What are you doing here?" the man asked again.

"Nothing." I figured I'd better answer since he was still pointing a gun at us. "We found her like this."

The man's gaze shifted to Nikki's still body then back to me. His expression did not seem too believing.

Suddenly, flames appeared on the sleeve of his coat. I gasped, and my eyes bulged. They had literally appeared out of thin air. The man's reaction was delayed as well, and he lost valuable seconds before starting to shrug out of the coat. Carly rushed forward and easily stripped him of his weapon. She hit him on the head with it, and he fell to the floor.

"Come on!" she yelled.

I spared a glance at the jacket lying next to the man. The flames were smoldering, making me fairly confident the man was safe from them.

I followed Carly to the Jeep, reaching it just as another car pulled into the parking lot near us. While I hadn't recognized the man in the townhouse, I definitely recognized this man. It was Vic.

I halted for a brief moment, and our eyes met.

"Sophie!" Vic unstrapped his seat belt and opened the driver's door.

"Get in the Jeep." Carly already had the engine running.

Shit. What was Vic doing there? If he was there, then it was likely the man in the townhouse had also been a guardian. Just as I looked back toward the front door, he appeared.

I looked back at Carly, who had one hand on the steering wheel. The other pointed the gun at Vic.

I flung open the passenger door and put my body between the gun and him. "No. You promised."

Carly didn't lower the gun as she backed out of the parking space. Vic stood with a helpless look on his face. No doubt he was worried I was in danger. Strangely, I was probably safer with Carly than I would have been with any guardian, except maybe Aidan. She would do whatever it took to protect me.

I quickly rolled down my window. "I'm okay!" I shouted. "Everything's okay!" It wasn't sufficient, but it was the best I could do as we careened out of the parking lot. I turned in my seat to catch one last glimpse of the man who was like an uncle to me.

"Who was that?" Carly asked.

"Family," I said miserably. Carly flinched. I hadn't said that to hurt her, but it was the truth. Vic was more family to me than she would ever be. Aidan had said guardians were headed my way, but even still, seeing Vic was a shock and a stark reminder of the loved ones I'd left behind.

Carly kept her eye on the rearview mirror. "I wish we had taken her laptop."

If we'd had more time, we probably would have, but it was probably pointless. "If there was anything useful on there, whoever killed her would've taken it."

"Maybe."

"Any ideas who killed her?"

"It can't be a coincidence that she was killed right before we came to see her," Carly said grimly. "I have to believe it's related. Shit. Wanda."

"Call her," I said.

Carly's phone was connected to the Jeep's sound system, so she was able to dial using the touch screen in the dashboard. It went straight to voice mail.

"Her address is saved on my phone," Carly said. "Pull it up and put it in the GPS."

I did as she asked and snapped the phone into the holder mounted on the dashboard. Five minutes later, we tried calling again, but there was still no answer.

Carly's knuckles whitened on the steering wheel.

In my mind, I replayed the scene at the townhouse. A table seemingly moved on its own, and fire appeared out of nowhere on the man's coat. "What the hell happened back there?"

Carly's gaze slid over to me as she ran a red light. "What do you mean?"

"Cut the bullshit. You know exactly what I mean." Aidan had told me some people had reported that Carly was telekinetic. I'd thought that was just another exaggeration that went along with all the other Cruel Carly stories, but now I'd seen it with my own eyes. She shouldn't have been able to do what she'd just done.

"Elements are all around us all the time."

"That table flew across the room without so much as a gust of wind."

"I didn't use wind. The table is made of wood. It's from the natural world, or most of it at least. Just because it's no longer a tree in the forest doesn't mean it won't connect with your powers."

"I can't command trees." It was a weak response, but it was the first logic my mind jumped to. I couldn't do it, nor had I ever seen anyone else do it. Heck, I'd never even *heard* of anyone doing it except for the reports of Carly's supposed telekinesis. I'd assumed it was part of the Cruel Carly urban legend mythology.

"Have you ever tried?"

I hadn't because even though trees were part of the natural world, they weren't elements. We were elementals, not naturals. "That doesn't make any sense."

"I don't know why the council works so hard to limit us," Carly said. "We've been forced to ignore our powers for so long that we're losing them. What I did back there didn't used to be all that uncommon."

I wasn't so sure about that either. That kind of power wasn't in any of the elemental history books. An image of a poster in my English classroom sprang to my mind. *"He who controls the past controls the future. He who controls the present controls the past."* The quote was from 1984. I shook the thought from my head. Surely I wasn't comparing the EA to Big Brother.

"You created fire out of thin air. That shouldn't be possible."

"Obviously, it is," Carly spoke slowly, as if I were simply too slow to understand. "Think about it. It's not so far outside of the realm of possibility. The components of fire surround us every day. All I did was pull the needed ingredients and put them together."

"Could you teach me?" The request was out of my mouth before I realized what I was saying, but I was drawn to the possibility. I didn't want to become lumped with the elementals who'd lost their abilities. I'd finally realized that being normal wasn't enough for me, not when I could be so much more.

"It's hard, even for me," Carly admitted. "But you're my daughter, and with your lineage, I see no reason why you couldn't learn too."

That was the second time she'd referenced my lineage with regards to how powerful I should be. I desperately wanted to know what it was about my father that made me have a greater potential for power.

Carly ran another red light and took a turn so recklessly, we almost crashed into another car.

"I'll try Wanda again," I said. She didn't answer. *Damn it.*

I really wanted to call Aidan or Vic, except I didn't actually have Vic's number. It was so stupid not to have programmed it into the phone I was carrying around with me—the phone Carly had given me. I hadn't anticipated needing or wanting to communicate with anyone besides Aidan. But now I wanted to explain things. I could only imagine what must have been going through Vic's mind. *Shit.* Wherever Vic was, Suze was usually not far behind, and she held Carly responsible for the death of her sister.

I wasn't so sure I did anymore. Carly certainly wasn't innocent, but if she'd been telling the truth, she hadn't forced or even coerced anyone into anything. Many people had died as a result of their own decisions, and while Carly had been involved, that didn't make her responsible.

Though if Wanda and her son... *Double shit.* I'd forgotten she had a twelve-year-old son. My gut clenched. If they'd met the same fate as Nikki, that was on both of us.

"Hurry," I said, and Carly pressed harder on the gas.

Chapter 17

WANDA LIVED IN a working-class neighborhood with tiny houses situated very close together. Large trees lined the street, which had no sidewalks. A few of the trees looked as though they were about to keel over. When they finally gave up, they would most likely take out two or three roofs. Carly pulled to a stop a few houses down from Wanda's and parked behind a large white van.

A pickup truck was parked in Wanda's driveway, and I recognized it from when we'd followed her to the coffee shop. But only one car parked in the driveway meant nothing, especially since the street was lined with parallel-parked cars. Besides that, if someone meant Wanda harm, he would be stupid to leave his car in the driveway like a calling card, and so far, the people we were hunting hadn't been stupid.

Carly opened her door. "Stay here."

"We both know that's not happening," I said. "So let's not waste time."

Carly narrowed her eyes at me for a moment, but I didn't flinch under her scrutiny. "Then take this." She handed me the gun she'd taken from the guardian at Nikki's house. "I trust you know how to use it."

"Of course." While my training with Aidan had mostly been physical, he had also taught me other things. I didn't have much experience with guns, but I knew the basics. That would have to be enough.

"We're going to go around the back." Carly pointed to a house that was three houses down from Wanda's. "We'll hop the fences and go in through the back door. You can jump a fence, right?"

I snorted in response. She was talking to a girl who used to climb out her second-story window for secret rendezvous with her boyfriend, but of course Carly would have had no way of knowing that. After making sure the gun's safety was on, I tucked it into my pants. I followed Carly through the neighbor's backyard and over several chain-link fences. Luckily, as we climbed the final fence into Wanda's backyard, there was an oil tank between the fence and the house, so we were able to take cover behind it.

"How are your power levels?" Carly asked.

I flexed my fingers as if I expected to see sparks shoot from them. It wouldn't have been the most surprising thing ever, not with the strong currents of energy that were flowing through my body. With every fence we'd jumped, my adrenaline had spiked higher and higher. As a result, my power had also grown and grown. "I'm good."

"I'll go in first. You come behind me, and if anybody approaches you, hit first and ask questions later. Understood?"

Aidan would've approved of Carly's game plan. Where my safety was concerned, it was always "hit first and ask questions later." I was more than okay with that. I only hoped I wouldn't be forced to shoot anyone.

"Got it."

In a crouched position, Carly dashed toward the house. I half expected her to use wind power to try to blow the door open, kind of like the Big Bad Wolf, but instead, she flattened her body against it and tried the doorknob. It turned, and she slowly pushed the door open. She motioned for me to come forward. Halfway between the oil tank and the back door, I heard Wanda's voice. "What the hell? You scared me half to death! Did you ring the doorbell at the front door? That stupid thing must be broken again."

Carly shoved her hands in her pockets, and if I weren't mistaken, she actually looked a bit flustered. "This door was open." *As if that explains why we're sneaking in the back door like a couple of bandits.*

"Did you need something?" Wanda chuckled. "Sorry, that sounded rude. I'm just surprised to see you is all. Did you find Nikki?"

"We found her," Carly said vaguely.

"Is Stacey with you?" Wanda's voice sounded hopeful, and when I stepped into view, her face fell. I smiled sweetly at her as I entered the house. *Sorry to disappoint you.* Wanda was old enough to be my mother, yet she was jealous of what she perceived to be a close friendship with Carly. I wondered how she would feel if she knew who I was. "Well, since you're here, do you want to stay for dinner?"

The back door opened to a small eat-in kitchen. An empty box of frozen lasagna was on the stove, and the scent of oregano and garlic filled the air. My stomach growled. I'd been staying in hotels and eating fast food for almost two weeks, so a frozen lasagna would be a welcome change. But if Carly's former associates were being targeted, then it wasn't safe for any of us to stay there.

"Jasper!" Wanda bellowed before we could respond to her dinner invite. She turned to Carly. "I want you to meet my son."

Carly and I shared an uneasy look. It seemed she'd come to the same conclusion I had.

A moment later, a skinny boy with shaggy light-brown hair came into the kitchen. He wore a big pair of headphones that looked like a knockoff of a more expensive brand. Jasper was small for his age, as though he hadn't quite hit puberty yet. Ah, the joys of middle school, where the girls towered over the boys.

Wanda put her hands on his shoulders and beamed. "Jasper, this is my friend. You can call her Miss Carly. I told you about her, remember?"

Not taking any interest in Carly, Jasper nodded, probably just to placate his mom. Instead, his sights were set on me.

Since Wanda once again seemed to forget I was there, I stuck out my hand. "I'm So—Stacey," I hastily corrected. *Damn it.* At some point, I was going to mess that up.

Jasper snickered. "So Stacey?"

Smart-ass. But his comment drew me to him. It was something I would have said when I was his age.

"Just Stacey is fine."

"Is anyone else here?" Carly asked, seeming ill at ease. Her eyes darted behind Wanda toward the hallway.

"It's just us," Wanda said. "Tim might come by later."

"Who's Tim?" I asked.

"Just a man I've been seeing." By the way Wanda said that, I could tell that to her at least, he was more than just a man she'd been seeing. Perhaps she was making it sound casual for Jasper's sake.

"We need to talk." Carly's eyes darted to Jasper.

Wanda took the hint. "Jasper, why don't you take Stacey and go play some video games?"

I wanted to roll my eyes. I was closer to being an adult than I was to being Jasper's age, and I had just as much at stake in the adult conversation as they did, but whatever. It would be quicker and easier to follow along. I discreetly handed Carly the gun before smiling at Jasper. "Sure, I'll play."

Jasper jerked his head in the direction of the living room. I followed him, and when he stopped short, I almost ran into him.

He turned. "The, uh, Wii is all we have in here. The Xbox is in my room."

"Whatever you want to do." It had been years since I'd played any video games. Lena and I had never had a gaming console because neither one of us had been into it. But I had played with Aidan from time to time. I wondered if he still had his PlayStation. It had been in his room, and I hadn't been there in quite a while.

I followed Jasper down the hall, which wasn't very long. The house was small, and it reminded me of the one and only EA safe house I'd been in. I had mixed feelings about that safe house. On one hand, that was where Aidan had taken me after I'd been kidnapped. I had been in bad shape, both physically and emotionally—emotionally for obvious reasons, and most of my physical ailment had been a result of being drugged. That part of the memory wasn't pleasant. On the other hand, the short time I'd spent in the house was when I realized I needed to pay attention to the feelings I had for Aidan, the feelings I'd buried deep within me. It was the first indication I'd had that he might return those feelings.

God, I missed him.

Jasper's bedroom was tiny and messy. Before I could sit on the bed next to him, he had to clear off a bunch of clothing. I sat on the edge, not wanting to get too cozy in his bed.

Jasper seemed nervous all of a sudden, so I took pity on him. "What games do you have? I haven't played in a while, so I probably won't be any good." Not that I was good when I did play.

"I have the newest Madden."

Was that basketball? No, it was football. Aidan might have had one of those if I remembered correctly. In any case, he'd had some kind of football game. I'd been horrible at it back then, and no doubt my skills hadn't improved.

"Okay," I said. My instinct was to talk smack and let him know what he would be in for when playing with me. Unfortunately, I was the one who was in for a butt-whooping. I didn't like it. Though I didn't really care about video games, I was competitive by nature, and losing felt like swallowing a poisonous pill covered in spikes and doused with hot sauce. Hopefully, Carly would finish her talk with Wanda before I was forced to swallow that pill.

Jasper got the game set up, and when I told him I didn't care which team I was, he picked for me. That was probably a mistake. If he were a strategist at all, he could've given me a terrible team, and I would have been none the wiser. Sure enough, it became clear only two minutes into the game that it was going to be a slaughter. I wouldn't call myself a sore loser, but my interest began to wane when it was clear I didn't stand a chance of winning.

I kept my eye on the door, expecting Carly and Wanda to come by at any moment with the directive for Jasper to pack his things. I was surprised it was taking so long for Carly to convince Wanda to go into hiding when Wanda obviously deferred to Carly's every whim. Or at least she once had.

Jasper's eyes were glued to the screen. "So, are you a…" Though he tried to act casual, the nervous quiver in his voice gave him away.

"An elemental?"

Relief passed over his face. "Yeah."

"We both are." I figured he already knew that about Carly since Wanda had told him about her. "What about you?" I didn't know who his father was, and to be honest, I didn't know any elementals whose parents weren't both elementals. I didn't know how all that DNA stuff played out. I'd never thought about it before, but it was odd that every married elemental I'd ever known was married to another elemental. It seemed as though some of them would have married outside the EA community, especially since we lived spread out across the country. I wondered if there was an EA regulation forbidding elementals from marrying normal people. If there was, I'd never heard of it.

"Yeah, I am." Jasper sounded almost bored, which was interesting. He was the one who'd brought up the subject. I was proud to be an elemental, but he seemed indifferent.

"What can you do?" I asked.

He shrugged. "Not much."

I tried to figure out how to proceed. I didn't know if Wanda had taught him to hide his powers like I'd been taught or if they were more open about using them.

"What about you? What can you do?" He peered at me with curiosity, leading me to believe he hadn't seen much elemental power in use. Carly had said that Wanda wasn't very powerful, so that made sense, but I wondered if there were any other elementals close by that they associated with.

There were some pencils sitting on his dresser, so I flicked my fingers and commanded the air to hit them. They rolled off the surface and fell harmlessly onto the floor.

He jumped up. "Whoa!" He stared open-mouthed at the pencils lying on the carpet.

Really? That impressed him? That was nothing. I'd been doing that since I was a small child. It used to drive Lloyd and Belinda crazy, which was probably why I'd done it. In retrospect, I must have been quite a handful for the elderly pair.

"Can you teach me how to do that?" he asked.

I wasn't sure how to respond. I didn't want to undermine any rules Wanda had set out for her son. "It's probably best if your mom teaches you."

Jasper made a dismissive gesture with his hand. "She can't do shit." His eyes widened for a second as he used the curse word, as though he expected me to reprimand him. I would've been more surprised if he didn't use curse words. Though since I was almost an adult, I frowned slightly at him because I figured I was supposed to do that. Unlike some of my classmates, I didn't babysit, and I couldn't remember the last time I'd interacted with someone so much younger than me. Lena would have been much better in that situation. For the first time, for the other girls' sake, I was grateful Lena was with them. Aniyah was only eleven, and she must've been scared out of her mind. Hopefully, they were being kept together, and Lena would be a comforting presence.

"The only way to get better at using your powers is to actually use them." As the words came out of my mouth, I realized how much like Carly I sounded, and I hated it. But damn it, it was the truth. Though much of using our powers was mental, it was also like any other physical skill. If a person wanted to get better at it, he had to practice.

"I don't use my hands," he said. "Maybe that's the problem."

Instinctively, I tucked my hands under my legs and fought the blush that threatened to spread across my cheeks. "You don't need to use your hands. It's just a silly thing that I do." I really needed to work on that, especially if the kid had noticed it was different. "Do you have any other elemental friends?"

"No." Jasper sighed. "Mom doesn't want to associate with any other elementals. I think she likes to forget that she is one. The only time she seems happy about that is when she's talking about the time she spent with Carly."

Wow... how often does Wanda talk about her? It felt all sorts of wrong to press the kid for information on what his mom had told him, but I couldn't pass up the opportunity. "What does your mom say about Carly?"

"Mainly just how awesome she is," Jasper said.

I took a second to think, trying to come up with a way to press him for information without him realizing what I was after. But there wasn't really a subtle way to ask, *"Hey, did your mom participate in any murders back in the day?"*

"Dinner!"

My eyebrows shot up. *What the hell?* Carly didn't actually expect us to eat there, did she? We should have been helping them pack.

Jasper and I trooped back out to the kitchen, and I could tell by Carly's frustrated expression that her talk with Wanda hadn't gone as planned. "I guess we're staying for dinner," she said tightly.

The wooden table had been set, and the lasagna, in all its prepackaged tinfoil glory, was sitting in the middle. My mouth watered. I was so tired of burgers and fries from all the fast-food restaurants where I'd been forced to eat lately.

I crossed the room to Carly. "What's the deal?" I asked under my breath.

"She won't leave until she talks to her boyfriend." Carly seemed annoyed that she didn't have the influence over Wanda that she used to. "He didn't answer his phone, but he should be on his way here."

"We can't wait forever," I said.

"We'll wait for her boyfriend," Carly replied. "That's all we can do."

I studied Wanda to see if she seemed rattled. As she pulled garlic bread out of the oven, her hands shook. *Good.* I regretted that she had reason to worry, but I wanted her to take the threat seriously.

I eyed the basket of garlic bread Wanda set on the table. *Might as well take advantage.* Though I wanted to shove a piece of garlic bread into my mouth and dig in to the cheese-and-sauce goodness, I waited politely for Wanda to tell me where to sit.

A knock sounded at the front door before she was able to instruct us. "That must be Tim," Wanda said. "I'll be right back."

Jasper dragged out a folded metal chair from the cranny between the fridge and the wall and grabbed another plate. "You can sit wherever."

"Is Tim an elemental?" I asked quietly.

Jasper shook his head. "He's kind of a jerk."

Carly frowned. "What do you mean?"

"I don't like the guy." Jasper sat, and I claimed the seat next to him. He seemed like a levelheaded kid, so I took his word for it and prepared myself for an unpleasant dinner experience.

The minute Wanda came back into the kitchen, it was obvious why Jasper didn't like her new boyfriend. It probably had nothing to do with the fact that Tim sported a comb-over, even though he was a good bit younger than Wanda. It had everything to do with the gun he had pressed up against Wanda's side.

Jasper jumped up. "What the hell?"

What the hell, indeed.

Tim's arm wrapped around Wanda's neck. Because he was about the same height as she was, her knees were bent, and she leaned backward at an awkward angle to keep from falling. *Shit.* If she slipped and Tim was jumpy, he might accidentally shoot her.

"Who are you?" Carly hadn't risen from her spot at the table. Neither had I. While she remained calm and seemed in control, my reaction was more of a deer-in-the-headlights response. I foolishly hadn't even considered that Wanda's boyfriend might be the threat we'd warned her about. I couldn't tell if Carly had suspected him or not.

But Jasper had certainly pegged him correctly—the guy was definitely a jerk.

"It doesn't matter who I am," Tim said with a sneer. "But I know exactly who you are."

Shit. That was bad. I mean, any situation in which a man had a gun pressed into his girlfriend's abdomen was bad, but this wasn't any old domestic dispute.

The metaphorical headlight on my brain dimmed, and I started connecting the dots. Wanda hadn't said how long she'd been seeing Tim, but I would've bet anything it had only been a few weeks, since Carly had come out of her hidey-hole and killed my kidnappers.

"Hey, asshole, let my mom go." Jasper looked as though he were ready to charge Tim. I wasn't psychic, but it didn't take future gazing to see that wouldn't end well. I reached up to put my hand on the boy's arm, hoping he understood my silent message. *Chill out.* I admired his willingness to defend his mother, but though Tim wasn't a large man, he would easily be able to overpower Jasper. Oh, and he had a gun. There was that.

Seeing what her son was about to do was enough to snap Wanda out of her shock. "Jasper, no." However, the fear cloaking her mom-glare minimized its effect.

Carly put her hands flat on the table and pushed herself to a standing position. "What do you want?"

"Yes, what do you want?" Wanda's shriek sounded hysterical. Perhaps it would've been better if she'd stayed in shock. "Tim, why are you doing this? I don't understand. You..." Realization dawned in Wanda's eyes, and I saw the second she shifted from scared to pissed. I preferred *pissed* to *scared*, as long as Wanda could keep her shit together and not do something stupid. Her gaze settled on Carly, and in it was absolute trust.

Shit, shit, shit. Please let us get out of this without blood or buried bodies or chargrilled skin. As the tension in the air grew thicker, my powers grew as well. They swirled and pulsed, ready for me to call them.

"Jasper," Carly said softly. "Why don't you go to your room while we sort this out."

Tim swung the gun wide, pointing it toward Jasper. "The brat stays here."

Jasper's hands balled into fists at his sides, and I touched his arm again. He glanced at me, and I shook my head. He jerked his head slightly to indicate he understood. Again, I was impressed by the kid. Most preteens would have peed their pants by now. I hoped to God he simply had nerves of steel rather than prior experience with life-threatening situations.

"Tell me what you want." Carly enunciated each word slowly. God, I hoped Tim answered this time so we could get on with it.

Tim swung the gun in her direction, and I fought the urge to duck as it passed over me. "You need to come with me."

"Is that all?" Carly laughed. "Why didn't you say so five minutes ago? We could've been on our way by now." Carly stretched her arm in front of Jasper and me and pushed us back away from the table, clearing a path for her to walk around to the man.

"You're all coming." Tim swung the gun around again, pointing it at each of us in turn. He still had his arm crooked around Wanda's neck. Her nostrils flared, and her hands were fisted as her sides, her posture mirroring her son's.

Tim didn't issue any other directive and instead continued to wave the gun at us.

He doesn't know what he's doing. The realization that he was an amateur at this brought little comfort. I would've almost preferred that he were a professional. That way, at least he wouldn't shoot us accidentally. If a pro shot us, it would be on purpose.

Maybe the guy belonged to the group we were looking for. But it didn't make sense for the feared organization to send someone so inexperienced to deal with Carly, the deadliest elemental ever known.

Carly stepped in front of Jasper and me. "This would be a lot easier if—" Suddenly, a chair zoomed across the room, just like the end table had at Nikki's house. It collided with Tim's arm, sending the gun spiraling to the floor. His body jerked from the impact and knocked Wanda to the floor.

Carly tipped the table onto its side and shoved Jasper down behind it. The lasagna hit the floor, and red sauce flew everywhere.

I didn't hesitate and dove for the gun, easily scooping it up among the spilled garlic bread and shattered plates. Trying to keep my hands steady, I pointed it at Tim. I assumed my most menacing expression and hoped I didn't look as inexperienced as he had.

Aidan would have been so proud of me.

Wanda scurried to her feet and hurried to Jasper. She wrapped her arms around him.

Carly took a few steps toward Tim. "Now will you tell us who you are?"

Though Tim seemed utterly bewildered by what had just happened, he looked at me and started to laugh. "She won't actually shoot me."

Bullshit. And speaking of shooting people, I didn't see the gun I'd given Carly earlier. Though with her skills, she probably didn't need it.

"Try me," I said evenly. I wasn't a great shot, but at such a close range, I wouldn't miss.

I hoped to God Tim wouldn't actually make me prove my intent. I'd killed once to save myself, and I didn't want to have to do it again.

"She won't need to shoot you." A slow, sadistic smile stretched across Carly's face. "I'm here."

Then just as quickly as it had happened before, the table flew into the air and smashed Tim into the wall. The tabletop pressed flat against him, and I had to take a few steps to my left so I could keep the gun trained on him. He pushed against the solid wooden table, but it wouldn't budge. Though I'd seen it earlier that day, I could help but marvel at Carly's abilities. The table hovered a foot off the floor, as if it were suspended from the ceiling by invisible string.

Blood rushed in my ears, and my adrenaline spiked. My power surged. It flowed through me, on high alert. I focused on my breathing, trying to calm the forces within me. It would be bad for all of us if I lost control. *No, don't fight it.* After the lightning, I'd made peace with my powers, but giving in to them completely was still unnerving.

"What's your name, *Tim?*" Carly asked.

Tim pushed against the table, the muscles in his arms bulging, but it didn't budge. *How the hell is she doing that?* She'd already explained it to me, and I was seeing it with my own eyes, but it was still hard to believe.

Carly took another step closer. "This is the last time I'm going to ask you nicely. Who are you?"

"Bitch," Tim growled.

Carly chuckled and glanced over at me. "You can put the gun down. You won't need it."

Slowly, I lowered my arms. I didn't put the safety on the gun, though.

A choking sound came from Tim. His hands strained to reach his neck, but the table had him pinned to the wall. Then he gasped and sucked in air as if he'd just been drowning.

I knew exactly what Carly was doing because it was a trick we'd both used before.

"Who are you?" Carly asked. Throughout the entire altercation, her voice had remained low and even. The effect was scary, and I wondered if that was her intent. She almost appeared bored by the entire affair. If I didn't know how concerned she was for Wanda's welfare, I would have been fooled.

Tim still didn't talk, but he didn't call her another bad name either. Instead, he stared at her with venom in his gaze. *Bold move, Tim.* I winced, knowing Carly wouldn't tolerate his insolence.

The table pushed against him, and he grunted. Behind him, the wall cracked, and a concave space formed around his body, cocooning him.

"Well, that's not going to work," Carly muttered. The table moved back a few inches, and Tim took advantage of the opportunity. He shoved it with his hands, and it flew back a few feet. Instead of going for either Carly or me, he started toward the back door. That might have been a wise choice, except Carly raised the table and slammed it onto his head. The first blow dazed him, and the second sent him to the floor. After the third one, blood spurted from a wound in his forehead. Two more blows, and he was out cold. The table slowly lowered to the floor.

"I'm sorry about that," Carly said to no one in particular. I didn't know if she was apologizing to the twelve-year-old boy for the show of violence or to Wanda for cracking the wall and getting Tim's blood all over her floor. Something told me she wasn't apologizing to me.

"It's okay." Wanda's voice shook. She exhaled and released Jasper from her death grip.

"Do you have anything we can use to tie him up?" Carly asked.

"We have duct tape in the garage," Wanda said. "Jasper, go."

Jasper nodded mutely, his wide eyes focused on the heap of Tim at our feet.

"Mind the blood," Carly said cheerfully as Jasper inched toward the garage. "And the lasagna."

Jasper stepped over the tinfoil pan and disappeared from the room. I stared at the mess in front of me. *Damn it.* It was hard to tell what was blood and what was sauce. I wanted to kick Tim in the face because I would never be able to enjoy lasagna again without thinking of his blood.

"Can you close the blinds, please?" Carly asked.

Wanda scurried to follow her command. *Probably just like old times.*

Jasper came back and held out a roll of duct tape. "Is he dead?"

"No," I assured him. "He's breathing."

Jasper's face was pale as he swallowed. *Poor kid.*

I stayed out of the way while Carly bound Tim's wrists and ankles. Jasper's reaction made me realize how nonchalant I was being about the whole thing. I didn't like that I was becoming desensitized to violence and not in the way that people feared kids who played too many video games would. Actual bloody and deadly violence was right in front of me, and I wasn't fazed one bit by it. If anything, I was merely intrigued by what I'd just witnessed.

Carly wrapped one final piece of duct tape around Tim's ankles. "Wanda, we'll take it from here. You should take Jasper and go. I'll be in touch."

Wanda nodded and dragged Jasper out of the room. Five minutes later, the front door slammed, and a car backed down the driveway.

"Now what?" I asked Carly, afraid I already knew the answer.

She leveled her gaze at me. "Now we get the information we need."

Chapter 18

Carly and I pulled Tim up into a chair, ironically the same chair she'd used to hit him. We wrapped him with duct tape to keep him in place. At first, I wanted to put a piece over his mouth so the neighbors wouldn't hear him, but it didn't take me long to realize that made no sense. He couldn't tell us what we needed if he couldn't talk.

While we waited for him to wake up, I stared longingly at the lasagna on the floor. It was such a shame, and I found myself scrounging in Wanda's pantry for food.

"So you knew the guardian at Nikki's house?" Carly asked.

"The one outside, not the one inside." If it hadn't been obvious, I wouldn't have admitted it. Though I had an uneasy trust with Carly, I didn't like her knowing Vic was important to me. It was bad enough she knew about Aidan. I wouldn't put it past her to use them as leverage against me if it served her purpose.

It seemed as though she wanted to discuss it more, but Tim was rousing.

"Wake up, sunshine." Carly smacked him across the face. *Whoa.* I didn't see that coming. Carly was violent, but she usually preferred to use her abilities.

Tim groaned. Carly smacked him again, and I cringed. "Is that necessary?"

Carly whirled toward me. "Do you want to find your friend or not? Greta slipped through our fingers. I'm not making the same mistake twice."

I clamped my mouth shut. There was nothing more important than finding Lena, but I wasn't used to such savage methods to get what I wanted. I couldn't decide if that was a weakness or a strength.

When Carly smacked Tim a third time, his eyes opened. He cursed at her, so she smacked him again. I turned away. Now she was taking out her frustrations on him.

"We'll start with an easy question first," Carly said. "Is your name really Tim?"

He cursed at her again and earned another smack. Tim—if that was really his name—didn't seem to understand the concept of cause and effect.

"Your name."

It didn't matter what his name was. Though I didn't voice my opinion, she turned to me and shrugged. "I like to know who I'm dealing with."

"Then let's look in his wallet." Wanting to speed things up, I reached over to get into his back pocket, where I assumed his wallet was. He jerked his head back, and it collided with mine.

For a moment, I was stunned, and my line of sight darkened. *Damn it! That's twice now!* It was my own damn fault. When my vision cleared, Carly was standing in front of him. She dug her fingernails into his neck.

"You know," I said, "she killed the last person who hurt me." I retrieved his wallet with some difficulty since he was sitting on it and opened it. "His name is Thomas."

Carly removed her hand from his throat, leaving behind little moon-shaped indentations from her fingernails. "You changed it from Tom to Tim? Seriously? That was the best you could do?"

He wasn't very imaginative, but it didn't matter. "Who are you working with, Tom?" I asked.

"You can do what you want," he wheezed. "They scare me more than you ever will."

Greta had said basically the same thing. Fear clutched at my insides. If their own people were afraid of them, then that didn't bode well for their prisoners. I spun so he wouldn't see the tears gathering in my eyes. What if all of this was for nothing? If the girls had already outlived their usefulness, they could have been cast aside.

I caught Carly watching me as I struggled to rein in my tears. Her gaze was both sympathetic and angry, and I knew what she was thinking. This group might not have hurt me physically, but they'd definitely hurt me, and that was not okay with her.

"Then you don't know me very well." Carly's voice was low and had an edge to it that sliced like a razor.

Oh God. Here we go.

CARLY SINGED THE man's hair on his head and arms, slowly igniting flames and putting them out when they reached his skin. She toyed with him, taking her time. And dare I say it— she enjoyed herself.

Tom remained stoic for most of it, only clenching his teeth and breathing heavily through his mouth when the flames licked at his flesh.

I didn't know if it was that or the smell of burnt hair that made me sick to my stomach. I'd caught a glimpse of this side of Carly in the woods with Greta, but that was nothing compared to now. I hung back, watching silently. My birth mother was also silent, not asking him any questions. I got the impression she was waiting for him to speak first, to beg for mercy. So far, he wasn't cracking. *Damn.* It was taking too long. Only thirty minutes had passed, but his people could have been waiting for him. Would they send backup when he didn't return?

We already had more information than when we'd arrived—we had his name and address from his license. Other than a few credit cards and fifty-seven dollars, that was all we'd discovered. It wasn't much to go on, but my time would be better spent trying to learn more about him rather than observing Carly do her worst. And frankly, I didn't care to see it, though I was eager to reap the benefits. *Hypocrite.*

"I'm stepping out," I said to Carly, who continued to circle Tom like a panther circling its prey. She nodded.

I headed to Jasper's room. There had been a computer in there, and I was hoping in his and Wanda's haste to leave, they hadn't taken it. Luck was on my side because not only was it there, but there was no password to log on.

Thomas Schlenker. At least the man had a somewhat unique name, making him easier to find. He was listed as mechanic of the month at a local car dealership almost three years ago. But other than that, there was nothing.

I wanted to scream.

Tom did scream, again and again, the kind of scream that a man being tortured made. I pushed away from the desk and ran back to the kitchen.

The smell hit me at soon as I walked into the room—Tom had lost control of his bladder and his bowels. The table had been pulled over to him, and his right hand lay on top of it. All five fingers were crushed. Carly twirled a meat mallet in her hands.

Holy shit. "What did you do?" It was a stupid question. Obviously, she'd pulverized his fingers.

Carly leveled her gaze at me. "One finger for each of the missing girls."

"There were six. One died." I hadn't meant to speak out loud, but my body was one step ahead of my brain.

"In that case." She swung the mallet like it was a golf club, making contact with his kneecap, which made a sickening crunch. Tom yelled. She dropped the mallet and reached on top of the refrigerator for a plastic bottle of vodka. "I wouldn't want your wound to get infected." I watched with wide eyes as she uncapped the bottle and poured the liquid over his fingers. His eyes rolled back in his head.

"Stop!" I yelled. "He can't tell us anything if he's unconscious."

Carly tossed the empty bottle aside. "Don't worry. Tom's about to give me an address, aren't you?" She leaned close to him. His mouth opened and let out the same horrific scream I'd heard before. Then suddenly it stopped. "Tell me."

He mumbled something, but I was too far away to hear.

"Thank you," Carly said primly, as if she were a schoolteacher thanking a student for providing a correct answer. Then she picked up a frying pan from the stove and bashed him over the head with it. His head lolled back, and blood streamed out of his nose and ears.

"What did you do to him?" I whispered. His agonizing scream would forever be etched in my memory.

"Sixty percent of the human body is made of water." She didn't finish the explanation, but she didn't need to—water was an element she could control. I couldn't begin to comprehend what she'd done to his insides.

Turning away, I squeezed my eyes shut and tucked the scene back into the deep pockets of my memory. I would process that nightmare later.

"What's the address?"

Carly pressed a gun into my hands. "Call your guardian friends to come deal with this. If he gives you trouble, shoot him."

"What?" I stared down at the gun in my hand, not comprehending what she was saying. My split second of confusion was long enough for her to dart out the back door. A loud crash followed.

I dashed after her, but a tree blocked the back stairs, which must have been what the crash was. By the time I climbed over it and ran around to the street, Carly was already in the Jeep.

"Call your friends!" she yelled out the window as she peeled away.

Shit, shit, shit. What had she done? Where was she going? Dumbfounded, I stared after the Jeep until it turned. Then I rushed back to the house to call Aidan.

AIDAN PICKED UP after the second ring. "Are you okay?"

I closed my eyes at the sound of his voice and let the deep baritone fill my heart. "I'm fine." There were so many things I wanted to ask him, but they would all have to wait. "I need to get in touch with Vic."

"I'm sitting right next to him."

I definitely wasn't expecting that. "What?"

"They were keeping me under close watch, but when Vic saw you today, we set out on our own. What's going on?"

"I think..." I paused, hoping the words I was about to say were true. "I think Carly's going after the girls on her own."

"What do you mean?"

"We've got a guy here, and she—" I stopped myself from telling him the gruesome details. He would see it for himself soon enough, and I didn't have it in me to voice what my birth mother had done. "Anyway, she got an address out of him and then took off, but she didn't say where."

"She left you with the guy?" Aidan's voice was filled with alarm.

I thought about Tom, who was a soiled, bloody mess. He wouldn't be a threat to anyone for a long, long time. I'd expected dinner with him to be unpleasant, and it had turned out to be worse in ways I never could have imagined. "He's... secure."

"Where are you?"

I hesitated. "It's just you and Vic?" I wanted their help, but I didn't want that to come along with an army of guardians. Carly hadn't managed to turn me against the EA, but I was definitely wary of them. If they showed up, no doubt they would want to question me, then there would be a debriefing and then a strategy session. We didn't have time for process and protocol. We needed to get things done.

"For now, it's just us."

I gave him Wanda's address, and he said it would take them about forty-five minutes. I needed to be prepared when they got there. Going back into the kitchen, I was both afraid and hopeful that Tom would still be unconscious. It would be easier, though more cowardly, to wait for Vic and Aidan if he were. They were fully trained guardians with the skills needed for humane interrogation.

Though this particular prisoner didn't deserve it. What Carly had said about not all humans deserving respect resonated with me just then. I never thought I would sink so low to think that some people deserved to be tortured, but there I was.

The blood had congealed around Tom's ears and nose. Though his eyes were closed, I wasn't taking any chances. I picked up the gun and turned off the safety. Not wanting to touch him, I grabbed a spatula off the stove and poked him with it. "Hey," I said loudly. He didn't even twitch, so I tried again. Still nothing.

My lessons with Aidan hadn't prepared me to revive a person who had been tortured into unconsciousness, so I did the only sensible thing—I did an online search. The number-one solution to my dilemma was smelling salts, but I doubted Wanda had any of those lying around. So my next step was to search for smelling-salt alternatives. Lemons came up. I scooted around Tom to get to the refrigerator. There were no lemons, but there was a bottle of lemon juice. It was worth a shot.

I balled up a paper towel and doused it with lemon juice. Putting it up to my nose, I cringed at the strong odor. "Here goes nothing," I muttered.

I pushed the paper towel right up against his nose. Nothing happened for a few seconds, but then his head jerked up. *Success.* When his eyes opened, it took them a moment to focus. A gun pointed at his face was the first thing he saw, but it didn't seem to concern him much.

"Where is she?" Apparently Carly had made an impression.

"You tell me."

The man swallowed thickly. "No."

Are you kidding me? "I *will* shoot you."

"No, you won't." His voice was hoarse, as though he were having difficulty speaking. "That gun looks unnatural in your hand. You've never shot anyone, and you won't shoot me."

I placed the gun on the counter. "Fine. You're right. I won't shoot you. I'm much more comfortable with my natural talents." Understanding flashed in his eyes a second before I sucked the air from his lungs. I counted to ten before releasing it. "Please don't make me torture you." The plea was as much for him as it was for me. I could've suffocated him until he'd turned blue in the face, but I didn't want to—I just wanted to make the point that I could.

His laugh came out like a cackle, sounding painful. Fury seared my insides. Carly had tortured him until he'd pissed and shit himself, yet he didn't take my threat seriously. I was a joke to him. As he continued to look at me with his defiant stare, my power stirred, multiplying at a rapid pace. My fingers shook as adrenaline spiked through my bloodstream.

This time, instead of sucking the air from his lungs, I pushed it down his throat, imagining his lungs expanding like balloons, and I wondered how much pressure it would take for them to burst. His eyes bulged, making him look like a frog, and his chest puffed out. His hand that still had intact fingers gripped his thigh.

Abruptly, I released my hold, and air rushed out of his mouth in a gust. Leveling my gaze at him, I stepped closer. "Do you believe me now? I am my mother's daughter, and I will do whatever it takes to get what I want from you."

He swallowed. "She's your—"

I picked up the frying pan Carly had hit him with and smashed it down on his already pulverized fingers. "Where is she?" I raised the pan, preparing to hit him again.

He said an address so quickly that it took me a second to register the fact that he'd answered my question. I put down the pan in favor of my phone. "Say it again. Slowly."

As he repeated it, I entered it into my phone. *Twenty-seven miles.* Lena was only twenty-seven miles away.

There was a knock at the front door. I was pretty sure I knew who it was, but just in case, I ripped off a strip of duct tape and pressed it over Tom's mouth. I scooped up the gun before running to the living room and peeking out the window.

Aidan and Vic stood on the porch. My fingers shook as I fumbled with the lock and flung open the front door.

Aidan's eyes met mine. How was it possible I'd forgotten how blue and perfect they were? With a choked sob, I launched myself at him, and his strong arms enveloped me, his hands gripping my waist. I tucked my face into his neck and inhaled. *Everything will be fine.* Aidan was there, and together, we would figure it out.

"Are you okay?" His voice was thick with emotion.

Though I wanted nothing more than to stay in his arms, I pulled away. "I'm fine. I know where they are."

As soon as I told them the address, Vic made a call, relaying the information to his fellow guardians. His words grew heated, and he turned away. He was probably being reprimanded for taking off with Aidan. My resolve to avoid the guardians grew greater.

"Where's your source?" Aidan asked.

I jerked my head. "Kitchen." I led him there.

"Holy shit," he said. "What the hell?"

My perspective suddenly shifted, and I saw the scene as it must look through his eyes—Tom's bloody, crushed fingers, the streams of blood dried on his ears, the damaged furniture and wall, and the stench mixed with the lingering aroma of the ruined dinner on the floor.

My gaze rested on the frying pan both Carly and I had used—it was covered with splashes of blood. I was as much a part of this as she was. *I am my mother's daughter.* Now that I was with Vic and Aidan, that statement took on another meaning. They—and the rest of my family—represented the good and the moral while Carly existed in various shades of gray. I no longer knew what to think about that.

I squared my shoulders, refusing to apologize. "We did what we needed to."

Aidan's expression remained neutral, but even still, I knew he understood what I was telling him—Carly wasn't solely responsible. "Who is this guy?"

"Tom, but he's not important right now," I said. "We need to go."

Aidan leaned close. "Will he implicate you?"

My breath caught as I prepared to admit something that would forever change me in his eyes. I knew it in my soul, but I refused to lie to Aidan. If we were going to figure us out, if he was going to love me, then he needed to love *all* of me. "If he tells the truth."

Aidan stepped back. "Damn it." I tried not to read into his response. I couldn't tell if he was concerned that I might get into trouble or if he was angry about what I'd done.

"Aidan, please," I pleaded. "We need to go. Who knows what Carly walked into? She's strong, but she's got to be outnumbered."

"Guardians are probably already on their way."

"What will they do if they find her there?" I bit my lip, and tears filled my eyes. "They'll try to kill her, Aidan. We need to beat them there. And Lena is there. I know it. *Only twenty-seven miles away.*"

Aidan's expression was pained. I was right, but he knew how dangerous it would be for us to go on our own. As the first tear streaked down my cheek, he closed his eyes briefly. "Let's go."

"What about Vic?"

Aidan's lips thinned. "Hopefully, he'll forgive us."

WE CALLED VIC from the road and were treated to a long string of cursing. I felt horrible doing the same thing to him that Carly had done to me, but we couldn't risk that he would insist on following protocol and waiting for backup. I also didn't know how he would react to seeing Carly, and I didn't want to make him choose between letting my mother live and killing the woman his wife held responsible for her sister's death.

Once Vic got his anger under control, Aidan told him Tom might implicate me. There was a brief pause. "I'll take care of it," Vic said gruffly. Then the line went dead.

Shit. I didn't know what he was going to do or how far down I was going to drag my loved ones. I swallowed my regret. It was not the time to worry about that.

"Why are you here?" I asked Aidan. "I mean—"

"I know what you mean," he said, and I was reminded of just how well he knew me. But my time with Carly had also changed me. How would that affect things? Only time would tell. "Once they found Greta, a team of guardians was sent in. They brought me because they were sure you'd contact me eventually."

"We didn't kill Nikki Blanchard. She was dead when we got there." I felt the need to make that clear.

"I know." Aidan glanced at the directions and signaled a lane change. "After Greta, we started checking up on Carly's old followers who were nearby. We found another one dead—Brad Zuritz. He'd been dead a few days."

Another one dead. When will it end? Hopefully shortly—just sixteen more miles to go.

"Carly was worried we led them to Nikki," I said, "but if the other guy had been dead for a few days, then it couldn't be because we were asking around. They were already targets."

"It seems that way."

We were quiet the rest of the drive. The gravity of the situation started to set in—we had no idea what we would find at our destination. Tom could have given Carly the wrong address, though I didn't think so. His mind had been too full of fear to concoct a plausible lie. He easily could've lied to me, but he had nothing to gain by doing so.

Carly was fearless and formidable, but she wasn't bulletproof. I didn't know what she had walked into. I didn't know what we were walking into.

Aidan slowed in front of a gated community. I double-checked the address. "Are you sure this is it?"

"This is the address." Aidan eyed the closed gate and the guard at the security checkpoint and kept driving. "We'll have to find another way in."

As intimidating as the front of the community was, it wasn't difficult to find another point of entry. The neighborhood was new, and houses were still being constructed, so all we had to do was sneak through one of the open lots.

The address we were looking for was for a large brick house with a huge lawn. While the neighboring houses weren't super close, they were close enough that the residents would have noticed a slew of abducted girls being brought in. I'd expected the place to be isolated or a warehouse or something, not located in a posh, gated neighborhood.

Did Tom lie to me? Then again, how would he have come up with this particular address? Several vehicles, including a large van, were parked in the driveway. That was the only indication that we might be on the right track. But the residents could be getting carpet installed for all we knew. We observed from across the street, but the blinds were all drawn. After a few minutes, it became evident we would be going in blind.

Aidan took the safety off his gun, and I did the same with the gun I'd taken from Wanda's house.

"Let's go around back," Aidan said.

Before we could circle around, the front door swung open, and Carly appeared. She waved.

I gasped and took off running toward her.

"Sophie, wait!" Aidan warned, but I ignored him. He cursed, then his feet pounded the pavement behind me.

I skidded to a stop at the front door as the smell of burnt flesh assaulted my senses. The source lay on the floor of the foyer—a body that was charred so badly I couldn't tell if it was male or female. I backed out of the house, bumping into Aidan. He protectively tucked me behind him and stepped into the house, gun drawn.

Trying to breathe through my mouth, I followed him. In the living room lay two more bodies, both bent at unnatural angles, both dead. We continued through the dining room. A man lay on the dining room table, his unstaring eyes trained up at the spot where the chandelier should have been—the twisted metal of which was now slicing into his neck, partially decapitating him. My vision blurred as I looked at him as if my eyes were protecting me from the ghastly sight.

Where is Carly?

A door slammed at the back of the house, and I rushed toward the sound, once again leaving Aidan behind. He chased after me. In the kitchen, I paused only briefly at the sight of the massive refrigerator on its side with two feet poking out from under it like the Wicked Witch of the East.

The back door was ajar, and I pulled it the rest of the way open. Carly lingered at the edge of the yard.

"Carly!"

She turned, and her expression stopped me in my tracks—sorrow, regret, and envy. Her chin quivered. She raised her hand, and I thought she was going to wave again. Instead, she blew me a kiss. Then she ducked through the line of bushes and was gone.

But...

Aidan grabbed my hand and pulled me back inside. "Let's finish checking the house."

Lena.

"It's safe," I said. "Otherwise, she wouldn't have left."

"Probably, but we still need to check."

Although there were six bedrooms upstairs, no one was up there. That included no more dead bodies. *Thank God.* But there was no sign of the girls either.

They *had* to be there. Carly couldn't have killed all those people for nothing. She couldn't have left me behind for nothing.

We went back downstairs, and Aidan headed into the garage. Feeling as though we had to have missed something, I circled the downstairs, carefully averting my gaze from the death and destruction. I was right—we had missed something. Two more bodies were lying under the breakfast table, and another one was sprawled in the pantry. But that wasn't what I meant. Lena was there. I felt it in my bones.

I started opening every door I could find, looking for some kind of clue. I went to the kitchen and opened the pantry door.

Except... the pantry was on the other side of the room. I ran my hand along the wall, feeling for a switch, and flipped on the light. Five feet into the space was another door. There were two crudely attached padlocks. I pounded on the door—it was solid.

I stuck my head out of the outer door. "Aidan!" He appeared within seconds, and I pointed at the door. "Do you know how to pick a lock?"

"With the right tools, yeah, but we don't have those. Hang on." He slipped out of the space.

I returned to the kitchen and looked in drawers for anything that we might be able to use. While the pantry was well stocked, the rest of the kitchen wasn't. Paper plates and plastic utensils weren't going to do us much good.

Aidan came back, holding a chain saw. I didn't even want to know why the people had one of those but no pots and pans.

"Stand back." Aidan went through the outer door and yanked on the string that started the chain saw. It whirred to life, and he sliced through the door right above the top lock. He made a square around both locks and turned off the chainsaw. I rushed forward and yanked open the door.

A dim overhead light faintly illuminated wooden stairs. *A basement.* It hadn't even occurred to me to look for one because our house in Tidewater was too close to sea level to have one. I felt along the wall for a switch but found none. Cautiously, I started down the steps, not bothering to wait for Aidan, who was hunting up a flashlight. Somewhere in the darkness below me, I heard a scuffing noise followed by a sharp intake of breath.

I rushed down the rest of the stairs and peered into the darkness. I was barely able to make out five shadows huddled against the wall.

"Lena?"

There was a choked sob. "Sophie? Is that you?"

About the Author

Jessica lives in Virginia with her college-sweetheart husband, two rambunctious sons, and two rowdy but lovable rescue dogs. Since her house is overflowing with testosterone, it's a good thing she has a healthy appreciation for Marvel movies, Nerf guns, and football.

To learn more about Jessica, visit her website jessicaruddick.com. Connect with her on Twitter at @JessicaMRuddick or on Facebook at facebook.com/AuthorJessicaRuddick.

Other Books by Jessica Ruddick

The Elemental Saga
> *Undefined (Book One)*
> *Untamed (Book Two)*

The Legacy Series
> *Birthright (Book One)*
> *Retribution (Book Two)*
> *Sacrifice (Book Three)*
> *Redemption (Book Four)*

The Love on Campus Series
> *Letting Go*
> *Wanting More*